Memories of a

I was standin
floor-length fu
360 SL conver
blonde and ar
from her throat. Supra-Aryan. She fired the motor before winding down the window and then sat there looking me over with that special arrogance only rich and reasonably beautiful women can afford – like she was doing the shopping and I was a cabbage on a market stall. Finally she nodded at my Bultaco.

'Yours?'

'Mine,' I agreed in a dead flat voice.

'Where do you live?'

'Ibiza town.'

She pushed her door open and was already halfway over into the passenger seat before she said, 'Get in.'

Also by Simon Gandolfi in Sphere Books.
THE 100 KILO CLUB

The Reluctant Stud

SIMON GANDOLFI

SPHERE BOOKS LIMITED
30-32 Gray's Inn Road, London WC1X 8JL

First published in Great Britain by Sphere Books Ltd 1981

Reprinted 1983

TRADE
MARK

Set in Lasercomp Baskerville

Printed and bound in Great Britain by
Collins, Glasgow

This is a work of fiction. It is dedicated with apologies to those who mistakenly believe themselves portrayed . . .

Chapter One

AUGUST! What a great month to be hospitalised. Admittedly I'm not missing much. At least, considering my condition, I'm not missing much. And I do have a window alongside my corner bed. From this window you can see the blue Mediterranean sky and the blue Mediterranean sea and the extreme western end of Malta's yacht marina, where the catamaran I brought in from Italy this morning lies stern to the quay. Are those two French girls who sailed over with me still on board? Or did they catch the afternoon flight to Tunis where they have an architect friend with a summer house along the beach? Palm trees. Possibly even a few camels. Romantic! Which is more than can be said for me.

There *are* romantic medical catastrophes. Tubercular poets used to be in vogue and may still be in vogue, for all I know.

Broken legs displayed in the ski lodge can be romantic if the legs got shattered jinking down a pine-stumped precipice so the lady can goo an appreciative, 'Crazy! I mean, wow, well just CRAZY!' Except she doesn't know how accurate she's being.

Nowadays, some teenage ladies find acid casualties romantic as in those daughter-to-mother dialogues, 'But, Ma, he has this beautiful head.'

Ma looks at the head disgracing her neatly-trimmed lawn. What she sees is wild hair, pimples and a definite negative in the career stakes.

There was even once a lady in my life who inhabited an anodised aluminium wheelchair. She was definitely romantic in my eyes – perhaps because she was untouchable due to a cracked pelvis. But there was always the knowledge that I might touch her if I could only find time to hang around for a few weeks. This is questionable for any lady willing to stay around my hospital bed. Not that I'm dying – which could be romantic

No, all that is wrong with me is this little matter of my left testicle deciding to get competitive with an ostrich egg. This is not romantic, but merely funny, particularly as I only have one testicle. The other one got squashed twenty-five years back when I was twenty years old and a serving officer in Her Britannic Majesty's cavalry. Not that I was doing anything courageous. I was simply attempting to take a nervous mare over a triple fence. The mare twisted in mid-flight, down I crashed on the saddle's pommel, and there was one-ball Tobias. Painful rather than romantic, this incident caused a certain amount of laughter amongst my brother officers, which is roughly how things stand in this present crisis.

Appearances and reality, that is what I lie here considering. There was a line of dialogue I caught this morning down at the marina. 'Some people have all the luck.' The remark concerned me but was not addressed to me. It was part of an exchange between two elderly gentlemen eating bacon and eggs for breakfast on the afterdeck of a seventy-foot motor yacht. The luck was my having these two French ladies on the catamaran. Even the customs and immigration officials exchanged bright asides. All these men were considering me the big stud, while the truth was that I hadn't been able to ball for the past two weeks, nor had I even known why I couldn't ball until finally the reason became obvious. Suffering an ostrich egg hanging between your legs is definitely obvious.

We sailed in at nine o'clock. This is another example of appearance and reality. A forty-five-foot catamaran is not the easiest type of yacht to manoeuvre under sail. Everyone watched us: me at the helm, these two young ladies standing by to let go the sheets and pick up moorings, plus a great big outboard engine sticking back over the stern. My not using the engine impressed our audience. Certainly I looked calm. Who wouldn't when doped up on heavy pain-killers? Not that ignoring the engine came from confidence; the mother refused to start.

Thank God the yacht agent came by with her car. She takes one look at me and remarks, 'Jesus!'

'Yeah,' I admit.

'What's wrong?'

I tell her. Hiding her smile behind a lace handkerchief, she looks at my crew as if this problem could be their fault . . . or at least something they should know about (flattering to my sexual reputation).

'Does he have a fever?' she wants to know. This is how women tend to be if there's more than one of them on the scene of a male emergency. The man gets discussed. I am uncritical. A few thousand years of human experience has taught them they are correct.

'We don't know,' responds the elder of the two French ladies, twenty-three years old but definitely wise in male psychology. 'He's too scared to find out.' True – they have been trying to force a thermometer into my mouth for the last four days.

'*Terrorise*,' adds the younger French lady, while the yacht agent gives me the look Mum wastes on her five-year-old who has just thrown up on a rich aunt's Persian carpet from eating too many ice creams.

'Fool,' she tells me . . . even the tone of voice is the same. 'Let's get you to the hospital.' So here I am and I do have a fever – one hundred and two point four. I am also slightly delirious. Nothing serious, though serious enough to have me scribbling away in this notebook. I'd rather be reading but I left my spectacles on the cat. Not that there are any books in here. A Catholic priest has been by with a promise of the New Testament. He's a young priest. If he had been older I might just have begged prayers for my testicle. Being young, he'd have been embarrassed (I think). An old one would have simply got on with the praying without wondering if I was teasing. Not that I would have been teasing. This testicle is a very serious matter as far as I'm concerned. Fortunately, it also seems serious to the surgeon. Yes, indeed! I'm in the *surgical* ward. If you think this makes me nervous . . .

The surgeon is pale brown-skinned and definitely not Maltese. I guess him to be in his mid-forties. He has a drooping moustache and large brown eyes which appear doleful while he examines my testicle. I ask him where he comes from.

'Pakistan,' he tells me.

'Which part?'

'Peshawar.'

'Pathan?' My question prompts a delighted smile. Even if he is not Pathan, he is pleased to be taken for one. So he should be. He should also be amused to consider his position and my condition in relation to the past history of our two nations. The Pathans are those tall gentlemen who inhabit the North West Frontier District. This separates Pakistan from Afghanistan (the Khyber Pass) and used to be where British Military spent an uncomfortable century being separated from their balls, despite impressions you might have had from Errol Flynn movies on late night television.

I am British and I am having this conversation with the surgeon to show him how calm I am. He is having this conversation with me while holding my testicle. 'Pathan,' he agrees and smiles for the second time. 'I think we should take a look at this in the morning.'

When a real-estate agent describes a country cottage as full of quaint old-world details, you can bet your last dollar he means the beams are so low you're going to crack your head three times each run you make for the can – and there's going to be a lot of runs to the can because you are going to get amoebic dysentery from the outdated plumbing. I know about real-estate agents. I also know about surgeons. 'Look' is surgicalese for getting both hands in among the carving knives.

'Wait a minute,' I squeak (though still not actually castrated). 'That's the only one I've got.'

He checks. I'm right. One tends to accuracy on such a matter, though given the necessity, I probably would have lied! The surgeon goes into a football huddle with two other doctors, one of whom is also Pakistani but definitely not tall enough to be Pathan. The third turns out to be a Czechoslovakian who is short on English. Their graphic sign language scares the shit out of me. If my ball wasn't so tender, I'd cross my legs.

'We'll try antibiotics,' the surgeon finally tells me. I thank him. He smiles. 'Don't worry.'

'Jesus,' I mutter and close my eyes. They've got me doped

up to the eyeballs. Not that I'm complaining. It's good dope. Kind of dreamy. And an older priest has just been by. Weird how there should be all these priests in at the probable end of my sex life. There were priests in at the start of it. Or at what the priests thought was the start of it. This was back when I was an eight-year-old being educated at a Jesuit prep school. I kept rabbits. Racing from breakfast down to the hutches and back for first period left no time to get to the can. I'd sit through first period as if it were purgatory. 'Please Father, can I go pee?'

'You should have gone before class.'

'But I need to go pee.'

'Why didn't you go before class?'

'Because of my rabbits.'

'If you can't keep rabbits and also pee, then you'll have to get rid of the rabbits.'

One of these conversations was sufficient. That's the good of an expensive education; the lessons stick. I would sit through first period praying I wouldn't pee in my pants while trying to twist my dick into a knot. Finally the priest sent for me.

'You like playing with yourself,' he accused.

Note that playing *with* rather than *by* myself. The priest was new to the school. He was Irish. I presumed he was weak on grammar. Also I had learned that when a priest said you liked doing something, you said yes. When he said you didn't like doing something, you said no. Never argue. So I said, 'Yes, I like playing with myself.'

'And what do you think about when you play with yourself?'

Having no idea what he wanted me to answer, I remained dumb and looked scared.

'Do you think about other boys?' he asks with a sad sigh which suggests I probably shouldn't think about other boys.

I play safe. 'Sometimes.'

'And girls?'

'Sometimes.'

'Now you know that's wrong.'

Of course I know it's wrong! Whatever it is, if it wasn't wrong I wouldn't be summoned to his office. What's worrying me is not what it is that is wrong, but how to *admit* to whatever it is that is wrong; and I must do this fast to avoid the priest getting further irritated. Irritated Jesuits beat the shit out of small boys.

'It can ruin your whole life,' he warns.

So it is serious. A minimum of ten strokes on the ass. And that's optimistic. I hang my head and say how I know and that I'm sorry. You have to know. That is religion. KNOWING. If you don't know, then you're a sinner for doing or not doing whatever it was I had or had not done. Confused? So was I.

But not the priest. He leaned back in his chair, very solemn, and lit his pipe, while I prepared myself for the inquisition. Here it comes.

'What do you think about while you think about boys?'

Silence.

'What do you think about while you think about girls?'

Silence. To Father O'Reilly my silence is proof of stubbornness. Stubbornness is a further sin. I know this is what the good Father is thinking but what can I answer? Me who can't even guess at what I'm meant to be thinking or not thinking.

In desperation I mumble, 'Well . . .' with a guilty look at the carpet (brown so it won't show blood stains – my blood). Shuffle of the feet. 'Boys . . . ?' I try and get no response. 'Girls?'

'Yes,' says the all-knowing representative of a punitive God, and sets his pipe aside to better deal with so much sinfulness. 'I'm going to have to punish you.'

Have to! But he does. Twelve strokes on the ass. I weep. Even scream a couple of times. To which he says, 'Be a man.'

Men play with themselves. That's what I should have snapped. Except I didn't know. And I had no idea why I'd been beaten. All this playing with myself – something to do with having insufficient friends was as close as I could get. I decided to become a highly social child.

Eight years old and already I'm picked out from the mob as a potential sex maniac. That's how it started. Or that is how the priests thought it started. So maybe I should discuss all this with one these hospital priests while waiting for the

Pathan to knife off my remaining testicle. Gloomy thought Maybe I should give the priests a miss and simply ask this great looking night nurse (black hair, dark eyes sweet with love for suffering humanity) for more dope.

'Nurse . . .'

She looks, finger to her lips. Beautiful lips. 'Shhh . . .'

'Could I have a pill?'

She stoops to study my chart. I glimpse a golden shaded valley between her breasts and, naturally, a crucifix. With a faint smile which she quickly hides, she asks of this future eunuch, 'What kind of pill?'

'Something to take the pain away.'

She takes a second look at my chart while I study her face not for beauty, but in wonder at how she could be so immediately suspicious. Do I look like a dope fiend as well as a sex maniac? But then I don't look like a sex maniac – not to a nurse who has read my chart. 'You've already had four,' she whispers with a hint of accusation.

I try the truth. 'I'm scared.'

This pleases her – not that I'm scared, but that I've told the truth. She smiles at me and doesn't have to hide her smile. 'What are you writing?'

'My memoirs.' This sounds kind of final so I grin a disclaimer.

'Librium,' she suggests.

'How about something with a little more dream to it?'

She blocks her giggle with a quick frown. The frown is ineffective since we both know about the giggle. 'I'll see,' she promises and gives up on the frown.

She tiptoes down the ward as if intent on robbing a bank, rather than sneaking one illicit pill. That she should feel this guilty makes *me* feel bad.

She returns with the pill, watches while I swallow, and warns, 'I'm off tomorrow for two weeks.'

'I hope the weather stays good.'

'Thanks,' she whispers and is gone. So am I. It's a great pill. I feel happier, not only from the pill, but because she and I related, if only for two minutes.

Relating *with* rather than relating *to* is what I've been working on these past months. This is fortunate considering my present state and how my past has revolved around sex. Having sex. Other people have relationships. Not me. Or not in what seems like a long time. Except once this year, and I blew that from lack of practice. Or believe I blew it. Though there just might be a letter.

And if there is a letter? One ball is better than no balls. But what's no balls better than? That last relationship was probably my last chance and that's a drag considering how much I care and how much she cared before I blew it. This is definitely not something I can write about, or not without sneaking up on it. But at least I now admit for whom I am writing: Sister Bear – and what a crazy name for a lady.

What would Sister Bear say of my present situation?

'Serve you damn well right.'

Perhaps.

And how would she view my present thoughts on relationships?

'About Goddamned time.'

Yeah, I can see her making both these remarks, hands on her hips and a toss of her head. She is short on faith regarding my ability to relate.

Other people have relationships. Not me. Women look at me and decide, *Yeah, he'll do for now. He's a nice friendly Aquarian, he won't get too heavy, and when something better comes along he won't mind too much if I split.*

At least that's what I presume the ladies who have climbed into my bed decided about me in the last years of my marriage and the six years since my wife and I finally broke up. They have certainly acted that way. And I co-operate. A thirty-five-year-old French lady living in Paris used to accuse me along those lines.

'I could never love you,' she used to complain. 'You're too easy.'

My wife, too. 'It's not your balling other chicks,' she'd accuse, 'It's the chicks you ball. Real drags. Think of my pride.'

I did think of her pride; but I would also think of the drag's pride, all the way over in Ibiza, Spain, for a summer ball and no one available to ball her. It's not that I *want* to ball all the time. It is not that I am even that good at balling.

It's simply justice that someone should service the drags and, if no one else will . . .

We are brought up believing men want to get into every girl's panties; if a man doesn't want to get into a girl's panties, then either he's gay or there's something wrong with what's in the panties. This is a drag for ladies. It is not that they necessarily desire to get balled, but merely that they want men to want them as evidence that they are all right.

If a lady discusses how she feels rejected, then she's going to get balled, which may not be what she wants. And she is going to wonder if she's getting balled just because the guy feels guilty about having made her feel rejected; so she will *still* feel rejected. And has been balled into the bargain by someone she didn't want to ball . . . it is complicated, and possibly a little difficult to follow. Keep with these memoirs and both you and I may end up understanding. Of course, we may end up not understanding, but that, at least, is no worse than how we started out. Or how I started out.

Chapter Two

I started out on a passenger liner sailing away from a pleasant English spring towards a rainy autumn in South Africa. I was fifteen years old and fresh from my second private school (this one run by Benedictine monks) and from vacations at my parents' house in the extreme north of Scotland where there were no women except for my mother, who didn't count.

Back then, sex was what woke you up with a sore back in the middle of orgasm and forced you to quickly wipe up the mess before the sheets got stained. By the time you'd finished wiping up the mess, you'd forgotten the dream so were never certain of what fantasies you'd had. Not that I called them fantasies. I'd been taught better.

'Father, forgive me my sins.'

'*Impure thoughts?*'

'Yes, Father.'

'Tell me, my son.'

'I can't remember . . .' but made them up because otherwise I risked being refused absolution. Absolution was vital. If I remained in a state of sin, God wouldn't help me beat shit out of Patrick O'Donovan on the tennis court. It was Patrick O'Donovan's backhand service return which put me in need of God.

So I wasn't totally innocent. Innocence is not knowing about sin. I knew about sin from the day a priest terrorised our class of twelve-year-olds with the knowledge that what we called playing with ourselves was actually the sin of SELF ABUSE. This came as a shock. Perhaps it shouldn't have – or not to me – considering the beating I'd taken from the Jesuit a brief four years back. But then I was too naïve to relate the pain of twisting my prick into a knot with the quick and recently discovered pleasure of creaming in my hand.

Innocent, but not of guilt: that's how I was on that ship.

Also relieved to have quit school. The priests were history, or so I hoped

There was one available lady travelling first class. She'd been twelve years in Hollywood attempting to make it as a movie star. Her attempts involved sleeping with all sorts of men she'd have preferred not to have known.

Weird what people will do for a career. Finally she had given up to marry a South African diamond king – or maybe a prince. Fat and fifty-five was how she described him. Lots of sweat.

'If you don't grab your old age pension before you're forty, it gets hard to find one' was another of her comments. This was back in the late 1940s and a more or less normal way of female thought. Possibly it remains a normal way of thought in those circles. I've quit travelling first class so I wouldn't know. Nor do I know how come she hadn't made it as a movie star. She was beautiful enough; honey blonde, mauve eyes and sweet lips. The eyes and lips were natural, while the blonde was black if you dug deep enough . . . and what I took for joy was probably a kind of hysterical disappointment at how her life had gone.

She was to be married the day after she reached Cape Town, and was having one last ball on the ship. She balled every man in sight. Admittedly, her sight was a little restricted: first-class passengers and junior officers. One night it was my turn. Not that she picked me out of a hat or even by eye. It was simply a night when everyone else was either too drunk or on watch.

'Aren't they dreadful?' she suggested of the drunks.

I agreed, 'Dreadful,' though my answer was short on conviction. Drinking was how real men lived; or so I presumed from these first seven days of adult experience. And I wasn't a man. Each time I tried, I'd throw up, to the amusement of the other passengers.

'Quite dreadful,' she emphasised.

The light touch of her hand on my thigh thrust me drowning into the matched whirlpools of her eyes and my own youthful hypocrisy. Jesus, was I happy! While she, sympathetic mother-sister, led me to her suite where we could discuss LIFE over hot chocolate and biscuits.

I swear to God she ordered chocolate. Admittedly, she added a slug of something sweet to my cup, a magic potion which had me swooning into ready hands which did all sorts of things to my body. Things I did not at first understand. Truthfully I don't think I ever understood – not till I found myself safely back in the corridor.

Then I realised! *I'd lost my virginity and was in a state of MORTAL SIN.*

What if the ship sank before I could get to confession? The terror of it!

My tie hung from my pocket, my shirt was open and I dragged my dinner jacket along by one sleeve (those were the days of black tie obligatory for dinner in the first-class dining saloon). The ship's chief cop stood by the head of the twin stairways. Wise in wickedness, he smiled. 'That's all right, sonny. You'll feel better in the morning.'

Epitaph to my virginity! As also epitaph to my certainty in sin. How could I belive such terror could condemn me to Hell Fire Everlasting? And could Hell Fire be that much worse than that which I'd just experienced?

I stayed locked in my cabin all next morning, scared to go on deck and be seen because I must look so different. You lose your virginity and the loss shows. That's what I *thought*.

Nobody noticed the change. Not even the ex-to-be movie star who I now suspect may have been as drunk as the rest of the passengers, which was how come she'd forgotten this momentous happening. Perhaps she was simply being kind. Forgetting was definitely kind. Except I had fallen in love. Naturally. And I had some insane idea she must be pregnant. I mooned after her with my mouth gaping, ship side and shore side. I got in the same horse-drawn carriage as she and her favourite lover (ship's doctor – bastard) which must have been a drag for them as we were driven around the island of Madeira.

She shivered in the sea breeze (or at my company). I shivered with joy and gratefully draped my jacket over her shoulders, thus nearly expiring of cold over the next two hours . . . while dreaming I *would* expire, though of tuberculosis (they presumably *praying* I'd expire or, at least, get lost). I longed to die while she knelt by my bed and mopped sweat from my fevered brow with a to-be-treasured lace handkerchief.

Could this delight in self-sacrifice be mortal sin?

I tried prayer but without much confidence. There were too many childhood scenes in my head. Memory of how I had nearly lost all faith back at pre-prep the first time I'd been selected for the school team. I'd wanted to serve mass The priest had laughed. I thought about that laughter Wanting a little help in scoring runs didn't seem too weird If God wouldn't help over such a small matter, how come he would bother over a task as difficult as saving my immortal soul?

Is this how all Catholics struggle from childhood through adolescence into adult status? Or am I a freak? Certainly this shipboard seduction was an inauspicious start to a sexual career. And it was only a beginning. The career has continued right up to this hospital bed. One ball down and one to go. Definitely not auspicious. And how will Sister Bear consider my predicament?

Sex and soul – they hang together throughout my life. I keep on tripping into God at the most inopportune moments. As with the red-haired stripper from Los Angeles who hit Ibiza my first winter on the island; me at twenty-six, with my first novel published.

I saw her sway down the gangway off the Barcelona ferry. Every man in town watched her. I write of the resident *extranjeros* of course – very segregated society, the Spanish and us, back in those far off days. The Spanish had not yet discovered they could ball foreign ladies so were still into long engagements made bearable by an occasional visit to the local whorehouse. (Once they did discover, the whores were out of a job which has made for some great washerwomen along the street where I live).

Funny about that ferry boat. We would all be standing on the quay in a friendly clump till we spotted a woman on deck. Immediately we would become mortal enemies. We would shift away from each other – give ourselves space to be picked out as individuals (prime for selection), stomach in, chin up, heels together. A real meat market! Except we didn't require a butcher to lay ourselves out on the marble slab. Prime beef.

The ship came in Sunday mornings. This special Sunday, in came the red-haired stripper, a gift from God. From every stud in sight, she picked me. That I looked the most timid and was not American was probably her logic. Certainly it was not the size of my biceps nor the length of the bulge in my pants. She wasn't into sex – or not as a first objective. She was intent on writing the great American novel. She also wanted to discuss literature, though not with a compatriot or even with an expatriot compatriot. She spoke no language other than American so a Spaniard or a Frenchman promised failure . . . nor would a German suffice, even if he could speak perfect English. She was Jewish and had a heavy down on Germans. This left me.

'Hey,' she opened, 'where can I find an apartment?'

There was my studio, of course. Great view over the port. Half a double bed vacant. Electric typewriter (Olivetti). Reams of white paper. Two-metre-long desk. Even a half-finished manuscript I'd been trying to get back to since late summer when panic had first set in. Panic at what would I do for company that winter (some call it writer's block). Hunt, hunt, hunt. No one can work under such pressure. And having been published was making writing tough. Once you're an author, you've got to really write . . LITERATURE. Jesus! The strain. So you can see it wasn't sex I was seeking. Me! No, madam. What I prayed for was a muse stacked with inspiration.

Not that I could ask this lady straight over to the studio. I could spot this would be a mistake. She'd have put me down with a hammer. So, super cool (despite the strain of having my stomach pulled in), 'Easy,' I told her. 'Want a coffee first?' Grabbing up her white Samsonite and Smith Corona portable, I headed down the quay for the fisherman's bar. This bar was a sound choice. Firstly, I lived upstairs. Secondly, I was the only foreigner to whom the owner gave credit.

Being alone with her failed to help. She was too wise and too sure of her priorities.

One cup of coffee and we were hunting her an apartment.

She didn't even allow me to pick up a sweater – not that I needed the sweater. However, she didn't need a tour of my studio. It was her own place she was after. All she required was a porter and there was no room in her head for advice – not even advice about the apartment she finally chose which was out by the airport. (The noise probably made her feel at home).

I tried to tell her the walls would be damp. The walls *were* damp. So were the sheets – and I'd had a tough day. You try lugging a gas heater and four outsize butane bottles a half mile on your back and then up three flights of concrete stairs – one by one – plus two crates of bottled water because, what with writing her novel, she'd have no time to waste going to the can with Spanish tummy; she told me this. And there was I with writer's block! Terrible. I *had* to be a waste of time.

We ate at her apartment, naturally and, naturally, I did the shopping and also cooked dinner – a leg of lamb, which had been hard to find on Sunday. How was I to know she thought lamb was what you fed your enemies? A real *gigot*. Garlic. Rosemary. Thyme. Even a leaf of fresh bay which I'd snipped from a tree a mere mile and a half from her kitchen.

'Shit!' she wanted to know on finding the bay leaf. 'What's this?'

I told her. She was unimpressed. No room for bay leaves in the great American novel. Nor lamb. I should have tried for steak.

She was impatient of conversation. Soliloquy was her trip. Literary soliloquies. Judgement values from Los Angeles evening classes. This is not a put-down. She'd read everything. She used to read in between stripping. Ten minutes to shed her clothes, one hour for Henry James. I was totally ignorant in comparison. All I could do was grunt out agreement and hope the grunt sounded brighter and more masculine than I felt.

'Want to stay over?' she finally invited while I stacked the dishes. Without waiting for an answer, she headed straight to shower (I'd fixed the plug on the water heater among other chores).

Naturally I wanted to stay over, while no doubt she had

ideas of getting me into town early next morning with a more complete shopping list. But I was scared. A real red-haired American stripper possessed of large breasts and hips that swivelled her ass so much she'd have left a trail of erections down Ibiza's main street in Cornucopia mid-July while this was the vacuum of mid-December. She was *heavy*! The first truly heavy American Jewish lady I'd ever come up against and for whom I knew I was in no way equipped . . . neither in literature nor in bed.

I lay there between those cold damp sheets, my prick shrunk to a terrorised centimetre, trickles of rain leaking through the walls, her in the bathroom, the door open, and me just certain it was going to be total disaster while all the time this reading list flowed towards me. And over me. And round me. Kafka, Nietzsche, Tolstoy, Dostoevsky, Freud, Jung, Rilke . . .

'You read?' she eventually demanded. Of course she wasn't interested – but talking while under the shower was getting water in her mouth.

'A little,' I confessed, and almost added that I also wrote. But had neither time nor courage. She'd have dispatched me through the rain to fetch a copy of my one and only book, and then would have read all night just so she could tear it apart.

'Who?' she wanted to know.

'Who what?'

'Jesus!' Her soaped-up head popped around the bathroom door. Green eyes regarded me as if I were a backward eight-year-old. 'Who do you read?'

Examination time. 'Oh,' I tried, 'this and that.'

'Yeah, but who do you *like*?'

What to answer? There was I, European (sounds sexier than English), lapsed Catholic, and without one decent hang-up to my name. Or no hang-up other than my hang-up over God. Would she understand? 'Graham Greene,' I suggested tentatively.

'Who?' came back from the bathroom.

Maybe she hadn't heard.

Maybe she *had* heard.

Christ, I thought (right hand grasping at what remained

of my prick). And was suddenly in total empathy with good Saint Peter the night Christ got busted by the Roman fuzz. Saint Peter got himself crucified out of guilt. Not me, I thought, so I said again, 'Graham Greene,' in a timid mumble stacked with avenues of retreat.

'Jesus!' spluttered out from under the shower. Had she gotten soap in her eyes? No such luck. 'All that God shit,' she judged. 'Like who believes in that crap?'

There was my master written off wih complete contempt. The last few millimetres of my prick fled into the shelter of my pelvic bow as, out of the hole in my beard, issued this castrato squeak. '*I DO.*' Grabbing for my woollen shirt, I crept down the stairs with my pants in my hand.

Bless me, Graham Greene. Though weak, I did not betray you. *Nor did I get laid.* Considering my present situation, I should have regrets. But I have no regrets because, if I had gotten laid, it would have been a mess. No erection. Of this, I am sure. This is the problem with faith. One is never certain if one holds to it out of need to escape, out of actual belief, or out of guilt-ridden loyalty. My hospital bed is a bad place from which to dig too deeply – particularly as there are no more drugs coming my way to make self-examination a pleasant pastime.

So bless me, Graham Greene. Even if my loyalty was out of fear of a night's impotence, I need blessing. Also I love you for what you've done for my head. This is more than I can say for Laurence Durrell. There's a fellow writer I truly hated.

My first visit to Greece was concurrent with the third volume of the *Alexandria Quartet*. Durrell was obligatory reading for anyone into culture, which I was trying to be while attempting my first novel, for which I'd gone to Corfu to give birth (how trite can one get?).

The summer invasion was on. The entire island was spread with American college graduates preparing their doctoral theses on Durrell. Everywhere you looked, copies of *Prospero's Cell* protruded out of Levi pockets.

A group of Oxford graduates had rented a villa along the beach. They'd just finished sitting their finals and all come out with Firsts except one lady who'd had a bad experience on the telephone a week before examination time. She'd picked up the receiver to hear her boyfriend rapping with her mother in a way that made clear her boyfriend and her Mum were afternoon bedfellows. Jane, her name was. She was very bright in the head and had a lovely nature, plus a body that reminded me of a modernised Rubens. Voluptuous curves but held together.

We met at a beach barbecue on full moon. Her boyfriend, ignorant of the overhearing, struck postures on a rocky pinnacle while she swam out a little way (the better to admire him, he thought).

I didn't know who was whose boy or girlfriend, but I did admire Jane enough to swim out after her.

She lay floating on her back. Her breasts rose like volcanic islands from the waves. Divine. Or, if not divine, certainly delicious. I swam up between her legs as if it was all ME when, if you stop to think about it, it was all her. They were her legs and *she* had let them drift apart. And it was she who remained silent.

She just floated there while I did what she wanted. Then she flipped over and swam back to shore without even a thank you. This left me moderately frustrated (though the sea cooled me down) and got the boyfriend cross. He had watched, and she must have known he was watching.

They split up a day later. Getting head in the sea was probably easier for her than a face-to-face, 'Mister Sunshine, go screw my mother.'

But let us return to Laurence Durrell. There were seven copies of *Prospero's Cell* in that one villa. Gifts from mothers, aunts and good British nannies; each copy was as full of deceit as the next. A grotto Durrell found full of rubies and diamonds, we found full of bat shit and used prophylactics. Durrell wrote how the sun struck jewels out of the grotto walls. We waited all day for artistic ecstasy and all we gained was paranoia from fear the bats would get in our hair.

This was only the beginning. The following week, the bastard nearly killed me. Jane and I tracked down this icon stuck in a cave along the coast where Durrell had thrown cherries into the sea for his lady to dive for. Great description of her plucking fruit off the sea bottom with her coral lips; perfect imagery but all crap. The icon was the top of a pre-World War II biscuit tin. As for the sea, I did the diving while Jane flung the cherries (basic difference between published and unpublished writers) First dive, I nearly broke my neck. Three feet of water at the deep end.

Of course it's possible that Durrell's lady was a dwarf. And also possible that I'd picked the wrong cave and the wrong grotto out of jealousy. Naturally I was jealous. Here was I, never published, while he (son of a bitch) was selling seven copies of one poetic travel book to a household of holidaying Oxford intellectuals. I hated him.

Kazanzakis was better. He helped me dream up mystical experiences while striding the Greek mountains in an attempt to clear my head of sexually manic thoughts of Jane and the way she'd looked that night in the sea with the full moon twisting her limbs through the wavelets.

She and I met up again a month later. She wanted to travel north through Yugoslavia to check out Byzantine murals from the second Iconoclast period. I bought a car. This seemed a natural decision at the time though I've always hated driving and she didn't know how. But this was love (mine for her). Love? Well, obsessional respect for her head allied to a desperate desire to get back between her legs. I wanted to lick her all over, not just ball. Had even fantasised her coated with that mixture of butter and honey Greeks serve up for breakfast . . . and still respected her head.

Jesus! that first day in the car. She had on a short skirt. I was trapped between fantasies of her thighs and a road map marked by the Yugoslavs with a four lane motorway. The motorway was Yugoslav fantasy. All we found was a dirt track. Cart wheels and rain had stirred the track into a deep gooey swamp. On one stretch we had to hire oxen to drag us out.

We made the hotel an hour after midnight by which time Jane was too tired. So was I – though I'd have tried. All I got was a nightmare. Laurence Goddamned Durrell balling her right alongside me, his head up so I could gain full benefit of the sneer he cast my way. I woke up covered in sweat and shivering.

Jane watched me through half-open eyes.

'You let Durrell fuck you!' I accused.

He'd become so much a part of our summer, Jane was unsurprised. 'How was he?'

'Busy,' I told her. 'Small, dark and busy.'

She yawned. 'I don't like small men.' And went back to sleep. Maybe I only fantasised him as small. In recent photographs he resembles a pompous whale. So there you are, I'm still jealous. Though no longer of his sales. But that he still has two balls. Bullshit baby, it's still his sales. *Confiteor omnipotens deus.*

Chapter Three

I've had two visits this first morning of my hospital incarceration. First came the football huddle The Pathan is still setting strategy. I am sure he is a highly competent surgeon as well as an excellent father and doting husband – nor do I wish to come between man and wife – but would definitely prefer for him to fondle my testicle out of homosexual lust than out of heterosexual desire to slice it open.

If only he were pale-skinned Caucasian! If he was Caucasian I could tell him to get lost. His being Pakistani awakens the worst of my liberal guilts. Yes! even to the point of disliking to frustrate the poor man's natural longing to handle a knife.

This is a little weird considering it's my ball which is at stake. Maybe I want to lose it? A subconscious desire to get the whole sexual problem free of my life – or my life freed of sexual problems?

Could I be that crazy?

Or do I simply suspect he'll prescribe me a fabulous pharmaceutical birthday gift out of gratitude for my letting him cut?

If I let him cut . . .

We shared a quick non-medical rap this visit. 'You know Pakistan well?' he opened.

'A little,' I admit.

He makes it obvious that he's noticing my beard and how my hair curls way down over where I'd have my collar if I ever wore one. 'Peshawar?' he suggests.

What Detroit is to the automobile, Peshawar is to the hashish trade. This being a pleasant thought, I smile.

'So you liked it,' he said. The black of his moustache exaggerates how white his teeth are as he returns my smile, and he nods agreement to his next question. 'Also the mountains . . . ?'

Which is where the dope grows. 'Swatt, I agree, 'Chindit . . .'

'Kashmir?'

'Both sides.'

His smile broadens into a grin of joy heavily spiced with brigandry. No number of medical degrees could rob a Pathan of this birthright. 'Good country,' he says and pats me gently on the back. 'You travel a lot.'

'Used to,' I reply.

'Ah . . .' One eyebrow raised, he waits.

Why not? 'I got two years,' I admit.

'Bad,' he says and pats me a second time so I'll know *bad* is what happened to me rather than his judgement on what I did to earn the two years. 'We must get you well.'

'That would be nice.'

'You are very welcome,' he assures me and away he goes down the ward to gloat over his knife-work.

Ten minutes later Babette arrives. At twenty-three, she is the elder of the two French ladies who have been sailing with me these past three weeks. She is small, neat and has one of those faces which are beautiful when young but will fall to pieces by the time she's forty-five. Babette knows this and already spends a great deal of time and energy on daily maintenance: almond oil morning and evening, hairs plucked from her legs, nails immaculate . . . yes! even on a yacht.

'Hullo there,' I greet her in French, 'where's Clo?'

'We didn't want to embarrass you,' she says.

'*Embarrass* me?'

'Shh . . .' she chides. 'Don't squeak.'

'Squeak!' I squeak, 'I'm *not* squeaking.'

'Yes you are.'

Now there's a classic example of male-female conversation!

'So I'll stop.'

'Squeaking?'

I give her the victory. '*Squeaking* . . . now tell me why I should be embarrassed.'

'Two of us,' she says with a flick of her head at the rest of the patients. 'You want them to think we were too much for you?'

I growl.

Babette grins, hesitates perhaps half a second with thoughts of how I may be contagious, then brushes my unshaven cheek with her lips. '*Ça va?*'

I smile and tell her, '*Très bien*,' and how the surgeon is a good man and knows what he's doing. 'Which is just as well,' I add and she giggles while taking a nervous look at my neighbour.

This neighbour is an old man the doctors have transformed into a flower bed for growing plastic tubes. The tubes are doing fine.

Babette shivers. '*Pauvre vieux . . .*'

I feel sorrier for the priests. This shocks Babette. She's a left-wing student from Paris and threfore hates all priests on an intellectual principle she thinks she inherited from Voltaire. Most likely it's merely a prejudice she has inherited from her once-Catholic and twice-divorced mother. Not that I suggest this to Babette when she asks, '*Pourquoi?*'

'Watch them,' I say.

She does, and miraculously locks eyes with a young Franciscan for all of half a second. The Friar flickers a sheepish smile before scuttling away like a scared mouse.

'See,' I tell Babette.

She studies me like I'm crazy and says, '*Quel con!*' which translates into my being a cunt.

Calling me a cunt is not derogatory in French. It's an expression used freely whenever the speaker can't think of anything better to say. Women's Lib would disapprove. Presumably they would also disapprove the French deciding cunt is masculine. As for prick, the common terminology is *la bite*. Feminine!

Perhaps the French consider cunts to be tough and managing – masculine traits? As for pricks, are these presumed female from the way they dress themselves up in fancy erections while actually being delicate and wilting?

Accepting this obtuse sexual logic, there is still no explanation of why the French should name the South Coast of their country le Midi – The Middle!

Personally I find all this very odd considering how Goddamned arrogant the French are on the subject of their faultless Gallic logic. This is a conversation I have already had with Babette more than once, so for now I merely remark that I am not yet a cunt – though may end up one if the Pathan gets his knives into play.

She grins and says, 'For all the good you've been . . .'

'I tried.'

'*Some* try,' she mocks and gives me a second kiss. 'Come visit us in Paris and we can try all over – hopefully with more success.'

'My pleasure . . .' If I end up trans-sexualised, she can start me off on her boyfriends. 'You play bait.'

'For you?' Her hair flows out like a shampoo advertisement. 'You're too old to change sex.'

I looked pained. 'So I've lost my looks?'

'What looks?'

'Nice,' I complain. 'I hoped you'd come by to cheer me up.'

'At least I brought you a present,' she says and dips into her purse for a flat parcel which has to be a book. She tries to hide her smile – too late – and there's no disguising the mischief in her eyes.

Why give her the pleasure, I decide, and say, 'Thanks,' as I lay the package carefully on my bedside table.

Babette looks disappointed. 'You're not going to open it?'

'Later,' I tell her.

'Coward!'

I grin. 'Don't squeak.'

Babette admits defeat. '*Ta gueule*,' she retorts, '. . . anyway it was a good holiday.'

'For me, too,' I assure her. 'If not Paris, maybe Ibiza next summer?'

'*Peut-être* . . .' She brushes my cheek good-bye. 'You'll be all right?'

'*D'accord* . . .' She gives one of those neat little Gallic shrugs. '*A bientôt*.'

'*J'espère*,' I say and watch her deliberately sway her ass down the length of the ward. She has trim ankles and beautiful calves. She also has a nice head even if her humour can be a little tough.

As she exits, one of my fellow patients lets go a moan of frustrated lechery and is immediately rewarded with a scowl from our ward's portly matron. Serves him right, I think, and reach for Babette's gift. I slit the wrapping with my thumbnail and draw out a book. Next moment I'm glaring down the ward. Bitch! There she is peeping around the door with an angelic smile curling her lips.

'*Connasse!*' I call.

She gives me a finger. That the victory is hers is my fault. All personal information is legitimate weaponry in the battle of the sexes. As for Babette's gift . . .

Goddamned Wallace, him again!

Gleefully I note his book has been remaindered at half-price. Wallace smiles at me off the back cover. All that charm! All those teeth! Two female bodies in his bed concurrently; that was his obsession back when I knew him on Ibiza. He didn't give a shit *what* women, just so long as neither was his current wife.

One summer he discovered two Jewish early twenties, fresh out of Brooklyn and direct off the Barcelona ferry. Sarah and Susan. Sarah was short and a little dumpy. Susan was tall and was twin to a Soviet PR man's fantasy of Mother Russia as a young woman: high cheek bones, flared nose, huge eyes and a mouth so damned generous you risked drowning in it.

They intended staying a week until my rat buddy enticed them into renting the one-room apartment below his studio on the pretext that they could type up the final draft of his new novel as a summer job. It wasn't a new novel. It was a six-year-old reject. He wasn't even *working* that summer.

IRS, hear me! If he wrote off that typing as a legitimate expense, you should sue the son of a bitch.

I tell you this, and I also tell you that I loved him. He helped me edit my first novel. I dedicated it to him and he still betrayed me. Betrayed my love for Mother Russia, Susan. She was everything I dreamed of that summer – total wisdom and total beauty. She'd leaped in one side of the New York drug scene and was out the other side by the age of sixteen, while here I was at thirty-something and all I'd managed to get into was a little grass and three mescalin trips.

Mescalin was legal – this was that far back! We used to write off to the pharmaceutical company. Back would come this cute wooden box with glass phials of pure crystal bedded down in the finest shavings. A questionnaire came with the box. Serious stuff:

> Did you see God?
> What colour was he?
> What colour were you?
> Which way did the blood circulate in your skull?

How could you *not* see God with a questionnaire like this? We took mescalin as if it were the Holy Sacrament out on Big J's terrace an hour before sunset so we'd get joy from the colours before going inside to meet God in the dark. Big J would have one candle in his apartment, Japanese temple music on the Sony tape-deck and a dozen sticks of incense perfuming the innocent sea air. He was our Guru that year. He'd just had his first pair of contact lenses fitted and had discovered the world. All six-foot seven of him. A shambling giant is how I remember him from those days. There he'd be, his round head cocked over a little to the left so he could see better, lank hair cut Joan of Arc fashion and his mouth always part open in permanent astonishment at how fucking *beautiful* everything was now that he could actually make out where the hell he was going, which he hadn't been able to do from behind the pebble lens magnifying glasses he'd worn the first forty years of his life.

He lost one of his new eyes while rapping seductive spiritual wisdom to a big-breasted Dutch girl up on the roof one night. Not that she needed seducing. But Big J had to interrupt himself and get down on his knees with a cigarette lighter. Ten minutes hunting his lens and the Dutch lady had given up on the Guru and was balling one of his disciples. This was cruel considering how much sincerity and effort Big J had put into his rap. But then he was new to the game . . .

And I must get back to the tale of Mother Russia, Susan . . .

I first met her up in my ex-friend, the writer's studio. I'd come visiting with tales of my most recent mystical experience. Susan let me in. Wallace was out. So I told Susan.

Then Susan *told* me.

Jesus! I sat at her feet for two hours and could have gone on sitting there for the rest of my life. Here was a lady who viewed tripping as casually as my mother views drinking tea (China and no sugar, please). She'd done so much acid that she spent the winter months of her fifteenth year rapping bi-weekly to an analyst on the problems she was having in recognising physical frontiers between her body and his couch. Six months later she was balling a black coke dealer on top of the beer crates in the cellar of his favourite bar because, if his steady had spotted them, she'd have sliced Susan's tits off.

'Not that I had much,' Susan mused while I sat mesmerised.

There I was on a Mediterranean island living with delusions of mystical adventure, two children and one wife. THREE measly mescalin trips and I'd thought myself hip! We'd *all* thought ourselves hip! Big J included; Big J who had been reading to us just that morning from Aldous Huxley's *The Doors of Perception.* Huxley recounting how he'd perceived the possibility of oneness through Van Gogh's painting of a kitchen chair. *Perceived* the oneness. Susan *was* the Goddamned oneness.

And, if we were square, what about my ex-friend Wallace, the writer? He didn't even smoke, and here he was deciding what pages of a six-year-old manuscript to give Susan and Sarah to type on his IBM while he planned methods of enticing them into his bed.

Entice my Priestess! I was ashamed to be sitting at her feet. I should be kneeling.

An hour later, I was kneeling, but in the downstairs apartment. The rewards of worship! Priestess, handmaiden and acolite all naked on two mattresses dragged out into the centre of the room, Susan, Sarah and me, while that chauvinist joke upstairs was plotting how to get into them together. Together! There wasn't a heartbeat they didn't share. And for one whole month they allowed me to share their sharing.

The three of us planned a trip to Israel for that autumn I flew up to London to fetch my VW bus. When I got oack, their apartment had been re-let to an elderly Finnish couple. Panicked, I charged upstairs to beg news from my fellow writer.

'Susan,' I gasped, 'Sarah – where are they?'

'Split,' he said.

I collapsed on to the bed on which he'd plotted to ball them.

'Split?'

'Right,' he told me and dug a couple of beers out of the refrigerator.

'Jesus!' My hands were shaking so badly I had to gulp or spill beer on the bed cover. 'Why?'

'My responsibility,' he stated with pride. 'I got rid of them. Cheap chicks like that . . .' He shrugged contemptuously. 'Not worth busting up a marriage over.'

'Cheap chicks . . .' I was too broken-hearted and bewildered to get uptight. So they had finally balled him while I was away. I wasn't jealous. No lady is my property, and certainly not two ladies. But, Lord, why did they have to split? Sick in the belly, I gaped at him like a beat-up basset hound. Was he that scared of his wife?

'I knew it was the right thing to do,' he said. 'Your old lady's a friend of ours.'

'*My* old lady . . . ?' It took a good ten seconds for my mind to work. Then I freaked. '*Shit*,' I shrieked, and hurled my beer can at his head. The can missed. It struck the wall, fell back on to his desk and spurted beer all over the manuscript he'd had Susan and Sarah type. Even broken-hearted and crazy mad, I was still a writer, and manuscripts are sacred, right? I grabbed for a cloth.

Wallace grinned. 'Don't bother . . .' that was when I learned that the novel was a six-year-old wash-out.

'Mother-fucker,' I cursed. If he'd stood up, I'd have hit him. As it was, I had to wait three years for revenge; by which time my one and only marriage had ended while Wallace was two years into his fifth.

Wallace collected two ladies at a New York luncheon. He was over there with his new wife for the publication of his latest novel. One of the ladies was his publisher's wife, which makes Wallace either brave or stupid – more likely, both. The other lady was a music mogul's daughter, Laura. A strange lady. She'd been on the coast modelling nude in a photographic studio for sad gentlemen equipped with rented Yashica Instamatics – not for the bread (though she did get paid) – but because she got off on getting the sad gentlemen off in their pants. A complicated kind of double reverse voyeurism, I thought at first, but later concluded it was merely the extension of a Jewish mother's generous nature.

Anyway, Wallace's wife stalked into their Chelsea Hotel rendezvous before Wallace had time to get either lady into bed. 'Yeah, well,' was all he had time to tell them, 'if you're ever in Ibiza . . .'

He hoped this invitation would bring the ladies back to the Chelsea at a more auspicious time. Instead they came to see him in Ibiza the following August. Their arrival was not exactly opportune. He was already putting up his new wife's ex-husband, the ex-husband's new wife and seven children of various ages from so many marriages I won't even attempt to explain.

Wallace told his wife, 'Look, we have to do something. How about I lend them my studio?'

To which his wife smiled sweetly. 'But *darling*, it's so *small*. And Fran *is* married to your publisher. How about asking Tobias to put them up?'

'Are you crazy?' Wallace said. 'We can't impose on Tobias.'

'Bullshit,' said his wife, and fed the two ladies an outsize martini before stacking them into her 2CV Citroen.

I was living out in the country then. Nice house. Lots of rooms. Even a swimming pool. It was the house where my wife and I were going to make our marriage work. We should have tried relating instead. But, at least building a house is better than starting a new baby, which is what a lot of couples despair their way into as a last resort. You can sell a house.

I was down by the pool tanning my ass when the three ladies arrived. Wallace's wife said, 'Hi, Tobias, I've brought you two house guests.'

It's difficult to look suave while grabbing for a towel I did my best. 'Great.'

Giggling, the three ladies came down the stone steps to the pool. Wallace's wife embraced me so she could get her lips close to my ear. 'Revenge for Sarah and Susan,' she whispered and, out loud, 'Laura, Fran – meet Tobias.'

'Hi,' we all said.

'Great looking water,' Laura added and yanked her dress off.

Wallace's wife grinned. 'I have to get back – all right if I leave their bags?'

'Sure,' I told her. 'We'll drag them in later.'

We had a swim before going up to the kitchen for a beer. Laura, the music mogul's daughter, swam naked while the publisher's wife kept on her pants and a bra. They were both Capricorns and had had their thirtieth birthday that January. We rapped a while down by the pool. Fran was small, pretty rather than beautiful, and very bright. She collected university degrees as a hobby. Laura was also bright but didn't bother with degrees. She collected orgasms as a hobby. Male orgasms. She didn't seem to be much interested in her own except as a matter of public record. Of course, I found out all this later.

I showed them around the house. There were five bedrooms for them to choose from. We came to mine last because it was at the end of its own staircase off the *entrada* (the useless formal room that all Ibicenco houses possess). Laura gave my room the once over, checked the bathroom and said, 'Nice, I'll fetch my bag.'

I said, 'Oh . . .' and looked at Fran.

Fran chose the small room directly below. She slept there the first night. The second night she came knocking on our door at two o'clock in the morning. 'There's something moving around,' she said.

'Something big?' I asked.

She tried to smile but only achieved a nervous grimace. 'I don't know.'

'I'll go check,' I said and left her sitting on the bed with Laura.

I scouted out the ground floor and had a quick look along the cloister. Nothing. 'Probably a rat,' I suggested on returning to my own room. This was a mistake. Fran lived on the fourteenth floor of an Upper East Side condominium where the only livestock were Pekinese, Shiatzu and pedigreed Siamese.

She clutched at Laura's hand, big eyes wide and her lower lip sucked in. 'Can I sleep with you?'

The bed was big enough, though it sagged somewhat with the extra weight. Also, Fran was a little strange. She always wore a nightdress – not that wearing a nightdress is odd in itself – but it did seem slightly eccentric to wear diaphonous blue nylon for two weeks of August heat while sharing a bed with two people sexually into each other.

Fran was a nice lady and certainly not shy. She used to giggle each time she found I had an erection. But she never took part herself or even watched. It felt weird having her there beside us while we balled – not unpleasant, but a little like having an aged Baptist housekeeper run blue movies through the projector while you play games with your latest lover.

Her being in bed with us also had an effect on Laura. When Laura and I were alone, all Laura wanted was to give me head. With Fran alongside us, she wanted me to ball her and would screech out all these orgasms she was having, except I don't believe she was having *any* orgasms. Not that I didn't try. To the contrary, I worked my tongue and penis to the metaphoric bone and we bounced hell out of the bed. By the time they left, the mattress resembled a loosely strung Mexican hammock.

I guessed Laura was demonstrating how she might not have a nice straight publisher husband, two kids and a summer house in the Hamptons, but she *was* having fun and ecstasy. It would have been nice to rap this out with her, but sex is a delicate subject.

Equally, non-communication had wrecked my marriage. Hadn't I grown in maturity?

Of course I had, I decided, while basking in the sun one

siesta hour. I peeked at Laura. She lay right side up on an air-mattress in the centre of the pool. The undersides of her breasts were getting a little pink from the sun – her problem. Mine was how to get the conversation started.

What are you, I sneered at myself, *a coward?*

Yes.

So be a man.

Huh?

Shit! Just this once.

Okay, I agreed, *just this once*, and strode around to the deep end to prove myself. In I dived and swam up to the air-mattress.

'Hey.'

'Hey, yourself,' Laura remarked with a lazy grin. 'You're rocking my boat.'

Great beginning! 'Having fun?' I asked.

'Want proof?'

'Yeah well . . .' and I tried to shrug which only served to get water in my mouth. 'I was thinking . . .'

'In this heat?'

'Jesus!'

'He walked,' Laura cracked while flicking spray off her belly. 'That's what the Good Book says.' She rolled her head sideways and opened her eyes so I could see she was not ready for a heavy conversation. 'Want to fetch me a drink?'

'Delighted,' I assured her and split for the kitchen.

Wallace drove up to find me chiselling ice cubes out of the freezer. His arrival was no surprise. He'd visited every day of Fran and Laura's vacation, much to their amusement. I was embarrassed for him. Curious that it never struck him that the two ladies could be allied to his current wife . . . but then he didn't know shit about women. He wasn't interested. All he was into was satisfying his ego. Whereas I . . .

'Hi,' he greeted me. 'How are the girls?'

'Fine,' I said. 'Want a drink?'

'So where are they?' he asked while helping himself to a beer.

'Laura's in the pool,' I said. 'Fran's having a siesta.'

He winked. 'So maybe I'll go visit with Fran.'

'Cool with me,' I told him and went back down to the

pool with a vodka tonic for Laura.

Two minutes later Fran stuck her head out of the bedroom window. 'Hey,' she called, 'guess who's here?'

'Wallace!' Laura shrieked.

'Right,' carolled Fran. 'I think he wants to discuss *literature*.'

'Bring him on down.' What a couple of wicked ladies! The poor bastard was only obeying a childhood indoctrination pattern. This is what I thought as Laura grabbed my head down between her thighs for propaganda. It was a good place for my face to hide.

'Hi,' Laura greeted him. 'You look like a hound who's forgotten where he's buried his favourite bone.'

'Yeah . . .' This from Wallace. Even with my eyes buried I could sense his uncertainty. 'Mind if I join you?'

'Come right on in,' Laura purred.

Wallace cheered up. I peeked out to see him dragging off his clothes. Fran was naked for the first time since she'd been at the house. Definitely heavy, I decided, and ducked back down into security as Fran dived in.

Wallace followed. 'Whoopee!' he yelled like a kid on a toboggan. The poor bastard didn't know how steep the slope was. Splash, splash and he was half on to the air-mattress with his knee thudding my skull.

'Jesus *God*, Wallace,' Laura snapped, 'what in hell do you think you're doing?' Her tone cut the pool temperature by five degrees.

'What . . . ?' Wallace stuttered and his knee quit my head.

'Do you think you're doing?' Laura prompted.

'When I tell Harold!' Fran cut in.

'Hey,' Wallace protested, 'I mean . . .'

'We can *see* what you mean,' shot Fran.

I looked. There was sad Wallace attempting to hide a ten-inch erection behind one hand while paddling to safety with the other. That finished Wallace, and the following night almost saw the end of Laura.

Big J the Guru dropped by for dinner along with his wife, Elizabeth. After dinner, we headed upstairs to the living-room with what remained of the wine and some fair quality Lebanese hashish that Big J produced. I had the living-room furnished with rugs I'd bought out East and a bunch of floor cushions. Sprawled out, we could see the full moon through the three arched windows. Maybe the full moon was why I chose a tape of Gregorian chant. It was an odd choice, given hindsight.

My head rested on Elizabeth's lap. The Guru's wife is that type of lady: a combination of mother-comfort and wisdom plus classic black-haired beauty traced with great little undertones of sensual invitation that you don't even notice till totally absorbed . . . not that we were thinking of sex.

I recall reclining there, calm and happy to be in my own home with a group of people I really liked, and happy that these two New York ladies were so obviously having a fine break from the city. A very relaxed evening.

Until Big J suddenly announced, 'Shit, I've got dust in my lenses,' and took them out. Without cleaning them, he tucked them away in their neat little case and remarked, 'Summer, there's always this damn dust.'

This may sound an innocuous statement to anyone ignorant of Big J and his experience on the roof terrace with the big-breasted Dutch lady who deserted him for one of his disciples. His wife and I knew the shedding of his lenses as a dreaded warning. Big J was on the sex path.

Elizabeth's right thigh developed a tic against my cheek while I thought *Oh my God* and studied our Guru. He *looked* calm enough. Maybe it *was* dust . . .

Anxious voiced, 'Fill a pipe,' I urged Fran and dug a quarter ounce of prime black Afghani out of my pocket. Get enough strong dope into Big J and he might stay cool.

Laura knew nothing of Big J. Relaxed and contented, she manoeuvred the Moroccan *julahba* I wore up a few feet so she could get on with her favourite pastime. Elizabeth's thigh gave a second twitch while I watched the Guru. Fortunately, he had the pipe in his mouth and his head back against a paisley cushion. He appeared lost in saintly meditation. Perhaps we were safe, I thought, and allowed Laura's mouth to draw me free of anxiety. 'Just perfect,' I murmured.

And right then our friendly neighbourhood Guru let out his war cry. 'What we need around here is an orgy!'

This was strange wording considering what seemed to be getting under way without any need for words – except it wasn't an orgy, but simply some pleasantly calm after-dinner sexual pleasure you might compare to the way the upper-class British used to circulate the port.

However, we should remember that Big J minus lenses couldn't spot a pregnant elephant at twenty yards. Let alone the few inches of tender penis Laura had in her mouth. Nor that my hands had disappeared under the lady Guru's skirt to roughly where my head was resting . . . all of which impelled Fran to giggle. Her giggle sounded like an invitation to Big J.

'Yeah, an orgy!' he confirmed and leapt on top of us. Six foot seven of him, two hundred and twenty pounds and size fourteen boots.

That ended the evening's entertainment. Not only did I lose my erection, I nearly lost my penis along with my treasured lone testicle. As for Laura, she was fortunate to keep her teeth and avoid concussion.

'Jim!' his wife yelped as he pitched over me with such force that his skull knocked the wind out of her lungs.

'Jesus!' I squeaked with his knee sliding off Laura's skull and into my crotch.

'Christ,' groaned Laura with one hand to her scalp to check for a fracture.

Even Fran stopped giggling. She raced downstairs to fetch ice for Laura's head and fresh steak for Laura's right eye. That eye was still black and swollen five days later when Wallace drove by at his wife's command to take my two house guests to the airport.

Despite her eye, Laura swore she'd had a great vacation. So did Fran, while I certainly enjoyed their company. As for Big J . .

Chapter Four

Big J, the involuntary near-castrator Guru, had lumbered through my sex life once before. It was during the time my wife, Joan, and I had an apartment in the Old City of Ibiza and were suffering our first try at separation. Joan had taken the children to visit her parents in England, leaving me loose in mid-July.

She'd been gone one week when I met a lady at Pasha's Disco. The hour was well past midnight and we danced one set before the lady announced her feet hurt. 'Why don't we go to your place?' she proposed.

Surprise had me answering, 'Why not?'

Now it was morning and I lay beside her wondering what her name might be. Names are unimportant in the build-up to balling. It's all, 'Hey . . . !' 'Wow . . . !' 'Jesus!'

Mornings are different. Calling each other *Honey* or *Darling* across the breakfast table suggests you're going to spend the day together, which may not be what either of you want except you're too weary to oppose the concept.

Morning: my right arm is numb. This is a product of instant romance. The lady falls asleep cradled in the man's arms in mutual pretence at deep affection. This is nice for the lady if she can stand the sweat but is hell for the man because the weight of the lady's head on his bicep cuts off the blood supply.

And there is also the problem presented by the erection a full bladder has produced. Shifting my arm may awaken the lady before I can get to the can: in which case we'll be forced to acknowledge the erection out of mutual politeness.

I ease my head over to see how she looks: black hair, a small nose peeping out from the flowing undergrowth, and her mouth is open. Perhaps snoring is an exaggeration, but she is definitely breathing heavier than the Sleeping Beauty.

My wife tells me I snore if I sleep on my back. She also says a kick in the ribs shuts my mouth. This is all right for marrieds, but you can't boot a lady whose name you don't know, even if she is in your bed.

Fortunately the doorbell comes to the rescue. I slide my arm free, drape a towel around my waist and set off for the door, whirling my arm in hope that the blood will return. It is a glass door and I can see two young ladies standing outside with bright-blue back-packs stacked at their feet. They are blonde, tanned and exceptionally fit-looking. They have snubbed noses, freckles and are total strangers to my memory banks.

'Exercising?' asks the taller lady.

'Circulation problem,' I explain and stop whirling my arm. 'Come on in.'

'Thanks,' says the shorter of the two. They drag their back-packs through the door and dump them on the pine dining table. 'Wow . . ' says Shorty as she checks out the open-plan living-room, 'out of sight.'

This is a compliment I am too confused to appreciate. Shorty decides to clarify the situation. 'We met this friend of yours on the train,' she says. 'He said we should visit.'

'Kind of grey-haired,' says the tall one. 'Neat-looking.'

'Talked yachts?'

'Right!' They grin as if we've solved the source of gravity.

I merely nod. 'Fantasy Pat.'

'*Fantasy?*' This comes from the tall one, though they both look uncertain.

'That's what we call him,' I say and add, 'Hi,' with what I hope is a winning smile for the lady from my bed who stumbles bleary-eyed into view.

The lady from my bed fails to return my smile. Instead she gives the two newcomers a look that says they are plague carriers. 'Who the hell are these?'

'I don't know,' I say.

'So how come they have back-packs?' demands the lady.

'A friend sent them,' I say. My reply lacks conviction for anyone unused to Ibiza life.

'So you run a hotel?' Her lip curls. '. . . or a whorehouse?'

I swallow twice before managing a defensive, 'Hey . . .'

She snaps, 'Hey yourself,' and heads for the bedroom with

her ass held tight as a budding stormtrooper's.

The tall newcomer says, 'Wow,' and throws me a sweetly forgiving smile.

I wonder what I've done that needs forgiveness.

She says, 'Maybe we're a little early.'

I say, 'Well . . .' You know? I mean this is 7.30 a.m. and I am suffering acute caffeine deficiency. I flip my hands. A whale stranded on a beach would appear more effective. 'Give me five minutes,' I say. Back in the bedroom I find my overnight guest dragging her pants on so fast she has both feet stuck in the same leg.

I say, 'You've got both feet stuck in the same leg.'

She says, 'Shit!'

I say, 'Yeah,' and then, 'Well,' and, after a good minute's deep thought, 'Look . . .'

She has her T-shirt over her head. The shirt has snagged an earring. 'How the fuck can I look?' bursts through the thin cotton.

Her head comes clear.

I wish it hadn't.

'So what are you?' she demands. 'Some kind of island stud?'

'Now, wait a minute,' I say.

'What the fuck for?' she snaps.

So I go hide in the shower. I stay in the shower till the hot water runs cold. I come out of the shower, dressed in a towel, and find the lady of the night has vanished. Not so the new arrivals. They have occupied the kitchen.

'Hope you don't mind?' says the taller one. She is not referring to the lady's vanishing trick but to having made coffee.

I say, 'Be my guest,' and lunge at a steaming mug. The first gulp untangles my mind sufficiently for me to take in how my guests look. How they look is clean, fresh, healthy, innocent and in need of curled plaits, a Bible class and blue gingham pinafores. This comes from their Nevada upbringing, I discover. I guess them to be nineteen or twenty – certainly not older. I figure perhaps I should put on some pants.

I feel safer dressed, and they've cooked eggs and bacon.

'Is it all right if we stay a week?' the tall one asks.

'Fine with me,' I reply through a mouthful of buttered toast.

'We've been in Europe ten days,' Shorty says like this is an event. It is to her, but I have an appointment for tennis in fifteen minutes.

'Look,' I say, 'the door's never locked and I'll see you this evening.' With this I head for the door leaving them looking hurt . . . but what can they expect? Am I supposed to change my life pattern for Fantasy Pat? Maybe he thinks he's rewarding me for five years of married life.

After tennis it's the beach till dusk, then back up to the apartment to find the two gymnasts dressed and ready to go out on the town. The tall one says it's her birthday (twentieth) so I give up a dinner invitation in order to feed them at Vincent Petit's, the only good restaurant in town.

We eat *moules farcies* coated in garlic, a fine *gigot* and chocolate mousse. Three bottles of champagne loosen us up. I even get to learn their names – Louise and Betsy. Betsy is the short one.

By the time we reach coffee and cognac, the conversation has become very relaxed or very uptight, depending on your point of view. 'How does it feel to have two chicks?' they ask and giggle all over the table.

This embarrasses the shit out of me considering I'm known to everyone in the restaurant. However, I smile and say, 'Just great.'

So it goes on . . . and is still going on when we get back home which is straight after dinner despite my invitation to go dance.

They are not interested in dancing. They are interested in Adventure. I can recognise this. It does not make me happy. What worries me is the certainty that this is their first sortie into this kind of trip – though they may have messed about with each other the occasional snowed-in winter's afternoon on the couch while listening to Frank Sinatra.

Back at the apartment, Louise and I seat ourselves in front of the empty fireplace while Betsy disappears to change out of her pink slacks which have gotten too tight from all she's eaten (so she says). This leaves Louise and I to neck. Betsy returns draped in a bath towel. She slumps down on the settee so I'm the filling in a flesh sandwich and she giggles, '*That's* better.'

The towel falls open so we can see all of her legs. This disturbs her friend who says, 'Why don't we go out to the patio so we can see the stars?'

There's a big sun mattress by the patio fountain. We lounge on the mattress, me still in the middle and feeling a little silly. They have decided we are going to do a threesome, but they haven't bothered to ask if that's what I want. They *know* it's what I want. *All* men want to be part of a threesome. There's some truth in this, but a man likes to have a say in *which* threesome. Also, though they have *decided* on a threesome, I doubt if this is what they *really* WANT.

These thoughts have me trying to play the scene light because if we do get into it, I want them to accept that it was their trip and their decision. And then Betsy in her bath towel flips water out of the fountain at Louise.

'Shit,' squeals Louise, 'you've soaked my dress.' Ten drops of water is excuse enough for Louise to yank her dress over her head. She is wearing those white cotton underclothes my sister would have worn back in the early fifties if I'd had a sister and if she had been fifteen years old and a hockey player. Fortunately, Louise has a beautiful body from so much exercise, which makes up for the underclothes.

Betsy giggles and offers her towel.

Louise accepts because the towel is already in her hands . . . fast lady, this Betsy! She also has a beautifully muscled body. I am impressed but stay cool while longing for a joint. The reason I don't roll a joint is for fear that my guests (guests?) will claim they've been drugged. Instead I suggest more champagne.

'Great idea,' says Betsy, and is off to the refrigerator.

Louise smiles at me and opens her arms.

I accept.

'Don't worry about me,' says Betsy on her return.

Louise doesn't, but I do, because I know Goddamned well Betsy is counting off the minutes to make sure she gets fair share of the eats. See? They aren't doing this together. They are competing. What's more, they are going to spend the next three years back in Nevada dissecting each second of this experience and then will never discuss it ever again because they will both be married to nice young men with nice houses in a nice suburb of their nice little town and have two nice children each . . . they will also hardly ever talk to each other because each will have taken comfort in blaming the other for this terrible lapse that happened back in Ibiza one July night with the stars shining down.

Knowing all this fails to put me in a romantic mood. Not even the stars help – nor the fountain spattering gently into the pool filled with my eldest son's goldfish. Shit! I think and decide on going to bed.

The ladies follow me without even an If you don't mind?

I should have stayed out on the sun mattress. The previous night it had been one head and one numbed arm. Now I've got two heads and a naked leg spread over me from each side. I also have an erection which is obvious to the ladies. If this continues, I'm going to get a Goddamned awful pain in my testicle. I have to do something – but what? Or, more accurately, to whom? The puzzle is too complicated. 'Look,' I propose, 'Why don't we take time out to consider?'

Two interrogative grunts are my answer. Not helpful!

'All this booze we've drunk,' I tell them, 'I'm not going to be much good.' This lets me out and lets them out.

They giggle and say, 'Yes . . .' and I didn't really think, did I?

Like hell I didn't! but am too relieved to enter an argument on honesty. 'Fine,' I say and add a good-night except it's soon clear I have no hope of sleep because my arms *are* numb and my ball *does* hurt. Also the big lady is already snoring. I slide my arm free of her head and use my ass to gentle her over on to her side. The snoring stops.

'Clever,' whispers Betsy.

'Yeah,' I answer and slip a hand between her legs.

She murmurs, 'Uhmmm . . .' and returns the compliment.

Five minutes later we are balling. Betsy has the gymnastic ability to keep her feet flat on the mattress beneath her ass so she's beating up at me like a steamhammer.

No lady can remain asleep alongside a steamhammer . . .

particularly when the hammer is blowing its safety valve. Unfortunately, neither Betsy nor I have brakes, so Louise is too late to take part. Nor does she want to watch. However, she does make her presence felt with a disgusted heave of her butt. I notice this. Betsy doesn't. Betsy is far gone. A weird noise escapes her nostrils . . . a kind of non-stop keening which reminds me of an Irish wake I once attended in County Mayo.

A wake is not the ideal memory for an approach to orgasm. Not that the memory stops me, but I do have it in my head . . . the way this nice old priest had looked as he consoled the women in between slipping outside for a glass of Irish malt with the men. A priest in the head is definitely a downer. Jesus! I think, either I get him out of my skull or lose my erection. I slam on the accelerator and come which is all right because Betsy has already done so twice despite congress orgasms being rare and out of fashion. That's Nevada for you!

I fall off only to discover my problem is not a priest in he head but that Louise is weeping . . . not real loud, but in real misery. I abandon Betsy to her supposed contentment and roll over to whisper something reassuring. This brings the saintly old priest back into play. 'There, there, Mrs O'Flaherty . . .'

Then I realise that Betsy is also weeping.

So I ask what the hell *she's* upset over.

She sobs, 'You never wanted me – you wanted Louise.'

Truth would have had me answering that I had mainly wanted to relieve a pain in my ball. I roll back to Betsy, kiss her and whisper, 'You're crazy.'

This upsets Louise. And now I'm upset. I am not that great a lover. Keeping one lady satisfied is tough; two is out of the question, unless the two ladies love and dig each other. These two are already starting to hate each other. Their tears leaking into my mouth give me a thirst and the Irish priest refuses to get out of my head. He seems to be laughing at me.

Thank God I hadn't yet met Sister Bear. She would have joined the priest in my head with a mocking, 'Those who live by the prick . . .'

Should I have announced tne priest's presence to Louise

and Betsy? Their knowing a priest was in the bed might have been a comfort to them. Maybe he could have helped me rid Louise of the feeling that I was rejecting her [illegible] doubt. There was only one reassurance she would accept.

So why didn't I get on with the job?

The answer lies in the mystery of the male erection. Have you ever met a lady who's read up on that subject? I haven't even seen a book which deals with it. There are best-selling paperbacks on the female orgasm and how it functions . . . but male erection? Certainly two Nevada gymnasts weeping their eyes out in my bed were not going to understand.

I tried giving head but this didn't satisfy Louise. She got my penis or I got her tears – while my eating Louise set Betsy back into her plaintiff role.

You try whispering condolences to one lady while you've got a mouthful of her friend. I'd about given up when the mystery of resurrection occurred. Lord Help Me, I prayed, embraced Betsy with tenderness in hope of damming her sorrow and immediately switched to Louise. Congress took place and continued for a good sixty seconds before Betsy became aware of what Louise and I were up to.

'Oh,' she wailed.

'Shhh . . .' I whisper and attempt to kiss her while still humping Louise.

This pisses off Louise.

'Hey,' I implore, 'we're getting it *on*.'

To which Louise sobs, 'No, we're not.'

'Yes we are.' *But we aren't.* The resurrection has gone limp.

'You don't love me,' weeps Louise.

Who's been discussing LOVE?

'Sorry,' I murmur and flee for the bathroom. At least this scene is keeping me clean what with running the shower tank dry for the second time in less than a day. Unfortunately, the cold water shrinks my penis into a quarter-inch insult to any lady.

Tip-toeing back, I discover the ladies resting hostile spine to hostile spine and separated by the maximum stretch of white-sheeted no-man's land. We are in for trench warfare. Courage lost, I creep off to the spare room where they have their back-packs stacked on the twin beds. But I know this won't help. The spare room may be a safe retreat for a one-night calamity, but it's useless against two ladies dug into my home for a week.

Most of this is that Irish priest's fault, I decide (though he may well be a holy man and was great on the whiskey). This leads me to considering that religion may be my only hope . . though introducing it rather than taking to it.

I drag on pants, shirt and a pair of shoes and slink out of the apartment and over the hill through the scary tunnel that pierces the fortress walls of the Old City of Ibiza. There are no lights in the tunnel but lots of phantoms. Only desperation would drive me this route on a dark night.

Big J agrees, because three o'clock in the morning is not a normal hour to receive callers - not even for Gurus. Fortunately he's home and is alone. This improves my spirits. 'Hi,' I start.

Big J responds, 'Huh?' with a few blinks which warn me he doesn't have his eyes fitted. Towering naked out of his doorway, he appears definitely unfriendly. Most of Big J's visitors at this hour are freaked-out junkies desperate to borrow bread for one last fix before they straighten out.

'Just this one time, Big J,' they plead, 'and I swear to God . . .' except it's been three times already this month which is the drag with junkies and really messes Big J's head as he can never decide which he hates most: the folk with the habits or being hit on for cash. As a combination they're purest poison.

I wish he had his eyes in. It feels crazy saying, *Hi Big J, this is Tobias*, when his head is only two feet from mine. Necessity being the master of men, I do say, 'Hi Big J, this is Tobias.' I am hopeful that my not being a junkie will lighten the atmosphere. 'Look, Big J, I have this problem . . .'

Big J lurches back on his heels. With this much urgency, I have to be about to hit him for a minimum of ten thousand pesetas. 'At three o'clock in the Goddamned morning, you'd *better* have a problem.'

I say, 'Yeah, well I have these two ladies in my bed.'

This shakes our Guru. 'Problem? Jesus!'

I waste a smile which he can't see and suggest he fits his

eyes. This is also a waste because he is already whirling in the direction of the kitchen counter and is fumbling for his eye box. It takes him two seconds and a couple of heavy winks to get the lenses straight. Then he's ready: six foot seven and two hundred twenty pounds of naked ready-to-go all-male enthusiasm. Good to see, this enthusiasm. Most men have grown casual about life – particularly at three in the morning. Most men aren't Gurus.

'Slow down,' I counsel as he grabs for his car keys. 'we have to get this thing rehearsed.'

Big J studies me like I'm Coach Hooper at Minnesota State and holding him out of the game with the score three down with eight minutes to play and Big J the star quarterback. 'So we can rehearse in the Goddamned car.'

Keen! And we *can* rehearse in the car, but not until Big J has on a pair of pants because I'm afraid my two lady guests won't believe Big J has dropped by the apartment out of spiritual fervour if he arrives in the nude.

His permanent look of multi-directional mistrust cut with general amazement makes it tough deciding whether my instructions are taking root, but he does grab up a book as he charges for the door. Into his car we go and he's off through the Ibiza streets as if this was the Monaco Grand Prix and Big J a maniac chasing Mario Andretti.

Back home, I strip and sneak into bed. Betsy is asleep, but not Louise. 'Where the hell have you been?' she demands in a guilt-making whisper.

'Showering,' I tell her.

'For three quarters of a Goddamned hour?'

'The drain got blocked,' I retort and add, 'Long hair,' in the hope of winning a point.

'Yeah,' she says, which is cue for the doorbell.

'Wow,' I declare with hostility. 'Who the shit can that be? It's half past fucking three.' Leaving the bed, I peep around the corner to the living-room. Big J is at the door. Surprise!

I scurry back to Louise and whisper, 'Damnit, it's this crazy Minnesota millionaire.'

Minnesota WHAT? signal Louise's eyes.

'Don't make a noise and he'll split.'

But those eyes of Louise are registering true love. *This* is the Ibiza she's come for . . . not some decadent lapsed Catholic middle-aged British sex freak, but a true Protestant millionaire from the heartland Midwest. Of course she hasn't yet *seen* him but she does manage to knock a lamp off the bedside table while trying to keep quiet.

Big J rings again.

'Shit!' I say and look glum. 'Now you've fucked up.'

Louise smiles a sweet, 'Jesus, I'm sorry,' while Betsy comes out of her coma to demand, 'What the fuck's going on?'

'Some weirdo friend of our host,' responds her bosom pal.

'Jesus!' protests Betsy – very religious conversation.

'I'll get rid of him,' I tell them, and make for the door while Louise sweeps up broken glass with one of my slippers. She's making so much noise, I'm scared she won't hear me protest, 'Like, Big J, it's four o'clock in the morning!'

Big J grins conspiracy and apologises. 'Yeah,' in a deep serious voice, 'so I was reading this text by the Maharishi and like, you know, well . . .'

'I say, 'Yeah . . .'

And he says, 'Right, man, I mean, well . . .' and gives a shrug of his huge shoulders.

So I present him with a further, 'Yeah . . .'

To which he comes back, 'Wow! I mean, well, WOW!'

'Heavy,' I agree.

'Very heavy . . . phe*wee*!' Big J whistles and mops a few drops of high-grade intellectual sweat off his forehead in case one of the ladies is spying. Two male chauvinist pigs fumbling Living Theatre.

'Wow!' Big J finishes.

'Wow is right,' I tell him. 'Yeah, you'd better come in.'

'Man,' Big J purrs, '*Thanks*, and I mean REALLY, right, know what I mean?'

'One hundred per cent,' I tell him – a guarantee which must give my lady guests the impression that I'm a telepathic – but this is all the dialogue Big J and I have rehearsed in his automobile. Now that we've run out, I tell him, 'So, right, man, sit a little.'

I come back through to the bedroom. 'You heard,' I tell the two ladies. 'There's no way I can get him out of the house.' Twisting a finger against my temple, I add, 'He's crazy!'

'I *heard.*' This comes from Betsy. She has sense.

Louise glares at us and protests, 'He sounds so sincere.' Perhaps *Louise* is sincere. She is already half into her dress and complaining, 'Jesus, the damn thing's still wet.' This is sweet considering how delighted she was when the dress GOT wet. Betsy picks up on this and shoots me an acid grin.

The acid is not for me so I grin back. We are communicating. Also we have lost Louise who sways through to the living-room wearing a smile that would have done credit to the Virgin Mary out visiting the sick.

'Hullo,' we hear her lisp. 'What's the book?'

I don't hear Big J's response because Betsy has her lips up against my right ear.

'And *she's* crazy,' Betsy whispers, so I know Louise hasn't passed on the information concerning Big J's wealth – while I haven't passed on the news that Big J's wife is holidaying at their country house with a Yugoslav backgammon professional.

I hush Betsy up so we can listen. Louise has Big J's book and is reading out loud. 'So *true*,' she purrs. Quite a switch for a lady whose ambition has been to oversee schoolgirls doing push-ups.

Betsy and I gape at each other. Betsy's mouth twitches.

'I can't make it out there,' I say.

'You think I can?' Betsy manages before we collapse giggling into each other's arms. Soon we're balling. Betsy is having fun at the expense of her absent pal. That's what I think at first, but I am wrong and evil to have had such thoughts. We dig each other, and the week turns into a definite success: yes, even when Betsy discovers the crazy is a millionaire . . . and particularly when she meets Big J's wife dropping by the apartment to pick up the housekeeping money and gets to tell Louise that the Guru is married. Threesomes . . .

Chapter Five

A murmur of pain rises from our two rows of bedridden males. Distracted from these scrawlings, I look up to see Clo, the second member of my crew. She is dressed in a T-shirt which is too tight, cut-down jeans and a broad grin. She struts up the ward with her heels thumping and her breasts bouncing. Her nipples thrust hard enough at the thin cotton for me to guess she's been playing with them preparatory to coming on stage. I recognise the T-shirt as Babette's and realise the whole show is deliberate, which explains Clo's smile. Great joker, our Clo.

'*Ça va?*' she asks with a lick at her lower lip. Her moistened lip could have turned me on if I wasn't scared of sexual excitement.

'*Très bien*,' I reply, while scribbling a quick note in the margin of these memoirs.

'What are you writing?' Clo asks.

'Whether getting an erection could set back my recovery,' I tell her. 'I have to check it with the doctor.'

'An erection!' Clo widens her eyes, the better to stare at where the sheet covers my trussed testicle. 'Is that a compliment?'

'You can take it that way.'

'How sweet,' she says and kisses me gently on the cheek. Her tongue flicks into my ear.

Jerking back my head, I glower up at her. 'Behave yourself.'

She grins. 'An old man in your condition should avoid excitement. Here,' she adds and extracts a rumpled edition of *Le Monde* from her shoulder bag. 'There were none in the shops,' she says, 'so I got this secondhand from a Frenchman at Air France.'

'So you're leaving?'

Clo glances at her watch. 'In two hours.'

'Tunis?'

'Naturally.'

'So have fun,' I tell her . . . though she hardly needs urging.

'What will you do?' she asks.

Having no idea, I shrug. 'Depends . . .'

'On your testicle?'

I smile and spread my hands.

'*Pauvre vieux* . . . .' She studies me a moment with her eyes almost serious. '*Bonne chance.*'

'Thank you,' I murmur and she kisses me good-bye. Watching her strut her ass down the ward, I find myself delighted she is an economics student. The science of economics will be better for her presence. She's bright enough to wind up advisor to some Government Minister, and that will be good for us all. There's too little fun in those circles.

She gives a quick wave from the door and another chapter is closed in the life of Tobias. What comes next, I wonder: a fresh start? Well, it won't be my first. There was the time I ceased being married.

I ceased being married two days after my thirty-fifth birthday. This is a frightening landmark in a man's life. You are suddenly no longer an up-and-coming man. Gone are the promises of a mythically rosy future. Judgement is on what you've already achieved. Scary!

Confronting myself naked in the full length bathroom mirror, I decided my only achievements were a paunch, bad teeth and a marriage which felt like a maximum security prison. Depressing! So I fled the house, had my teeth capped and lost twenty-two pounds in a health farm in two weeks out of determination to get my money's worth. The other inmates were like school kids the way they cheated, while I cheated only once and on my last night. This was at the local inn in the company of a forceful Australian lady.

The Australian lady did the inviting. It was her last night as well as mine. I was still pondering why she had come to a health farm considering she'd arrived thin as a rail. No one had told me about drying out. At the inn she drank double whiskies faster than I can drink iced orange juice on a hot day. She demanded I drink, too. I refused out of fear of calorie intake.

'So drink dry champagne,' she insisted. She was paying, so I accepted one bottle rather than get into an argument.

Driving her back to the farm wasn't easy. Leaving the car, the cold air hit. I'd had nothing to eat in two weeks except a half-orange for breakfast and a lemon for dinner. It was miraculous I could walk. The lady marched me to her room There was no disobeying a lady who could drink eight doubles without a quaver. I did the quavering. Stripped for execution was how it felt to be standing naked on the pale-green health farm carpet.

Lying on her bed, the whole room took a violent lurch to starboard and hovered a half-second before hurtling into a spiral dive. I was in the centre of a whirlpool and had to get out. I walked to the door. Crawled down the corridor. Heaved up my guts. You know the trip. Kneeling at the can with a finger down your throat and a prayer on your lips. Having to keep on changing to a fresh finger. Ugh! Definitely not fun. Particularly when you haven't eaten in fourteen days and have nothing to spit up but bile. But that's the altar to alcohol – white ceramic with the holy word inscribed at water level in pale blue.

Getting back was a trip. You feel kind of defenceless crawling on all fours down a health farm corridor at midnight. My room was in the next block. Flight would not have been polite. I got back to my feet before opening her door. The lady was waiting naked on her bed. Apart from being thin, she had spots on her chest.

'It's the citrus,' she informed me. 'Lemons give me a rash.' Is that remark designed to turn a man on? Lemons! while I stood praying for an erectile miracle.

Poor lady! She was going back to an Australian sheep station next day. One husband, three sons and six dogs. She had told me all about her husband down at the inn. He worked his ass off keeping her in furs, whisky and Rolls Royces. She'd drag him off in their twin engined Beachcraft to hear Joan Sutherland at the Sydney Opera House while he longed for sheep, tennis and golf. He still believed balling was what men did to women rather than the other way around.

Her kids weren't much better – at least not the eldest two;

horses and Australian Rules football, which is like American football without the padding. She was attempting to turn her youngest into a tall blond gay as far as I could understand, though I didn't tell her so. Why spoil a lady's fun? Video tape ballet on their sixty-inch TV and *DARLING, must you wear those dreadful jeans?* Odd, considering she used fag as an insult. But this came later in our night of love.

She lay there, waiting. I was also waiting, but without much hope. Weird how some women presume a man can produce an erection on demand. If he doesn't produce an erection, he's insulting them. Knowing all this filled me with guilt. So I gave her head. All I could taste was lemons. Every time I closed my eyes the room went into a whirl. Finally her belly shivered a little. Promising, except she started screeching for me to get into her.

Yes, but with what? Half an inch of floppy frankfurter? How could I tell her she was too thin for my hunger complex? Nor could I confess to being drunk – not to a lady who could down a bottle of scotch while all I drunk was dry champagne. I couldn't even kiss her on the lips for fear she'd taste why I'd been on the can so long. Nor could I protest a headache. Headaches are the woman's prerogative. These thoughts were getting me no nearer erection – but were definitely boosting the lady's anger.

In desperation, I tried man's last resort. 'I'm impotent.'

'You're *what?*'

'Impotent,' I pleaded into the lemon drench of her sacred grotto.

'Oh . . .' Or maybe only two dots seeing how short a time she required for consideration. 'You're a Goddamned *FAG!*'

'Yeah, well . . .' So *you* try staying cool with a lady ramming her feet on your shoulders. One almighty shove and I was flat on the carpet.

'Get out of here.'

To which I managed a pathetic, 'Sorry . . .'

'Sorry!' She leapt out of bed.

I was scared she was going to kick me. Instead, she hurled my clothes out of the window.

I told this story to Sister Bear one lazy afternoon at the

beach. She said, 'Jesus! I mean, what the hell did you get into her bed for in the first place?'

My answer was, 'She wanted me to, right? Think how bad she would have felt if I hadn't.'

'Great,' said Sister Bear. 'So think how badly she felt when you did and couldn't get it up.'

That's exactly what I thought about while crawling naked out of the lady's room, down the corridor and out across the lawn to my own block, my head heavy with guilt. But there are a lot of beds I've been in for the wrong reasons. Sister Bear has been busy teaching me this all summer.

The one that really got her angry was a lady in Brussels I told her about.

The lady was rich, bleached blonde and into art and other intellectual pursuits. She had bought an antique table from me. She hadn't paid for it and I was broke. This happened three years back, at the end of my first post-prison summer.

Getting locked up kicks the bottom out of your finances. Especially if you have a family on the outside who need support. You don't get paid worth a crap in jail, which may be justice, but is also why many jailees are back in a cell after a few weeks or months. Thieving is the only way they can see to get straight of their debts and into a new life. Except they don't get straight. But that's another tale. This one is of how I hitched up to Brussels in hope of collecting on the antique table.

The lady wouldn't pay. Logic was on her side. Her logic. First, she was broke (so she said). Second, two thousand dollars wouldn't last me worth a shit. Third, we'd been lovers back there in Spain a couple of times so why didn't I move in for the winter so she could pay me off with bed and board. Her bed. Ex-cons can't be choosers so I was stuck for four months.

The lady ran a snob's gallery for incomprehensible art which she sold at wicked prices to the new rich. She spent a lot of time with the rich. The disco scene each night, hairdresser three times a week, pedicure in her office, manicure, and a miniature poodle. The poodle was dyed a pale pink and shampooed every five days by a tall thin gay with rings on his fingers and a diamond stud earring. Yes, she was very respectable.

My being an ex-con, there was no way she could present me to her friends. Not even the ones I already knew. This was part of her trip: keeping a man so low down the social scale she couldn't afford to be seen taking him out for a meal. I was her winter sin hidden away in the cupboard with a fine collection of pornographic novels. She never brought anyone back to the house during those four months and I got to go out twice. Not that I minded. I got a lot of writing done. Except for Sundays. All week was waiting for Sundays. Saturdays were purgatory. Poised on the brink.

Sunday we spent the whole day in bed. Or she did. I'd have to get my ass down to the bakery for breakfast croissants, walk the dog, cook lunch and open the wine. Two bottles of vintage red decanted into a cut chunk of glass with a price label capable of keeping me in luxury for a month. Colour TV (twenty-eight inch) but no watching the football match. Not on Sundays – not until later.

Lunch eaten, she'd drag her robe over her head. This was the signal. Time for work (me longing for a siesta). What she liked was getting hit. And not just simple hitting but the whole trip of being put down by a slob. Abasing herself before a man so low she couldn't be seen dead with him in public. A criminal. A drug trafficker (retired). A man who beat up on women.

I'd do everything I could to keep the act more or less straight. Down I'd go on her and suck till she HAD to be tired. If I shifted up, I'd try to pin her arms flat each side of her head. Nothing worked. She was a Goddamned contortionist. One unguarded moment on my part and she'd be over on her knees with her butt stuck up in the air and her head hanging down over the bed edge so her nose rubbed the carpet. The pink poodle used to whine and go into the other room. Lucky dog!

In the end I'd get so mad at having to go through this whole Sunday scene that I'd belt shit out of her ass and she'd really scream.

'Master! Master!'

Think of my embarrassment. She so high and mighty (except for Sundays), her ass up in the air and screaming,

'*Oui, Maître . . . Oui! Oui! Oui!*'

She'd always manage to end up facing the TV set. Gave her an extra kick to feel I was watching the screen. But how can you concentrate on Amsterdam playing Liverpool in the quarter finals of the European Cup in a situation like that?

I'd always be scared of getting so embarrassed I'd lose my erection. This happened a couple of times and really got her mad. There she was all prepared for her Sunday sacrifice and no ZAP. She'd storm off to her study and spend the rest of the day working over the gallery accounts. I'd get back to writing, which was nice, except she wouldn't bring any food home for the next few days. I'd be eating dog biscuits along with some God-awful muck called whatever the French is for Gravy Train. The gravy was pretty good but the meat had the texture of a rotting sponge.

That's how I know that whores don't always eat well. Nor do they necessarily get paid. Because I never did get paid for the table. I was her lover, right? So it was write, write, write, plus a daily prayer to the muse. Finally there was enough manuscript completed for a call to my agent.

'Help,' I pleaded down the umbilical line to London. 'I can't keep this up.'

'Age,' mocked my agent (but sent me the bread for a bus ticket).

Age – is that what it is? I refer to this flagellation waltz. And not only flagellation, but the whole rape fantasy which seems to prevalent nowadays. Or is this merely that a lot of the ladies who *are* into this bag have chosen to pass my way these last few years?

There I'll be on the bed, head full of romance and a big vase of roses glowing on the bookcase, dim light, soft music. Next moment, the lady's arms are grabbing for the headboard in that 'tie me to the rack' position, her head lolling off to one side like her neck's broken and her eyes closed against the horror of what she's fantasising may happen to her if she only prays for it hard enough.

Here we go again, I think, with a guilt-ridden glance at my desk where the book I was reading pre-luncheon is lying open in invitation. There's age for you. None of this happened to me when I was young; neither the rape fantasies, nor my present desire for the comfort of an overstuffed armchair and a good book.

Has what my face suggests changed with age? I wonder about this while we ball; then, as soon as it's polite, head for the bathroom where I inspect myself in the mirror. Do I look sadistic? Or am I simply the sort of man who's content to suffer a lady's trip? Or is the lady fantasising a mythical male supremacy? If so, she's been had. Men have never been that tough. No, not even the brutish soldiery who, victorious, raped the entire female population of a city prior to putting the ladies to the sword. Why do you think the soldiers killed the ladies? So the ladies couldn't get to recount for history how few of the soldiers actually got it up.

Ladies and their fantasies of whip, rape and a twenty-six-inch penis blasting endless orgasms into their womb with the force of a rapid fire anti-tank rifle; why should they come to me? Me, the bewildered possessor of a five-inch prick which should remind them of the nozzle on a soft ice cream machine, the reservoir stocked with a neat blend of self-doubt and Catholic guilt rather than the prescribed five gallons of pastis-flavoured spermatozoa.

Do they bring their fantasies to my bed because I am a writer and writers are said to be sympathetic to fantasy? If so, I must learn to write better because, as a rapist, I am definitely past improvement.

Or is it my having served time that turns them on? Do they, along with the Belgian lady and her pink poodle, fantasise me as a super tough Mafioso fresh from two years in Top Security? A drug smuggler! Again I must disappoint them. What I got busted for was forty kilos of the worst hashish ever smuggled out of Morocco. Not only was it the worst hashish, but it was stashed under the floor of a ten-year-old 2CV Citroen so slow the cops ordered me off the highway.

The prosecutor called me a mastermind which was kinder than Sister Bear's comment. 'Jesus,' she said on hearing the story, 'For shit that bad they should have busted you for fraud.'

Chapter Six

'But why on earth *dope dealing*?' my mother wanted to know after I was out of prison. The answer was simple, though impossible to explain to her. There was nothing else I could do back in those years. Nobody was reading fiction, or at least not my fiction. Big J had pre-empted the Ibiza Guru position, and I didn't think I could make it as a pop star. So it was dope dealing. I wasn't much good at it, but at least dope dealers seemed to have fun.

And dope dealers got to travel – New York this week, New Delhi the next. There's romance! That's how I saw it while I was still on the outside. Kabul, Montreal, Copenhagen, Tangier, Katmandu, Los Angeles . . . I didn't know then that dope dealers don't really see these places. All they get to see are a lot of identical international airports and plastic hotel rooms. What they do most of the time is fly. It was a strange occupation for a man scared of flying.

Scared! I have to gulp Librium by the handful simply to get on a local flight. Back when we were together, my family refused to fly with me. My wife claimed my terror upset the children. My terror certainly upset me. It still does. And this was before the era of highjacking. Once that started, my life was transformed into total misery.

On one flight, I spotted a six-foot Japanese with shaven head, a scar on his right cheek, and a tweed topcoat brushing his sneakers. One look and I knew he was Red Army. The doors weren't even closed and he was already making for the can. I knew what he was doing there. He was stashing his machine-gun, three bombs and a couple of unstable incendiary devices.

Paranoia? If he had been by himself I might have risked the flight. He wasn't by himself. There were two Arabs watching him from the fifth row while pretending to put their briefcases into the overhead racks.

Admittedly, this was Bahrain and these two Arabs wore

dark blue suits, so they could have been OPEC officials going to Vienna. But why run the risk? Down the aisle I went with the sweat drenching my collar.

The ass end of a blue uniformed Goddess barred the road to safety.

'Miss,' I pleaded. 'Excuse me, Miss . . .'

We all know how far a timorous approach will get a passenger. I made five attempts before the Goddess inspected me over the top of her plastic-sealed clipboard.

'Yes.'

'Please,' I said and thrust out my ticket. 'I have to change flights.'

One pencil-thin eyebrow rose. '*You what?*'

'Change flights,' I begged.

Next moment I was face to face with the Captain and two fully armed Bahraini cops. 'Look,' I told them, 'I'm too scared to fly. That mean I'm crazy?'

'So you're going to walk?' the Captain suggests without much charm. 'No one tell you Bahrain's an island?'

I mean I was a paying passenger, right? Four hundred and fifty-eight dollars cash and I could see they were fantasising me as some kind of dangerous criminal simply because I wanted out of their DC something or other. 'Just give me an hour,' I pleaded. 'One hour and I'll have it together.'

The Captain eyed me like I was offal. 'You will?'

Fortunately the cops were more reasonable. Arabs, reared on camel transport, they understood how a man might change his mind about risking his life to the air. They led me off to the transit lounge where the airport doctor stuck a rubber plug over my heart so he could hear it beat. I was alive, he decided, which was a relief to both of us. But now I began worrying about whether they would search my bags for evidence of why I was nervous. So I told the cops about the Red Army. This produced action. They radioed the plane. The second pilot and two male stewards jumped the Japanese. This surprised the Japanese so much he pissed himself.

Buddhist monks shouldn't wear floor length topcoats. Nor should they suffer from dysentery. Their suffering from dysentery could give vegetarianism a bad name and this monk's dysentery certainly gave *me* a bad name. Pan Am threatened to blacklist me for life.

Other dope dealers worried about getting busted. I worried about getting blown up. Not even Librium helped. Getting busted would have been a holiday from terror. And the conversations! Listen in on a bunch of dope dealers. They're worse than wine snobs. And they all carry these pocket calculators which I could never learn to use. Profit percentages!

Plus there were the social put-downs. 'Yeah, well he's just a six-kilo man.'

And the hypocrisy. 'I mean, you know, like well all my folks are into is bread.' What in hell were dope dealers into? Love? Sure, but at what profit?

Visit a dope world banker. Joss sticks scenting the air and the man is sitting on a four thousand-knot-to-the-inch silk prayer mat. He's sitting in the full lotus with his curls hanging half-way down to his ass in a haircut that's cost two hundred dollars and you've got to be fast with your proposition because it's ten minutes to his meditation hour and he's asking three hundred per cent on his investment capital over two months! Peace, love and understanding and a white Porsche 911 Turbo parked three blocks down the street so the IRS won't make the connection, eight thousand dollars worth of hi-fi electronics eating at his floor space like a tropical jungle, three Haselblad cameras and a fifty-two card pack of no-limit credit cards.

Nor was I innocent. No Sir! I was as big a snob as the next dealer. Snobbery went with the job. Selling quarter ounces on the street was no better in our social register than being Tony with the ice cream van. Sell less than five kilos and you've threatened your social standing. Next time you drop by the Kabul Inter-Continental Pool Club the heavies will cut you dead. Even the runners will sneer.

You even have to be careful of *what* you deal. There's as much difference between running commercial grade Moroccan and running Bombay Black as there is between being a scrap merchant and a bullion broker. Fly in with a load of Moroccan and no one's going to invite you to their full moon party. They may buy from you if they're desperate, but that doesn't mean they want you in their house.

My mother lives the same type of social scene in the South of France, where it's how many Dukes you can persuade to sit at your dinner table. In the dope world, it's how many members of the Brotherhood come to your barbecue. On the Riviera they drip diamonds to prove they've made it. In the dope world it's a nose drip and a silver coke spoon from Tiffany's. The heavy aristocracy (Catholics) keep a tame priest. The heavy dealer supports a tame Guru. Both have habits except the Guru's probably comes out of a needle.

Then there's the clothes you have to wear. I was sitting in Frankfurt's transit lounge one summer afternoon in grey flannel trousers, brown brogues, a neat striped shirt with regimental tie and navy yachting jacket. I had the *Wall Street Journal* open at page six while down below were two false-bottomed suitcases changing flights from the Far East to the Far West without my help but with my baggage tabs.

I'd survived ten hours in a Boeing without one maniac leaping up with a Czechoslovakian machine-pistol clutched to his chest. Times like that you start to think it's going to be all right. You fantasise how God, in his mysterious way, may be on your side. You're grateful. You're relaxed. And you have swallowed so many Librium you could even sleep except that your next flight is leaving in thirty minutes. And that gives you time to start worrying again.

This sort of in-flight paranoia always made me feel good going through Customs. I was so happy to have my feet back on the ground and I looked so happy that the Customs men would take one glance at me and think, *Well, this one has to be innocent. He's pleased to see us.*

There I am in the transit lounge. I have one leg crossed over the other, brown brogues shining nicely, and I've just read how they've hit Spiro Agnew for cheating on his taxes. I have also read how a whole cargo of heroin has mysteriously disappeared from the New York police safe deposit.

Libriumised and happy, I hear this high-pitched shriek of what could be my name if I'd been born in the depths of the Bronx. I'm so deep into my act of junior partner in an

Investment Brokerage that deals only in Blue Chips that I don't even look up at the second screech. The third shriek I'm forced to look up.

The entire population of the transit lounge is watching this lady bearing down on me; an old friend with a fifty-inch bust and hennaed hair.

Normally I would have nothing against meeting this particular lady. So she enjoys dressing like a hooker, that's her bag. But why lay it on me when I'm going through the hottest airport in Europe with two Samsonites of the best Bombay Black? She is blowing my act. No partner (however junior) in any kind of Brokerage House would risk his public image by being seen in conversation with a lady dressed the way she's dressed.

'Well *Hi*,' she coos soft enought to send the maintenance staff scurrying to check out the plate-glass windows. 'Where have you been?'

'Here and there,' I say with a look any other lady would have read as saying *I love you but get away from me before I die*.

Not this one. She sits right down on my lap and ruins the *Wall Street Journal*. She also musses my made-to-measure grey flannel, fluffs up my glued to the skull hairdo and carols, 'But you look so square! What's *happened*?' Then, without waiting for a reply, she tells me the news. And what kind of news! Like who's doing what number out of which hash field and into where and of the ten dozen mutual friends we have who are serving time for doing what I'm hoping not to serve time for doing.

This is not the coolest conversation for Frankfurt Airport. It is not a cool conversation for any airport. Not even if you're totally straight. When you're working, it's instant assassination. But I can't even get her off my lap let alone gag her. Plus she's creasing my pants. And there's this sweet old lady opposite who's studying me like she thinks I'm into bondage.

Thank God there's a flight being called. 'My plane,' I gasp.

'Wow, she says and eyes me like I'm really weird. *Albania?*'

'A travel book,' I explain and race for the toilet to spit up.

Nine hours later I'm through and safe (though not in Albania). I dial the cousin of a close friend. 'Hi,' I say, 'your cousin Billy said I should call when I hit town.'

He says, 'Oh . . .'

This is not particularly welcoming. Nor is one of Bell Telephone's aluminium coffins the best place for objective thought. But I do take a few seconds out to consider Billy. There's nothing specifically wrong with Billy. It's simply he's stumbled over a religious experience in India and he relates this experience from the moment you meet him to the moment you flee – unless of course he's discussing dope.

Most people are into dope (the people I know). But having to hear how a friend's got himself zapped with the white light of total knowledge by a fifteen-year-old Indian kid into tax evasion . . .

See what I mean? So I say kind of casually, 'Listen, I've never even *visited* with the White Light Mission.'

The cousin says, 'Oh . . .' for the second time. However it is a better Oh. There may not be much enthusiasm but at least his immediate paranoia is fading.

'Never,' I insist, 'though I have been around that part of the world.' And add after a deliberate pause, 'Fact is, I've just come from there.'

'You have?' Cousin sounds almost optimistic.

Nice, but I'm running out of change. So I drop what you think is a strong clue. 'Yeah,' I state. 'It really teaches you how Black is Beautiful.' This should suggest that I'm loaded down with Bombay Black. Bombay Black *is* beautiful. All I get is a third Oh served up with ample ice.

'Look,' I hurry, 'could we meet for coffee?'

'Why not?' Which is still not specifically encouraging. 'When?'

'Like now,' I insist. 'I'll be in the downstairs bar at the Plaza International.' This is all I have time for before change runs out.

Cousin is easy to spot. He is a jazz clarinetist and having to be competitive with New York Black Draft Dodgers has got him dressed in a red velvet two-piece. He wears a wide-brimmed felt hat pulled down over his eyes and his hair is tied back with a silk ribbon. The ribbon is blue. Electric blue.

Loaded with dope, I try to be sufficiently inconspicuous so people will stumble over me like I'm not there. Cousin is not going to help this aim. If I had another address to call I'd be out of the bar and down the street. Having no second address, I up a copy of *Time* magazine and whisper from behind its protection, 'Billy's cousin?'

He hears nothing. This is an ailment of both pop and jazz musicians. All that nightly noise wrecks their eardrums. I poke him in the ribs. This makes him nervous. He's not at home in his fancy dress. He suspects everyone is suspecting him of being a gay hooker. He gives a leap and rounds on me with an all male scowl.

'Billy's cousin?' I repeat, which relieves him of having to defend his honour.

'Right,' he admits.

'Look,' I suggest, 'can we get the hell out of here?'

He gives the congregation a quick inspection and says, 'It was your choice.'

This remark has me doubting we can ever be true friends. Fortunately I'm wrong. Once we get outside into the safety of his six-year-old VW bus the whole scene straightens out.

I say, 'I'm sorry to drag you out of the house,' and offer him a Winston which I light while he feeds Coltrane into his tape deck. The noise is heavy, but it's great protection against the fuzz focusing on us with a directional mike. 'I have this dope,' I say. 'Eight kilos of Bombay Black.'

'Jesus!' he flips off the sounds as if silence is going to help him check out how I look. Weird how people not into the business expect a dealer to be dressed up in Indian pyjamas, an Afghan waistcoat and have his head decorated with a garland of freshly-cut jasmine blossoms.

I apologise for looking straight by reminding him I've just come on a plane. Actually there's no need to apologise. Now that he's got his head together, he's regarding me like I'm Saint Christopher striding through the raging waters.

'Bombay Black – *Wow*!' he says. 'Out of fucking sight!'

I grin and loosen my regimental tie while he continues,

'We haven't seen anything that good up here in months.'

So I've heard, which is why I'm here.

'All we get's Moroccan mule shit,' he tells me, which I've also heard.

His appreciation gets me high. 'So the price should be right?'

'Too right,' he says and adds that bad Moroccan's selling at a thousand dollars a pound. 'So let's find you a place to crash,' he finishes, sets off Coltrane again and un-parks the VW.

While he drives, I do a little abstract mathematics. The result suggests I'm going to find it easy to pay my kids' school fees for another year. They're at a Rolls Royce ghetto which preaches freedom and togetherness to the children of diamond decorated jet-setters into guilt that they don't spend enough time with their offspring. So I'm a jet-setter and guilt ridden . . . or was back then. Now I'm just guilt ridden and my kids go to a cheaper school. But back to Toronto . . .

We collect my bags from where I've stashed them at the central station, then cruise out to this pretty tree-lined street. My guide parks outside a red brick house with steps leading up to the front door. The door is painted half in white and half in red primer. My guide walks right on in with a bag in each hand and calls out, 'Hi, it's Tom.'

A lady answers that she's on the can.

Tom dumps my bags in the hallway before showing me into an outsize living-room that is furnished with a big brass bed and a half-dozen cushions piled on the polished wood floor over by the window. There's no music playing, which I find restful after thirty-six hours of jet travel followed by Coltrane.

We sit on the floor cushions while Tom rolls up a thin joint from a tiny piece of Moroccan. Tom lights up and sorts out who he's going to call. He's decided to set up an auction the following morning, which is cool with me so long as I don't have to be present. In the dope game each person you meet in the trade is a potential security risk – that's my belief.

'Sounds great,' I say. 'Want to take care of it?'

Tom has a quick think. 'Five per cent.'

'Five,' I agree and relax into hope of sleep. Then I hear what sounds like someone wheeling a bicycle down the hall. This surprises me. So does what comes wheeling into the room. An anodised aluminium wheelchair. There's a lady seated in it. What I notice first are her legs. Miles of legs. They are propped up on the footrest and are slightly apart and seem to go on forever. If God is a leg freak and created Eve on a day of high artistic output, then these are twins to the legs he sculpted for Adam's admiration. They are pure gold silk. There are no shoes on the feet and they are covered a third of the way down their thighs by a thin cotton dress. They have wheeled all the way across the polished floorboards right up to my face before I find strength to check out who they belong to. When I do look up, I find a pair of deep grey eyes studying me with a medium quantity of amusement and even a certain slight interest which is natural as she's never seen me before and this is her house.

'Hi,' she says. 'I'm Zee.'

'Tobias,' I introduce myself.

Tom adds that I'm in the business and need a cool place to stay.

'He can help you in and out of bed.'

'Thanks,' Zee says and gives me a closer inspection which takes in the travelling bags I'm wearing under my eyes. 'Right now it looks like he's the one who needs helping into bed.'

I grin. 'That would be nice.'

'Just so long as you don't roll over in your sleep,' Zee tells me. 'I've got a cracked pelvis.'

I say, 'Jesus!' and shake my head in awe. 'How come?'

'A Honda 1000 laid its head in my lap.'

'Shit!'

'Yeah,' Zee agrees. 'Shit's where it's at.' She gives Tom a nod, '. . . but no rapping deals over my phone.'

This wisdom makes me happy. 'So you know the business?'

Zee snaps a glance in my direction which informs me that I'm one more dumb male. 'No, but I've got brains.'

Turned into an embarrassed sheep, 'Sorry,' I mumble.

She grins. 'Just so you know.'

'I know,' I say. 'Ten hours sleep and I'll finish painting your door.'

I do paint her door. Painting is fine therapy for a dealer's nerves. There's little brainwork involved but it is a definite occupation, which is what you want while waiting to learn if you're going to end up ripped-off, beat up, busted by the fuzz or temporarily affluent. Also the hot water faucet on the tub had a permanent drip, there were two assemble-them-yourself wardrobes Zee bought the day before the Honda fell on her; and the kitchen window was seized solid. Fixing all this took the three weeks it took Tom to collect on my dope. Zee and I also had other kinds of fun.

The last many years of my life have been ball the first night and start working out over breakfast if you actually like each other enough to hold together until lunchtime. If you last through lunchtime, you try for a week. The week is fun, then you calculate you're working out some kind of a sunshine relationship. We have all sorts of frustrations in our lives, but few, if any, of these frustrations stem from not balling. Zee was a total switch.

Three weeks of having her swoop around the house in that aluminium wheelchair and we couldn't even touch except for a gentle kiss. Mystic! Sleeping in the same bed; helping her undress and dress; sponge-bathing her; massaging her limbs with almond oil. Jesus! We grew so into each other physically we were running on a permanent high from which we couldn't come down. Instead of exploring each other's orgasms, we had to explore the insides of our heads. This was how courting must have felt back in my mother's youth.

My last day the doctor said Zee could go driving so long as we went slow and very careful. We drove downtown in a rented Buick convertible with the top down and Zee picked herself out a celebratory dress she had planned on wearing four weeks later, which would be my next time in Toronto.

We had a whole beautiful trip planned – coast to coast. I got busted three weeks later. They let me out after two years and gave me back my address book. Names, streets, telephone numbers, cities, states, countries and continents

. . . all of these were jumbled in a non-system which I kept in my head. The cops hadn't found the book useful. Nor did I find it useful once I was free. Two years and I'd forgotten the code, so I haven't been able to write to Zee, but I'm sure she's doing fine. She is that kind of lady (or was): courageous in adversity, sweet sense of humour and a very together head. If my head had been as together as her's was, I wouldn't have gotten busted and we'd have made that trip. It would have been a great trip. Those first few weeks in jail I checked daily in the *Herald Tribune* temperature chart: sunshine all the way from the Atlantic seaboard to the Pacific coast . . .

Chapter Seven

My life history is filled with abandoned or mislaid addresses and telephone numbers. This has never worried me . . . perhaps because a state of loneliness has seemed too improbable.

Lying here in bed I imagine my penis as a telephone cable plugged into the main switchboard. Happy concept – except the phone bill has just arrived: pay up or get cut off. The drag is not knowing what currency the Telephone Company accepts nor had I expected to get billed for incoming calls. Failing to study the small-print clauses on the reverse side of the original application has proved an error.

Heavy thoughts, these, and they have been circling my skull ever since midnight. It is now four o'clock in the morning and there is no white-uniformed saviour willing to shoot me out of pattern with a pellet of instant action pharmaceutical peace.

Our new night nurse is graced with a permanent scowl and the beginnings of a black moustache. As she strides the ward she digs her heels into the floor tiles like an irate drill sergeant. She has refused my two requests for a sleeping pill. My nickname for her is Hitler. This is not original, but I am not feeling original. I am feeling old and scared of the future.

Perhaps looking into the past is also scaring me. Scribbling these memoirs maybe unwise. Memoirs may not be the best medicine for a man in my condition. Tobias of the ever-ready smile has been my favourite self-portrait. The smile has slipped. Of course, the nurses are pumping heavy doses of antibiotic cocktail into my ass at six hour intervals and antibiotics are depressants. The perfect excuse . . .

Come morning I shall complain to the management. 'Shit!' I will protest, 'even in jail we got dope.'

Smoke-type dope got smuggled in for the mentally fit while chemical dope was on issue to the mentally injured. Three times a day those prisoners incapable of hacking incarceration would line up for their happy pills. First a man gets locked up as punishment, then he gets issued dope so he can support the punishment. Logic?

Do fork-tailed demons issue dope to the damned?

If the answer is affirmative, how do the damned recognise they are in Hell?

Because they need dope.

Right now I need dope.

For a retired dope dealer to be incapable of scoring one lousy little sleeping pill in a surgical ward is sufficiently castrating for there to be no need for a Pathan surgeon. On this thought Brave Tobias presses the bell.

Hitler marches up the ward. 'Yes?' she demands with a scowl.

Shy to meet her eyes, 'Sister,' I plead, 'I need a bottle.'

Humility is food for the fascist and this one swells up like a six-six Amazon while actually standing five foot nothing. With a glower at my criminal bladder, she departs on her errand.

Returning, she leaves me with a bottle to fill. I fill it and ring again.

Back she stomps. 'Now what?'

She has taken up station to the right of my bed. I smile up at her with saintly purity, extend the bottle over to the left and murmur sweetly, 'Lady, get me a pill or this bottle gets dropped.'

'Don't you dare,' she threatens in a fierce whisper.

'Don't you bet,' I retort.

She bites on her upper lip – glances up and down the ward. Forty-one men sleep in ignorance of the approaching war.

'One,' I count, 'two, three . . .'

Hitler capitulates – but then I'm better armed than Chamberlain. Five minutes and she's back with a pill. I examine the pill with well-earned paranoia. 'What is it?'

'Seconal,' she admits with sadness at having found the poison cabinet locked. 'I'm going to report you to Dr Rahman.'

'Do that,' I tell her and, swallowing the pill, pass her the bottle. 'Good night, Sister . . .'

Courageous Tobias. Victorious Tobias. No! just plain *stupid* Tobias. You would presume a man who has suffered two of England's most expensive private schools, three years in the army and two years in jail would have wised up enough not to buck the system.

Six o'clock in the morning the night nurse shakes me out of sleep. I groan at the sight of her junior acolytes armed with a screen.

'Bed bath,' she pronounces with a sadistic curl to her lip.

The seconal has me too groggy to resist. Nor can I escape the needle she has waiting for me. She has spent the last two hours filing the tip flat on a cement window ledge. Yes, indeed . . . one way or the other they always get you. Is this paranoid thinking or a face-up to reality?

At least I am clean and combed to greet Ilsa, the yacht agent, who arrives an hour later. Our mother-type day nurse leads her towards my bed. They appear to be old friends. 'Hi,' I say.

Ilsa smiles, but not at me. The nurse also smiles. They are a female conspiracy of two and I am the nurse's possession – her toy. She is going to lend this toy to her friend for a strictly limited period on condition the friend promises not to damage it. She slides a chair up close to my bed, gives the yacht agent a parting look of conspiratorial warning and ghosts off with her starched white skirts flicking electricity.

The yacht agent waits till the nurse is off ward before giving me true attention. She is alone with me now and we can play – at least, she can play with me. Not that I mind being made to feel like a doll. Who am I to challenge the nature of women?

Ilsa says, 'Hi – how are the doctors treating you?'

'Fine,' I say.

'Yes?' She looks unconvinced. 'Perhaps you should fly to London?'

'London?' I ask. 'Why London?'

'Well, the doctors are on strike,' she tells me.

'Not the one who's dealing with me,' I say.

'But he's Pakistani . . .'

'I've noticed.'

She looks kind of anxious, which is natural. Most of us are

shy at coming out in public with our racial prejudices. This is why many blacks prefer dealing with Deep South Rednecks. The Redneck is honest.

So is Ilsa. She plays around with her fingers and asks, 'You're sure he knows what he's doing?'

'Look,' I say, 'for now he's kept his knife out from between my legs.' I grin. 'What more could I want?'

'Yes . . .' Poor lady, she is still fiddling with her fingers.

I feel for her. That she has betrayed herself shows she actually cares what happens to me. This gives me a warm feeling. I put a hand on her arm. 'Don't worry.'

'If you're sure . . .'

'I'm sure,' I tell her.

She gives my hand a slight squeeze.

'How's the catamaran?' I ask.

'All right.' She looks towards the window as if she might see the yacht. 'I've cabled the owners.'

'Maybe you should have called,' I suggest.

She smiles. 'The telephone company is on strike.'

'Along with the doctors.'

'And the banks,' she tells me.

That's nice. So I can't get any bread sent and can't call out. 'How about the mail?'

She giggles. 'Next week,' and digs into her purse. 'There's a letter for you.'

I check the stamp. British. Shit, I think and reverse the envelope. There is no name or address on the back. Not that I need this information. I know who it's from. Sister Bear. My knowing shows and whatever it shows is apparently serious because Ilsa gives my hand a second squeeze. 'I'll come by tomorrow. Anything you need?'

I glance at my bedside table. 'A couple of loose-leaf notebooks.'

'Newspapers?'

'No point,' I tell her and grin as I release her arm. 'Like if they're going to start a war, tough luck.'

'Yes,' she says and leaves me to my letter.

I am not sure I want to be left with this letter. I lie here fingering it like it's one of those bombs terrorists send their enemies for the fun of having their enemies need a new secretary because the last one has had her fingers blown off along with half her face. I am against terrorists. Unfortunately being against terrorists is of no immediate help so I check the postmark.

The letter is four weeks old. This freaks me out. What the hell is she doing in London? The easy way to find out would be to slit the envelope. Factually, I am an emotional coward and prefer memories to the here and now.

Immediate memory is of a German millionaire's wife. We met this spring. I had been dining with a couple of friends at a Catalan's restaurant fifteen kilometres from Ibiza town. We came out of the restaurant to find the rain pissing down. My friends offered to drive me home if I wanted to leave my bike, but I told them not to bother, the rain would stop. The rain didn't stop.

I was standing on the porch when this lady in a floor-length fur coat swept out and into a Mercedes 360 SL convertible with its top up. She was a tall blonde and around the thirty-five mark, judging from her throat. Supra-Ayrian. She fired the motor before winding down the window and then sat there looking me over with that special arrogance only rich and reasonably beautiful women can afford – like she was doing the shopping and I was a cabbage on a market stall. Finally she nodded at my Bultaco.

'Yours?'

'Mine,' I agreed in a dead flat voice.

'Where do you live?'

'Ibiza town.'

She pushed her door open and was already half-way over into the passenger seat before she said, 'Get in.'

Why not? I thought. She had lousy manners but her car would be fun to drive and it was still raining.

'Gerda Von Stilling,' she informed me as I eased the Mercedes on to the highway. Her tone suggested the Von Stillings were famous for something. I had never heard of them.

'Tobias,' I said.

'Tobias?'

'That's right,' I told her with equal snobbery – the snobbery which comes from being based on a small island for nearly twenty years. Disembark from the Barcelona ferry and ask any Ibicenco along the waterfront for Tobias. You'll get immediate directions just so long as you don't look like a straight and elderly relative or a disguised cop.

We are half-way to town before she poses her next question. 'You've been away?'

She's querying my heavy tan. 'Pyrenees,' I tell her.

'Ski-ing?'

'Correct.'

She relapses into silence. Presumably she is calculating my social class and possibly my occupation. Class is probably more important to her. She has that smell. She lights two cigarettes without asking if I smoke and passes me one.

I accept out of shock at spotting the bracelet on her left wrist. It resembles one of those studded dog collars people put on German Shepherds except the band is platinum and the studs are either excellent paste or the biggest diamonds I've seen. Whichever, this is a very strange piece of jewellery to be wearing on Ibiza. My mother would have judged it vulgar at a Nureyev Gala with everyone wearing evening dress. I take a quick glance at how this lady is dressed. The coat is silvery fur and open. Beneath it she has on a T-shirt which spots her nipples and a pair of jeans tucked into high leather boots. Great dress for a hippy paradise!

There is no further conversation till I halt the car outside the bar at the end of the quay. This is the fisherman's bar and this is the fisherman's part of town. The narrow-fronted houses are whitewashed, three or four storeys high, and rise in steeply stepped rows towards the Old City walls. The houses are old and beautiful but are not necessarily impressive to anyone into wealth or hygiene. In summer there is a slight stench of open drains. Fortunately this is early April and all we can smell is the jasmine and honeysuckle spilling out of flowerpots which decorate the balconies.

Gerda Von Stilling eyes the drunks propping up the bar and remarks without much enthusiasm, 'You live here?'

I point up through the rain at the third floor. My window is open and I've left the desk light on as warning to potential thieves that I'm home from the mountains.

She can see a rectangle of white painted ceiling beams and a triangle of wall that has a picture on it. It's not much to form a judgement on but presumably looks clean enough for her to take a risk. 'You must have a beautiful view?' she says.

'Correct,' I tell her, 'and thanks for the lift.' I have the driver's door already open and one foot on the ground before I realise she also has her door open.

'Don't forget the keys,' she reminds me.

Heavy! But she *has* saved me a wet ride, so I say, 'You're going to have to make a run for it,' and indicate the steps which mount beside the bar to the next street back. Then I think of her coat and nearly offer to bring her down a slicker but decide this would be pandering to her arrogance. 'Give me a couple of minutes to get my front door unlocked,' I advise and leave her to deal with her car.

My studio is small. You enter into a tiled kitchen with a round pine table big enough to seat eight if they're close friends. There is a shower and separate toilet off to the right of the kitchen, and there's the front room which faces on to the port.

This main room is fourteen feet by sixteen feet. The door is four feet in from the right side. There's a narrow wardrobe each end of the right hand wall and there's a pine slab desk running full length between the wardrobes.

Left of the door is a low bookcase which divides the work area from the rest of the room. Behind the bookcase is the bed which is seven feet by nine. The bed has an Afghan carpet for a cover and rug bolsters along three sides. This is mostly where people sit though there is an upright chair at the desk and one easy chair with a foot stool. The chair and foot stool are Charles Eames designed and were the only possessions Gerda remarked on as she entered at a fast trot.

'Nice,' she said as if surprised. 'Expensive.'

'Not to me,' I tell her. 'I got them cheaper than cheap off a dope dealer who had to split the island in a hurry.'

This stops her for a moment. 'A what?'

'Dope dealer,' I repeat.

Deciding this is a conversation she would be safer to

discontinue, she sheds her coat and gives her head a shake. Her hair is wet from the rain and I see her eyes are a deep green She is definitely beautiful. With her hair wet and without her coat, she looks almost in harmony with my home. If she'd dump her bracelet out of sight I could begin considering her human. 'Want a drink?' I ask.

'No time,' she tells me. 'My husband is waiting up.'

She has her belt undone before I can think of an answer – if there is an answer. I go back through the kitchen to close the front door.

'Please hurry,' she calls after me.

Ridiculous! Returning to the front room I find her naked and already on my bed. There's a drawer under the bookcase which holds the bedding. I take this out and say reasonably politely, 'I don't want to mess up the rug.'

She gets off the bed without as much as a *sorry* and watches impatiently while I roll out the thin cotton mattress in its fitted sheet. Immediately she's back on her back. For a moment I think of telling her to get out. But she's got me irritated enough to be aroused, so I strip off and get on top of her.

She doesn't want any preliminaries. Nor is she interested in having an orgasm. This is plain. All she wants is to be fucked. I have no idea why and don't much care. I come quickly and she's immediately up and making for the shower.

So she's crazy, I decide, and lie there looking out of the window at the fishing boats thudding their big one-lunger diesels seaward to lift the nets.

She comes back in and gets her clothes on like I don't exist. You can learn a good deal from watching women dress. A lot of wives behave as she does. Sometimes you've actually been making love rather than balling, but the time comes for them to leave and they are putting on their clothes like each item is a swipe of the eraser and it's you who are being rubbed out. You are a dream they've had. They've woken up to reality and reality is home waiting for them. You can see how totally concentrated they are on that homecoming. You say something and they don't even hear. It's not that they don't want to hear. They can't. They've gone deaf to anything outside their immediate future. Makes you feel great to be transformed into a non-person.

Gerda drapes her coat over her shoulders, gives her hair a final pat and stands waiting for me to do something with the door. Non-persons aren't good with doors. 'Let yourself out,' I tell her and reach for a book.

Bitch, she doesn't even slam the door.

Next time I see her is a week later. I am at the racetrack disco – not for the music, but because one of the barmen is a friend. If you're not into alcohol it's a drag having to pay out a dollar for a glass of synthetic orange. At the racetrack I get my orange free.

Dancing around by myself for a while, there's finally a French late-teenager swaying opposite. She is a little depressed at finding no one with whom she can talk: a recurring problem with the French because they won't learn languages and few people speak French these days other than the French and citizens of their ex-dependencies. We exchange a few words which cheers her up.

We've been dancing together ten minutes when Gerda Von Stilling comes in with a party of overdressed rich and acting rich. Gerda has her arm through that of an older man who is carrying too much weight. He is shorter than she is by a good six inches and seems uncomfortable in this haven for jump and noise freaks. He also looks permanently tired. Bringing up the rear of the party is a much older man who has to be Gerda's father. He is tall and moves with the condescending obsequiousness of an overpaid butler.

I cross over to the bar for a free orange and buy my dance partner a rum-coke. Gerda comes up behind me. 'Who's the girl?' she asks.

I say, 'French.'

'Yes?' She looks over her shoulder at the girl who has remained on the dance floor. 'Known her long?'

'I don't know her at all.'

'Oh,' she says and looks back at me. 'I'll see you in the morning.' She then drifts off to join her friends.

I presume she means we'll meet at the Cafe Monte Sol. Everyone meets at the Monte Sol around eleven o'clock to plan out what to do with one more beautiful day.

I'm wrong.

There's a heavy knocking at the door. The clock reads two minutes to six so I've had two hours sleep.

It is bad Karma not to open your door that early in the morning. There is probably someone outside with an urgent problem such as needing a doctor or someplace to hide. I disentangle my right arm from beneath the French girl and go open up.

Gerda! 'Hullo,' she announces. 'I had Daddy drive me in to buy fish at the market.'

I peer bleary-eyed over her shoulder for Daddy.

'He's waiting down in the car,' she tells me and walks right on in. She's clad in a tweed jacket along with jeans and the same boots. She has the jacket off before she's crossed the kitchen. The French girl's clothes are draped over the nearest kitchen chair. Gerda takes these in with a glance and strides through to the front room. The French girl is sitting up with the top sheet clutched to her throat. She looks both scared and bewildered. I am only bewildered.

'You,' Gerda orders the French girl, '*Out!*'

'Hey!' I protest, but the French girl is already off the bed and scurrying for her clothes. She has slim legs without much thigh. Seen from the rear as she bolts for the kitchen she resembles a scared hare.

Gerda looks at me and actually smiles.

Her smile is so right (however wicked) that I can't help answering with one of my own. Nor can I believe what's happening to me. I'm the hip island stud and this lady has transformed me into a square jelly bean. The least I can do for my pride is act casual.

'Want coffee?' I suggest. Now *that* sounds suave . . . or doesn't it?

Not to Gerda. Ignoring the coffee suggestion, she flicks the bedding with a sniff of distaste and asks, 'Do you have clean sheets?'

I gape. 'Sheets . . . ?'

'These are filthy,' she remarks.

'Oh,' I say as if it's my fault, and am down on my knees digging for a clean one from beneath the bookcase before I can stop myself. I'm naked, right? You try being suave while down at floor level when the lady standing over you is in jeans and boots. Nor do I have a clean sheet.

All I can find to say is, 'They're at the laundry.'

Gerda is unimpressed. '*Scheisse!*' She flips the thin mattress over by one corner as if scared of catching crabs. 'This will have to do.' Down she sits and off come her boots. Her clothes follow. Next she's on her back. And I'm still kneeling on the floor.

'Well,' she demands, 'are you going to stay on your knees all day?'

I get mad. *Fuck it*, I think, this time I'm really going to put it to her. Last time she didn't want any preliminaries. This time she's not going to get any preliminaries. *Wam!* She's going to get it right in up to her throat. That's how I see it happen in my arrogant little male head while still down there on the tiles. There's one small problem. I don't have an erection. Not that I notice this – I'm too damn angry.

Up I stand pregnant with all-male fury. Every muscle is tensed and throbbing – except for the one that counts.

Gerda looks me straight between the legs. 'Christ!'

The disdain of the lady is designed to hurt. *All* my muscles deflate. 'Look,' I protest, 'I've had two hours sleep.'

'How many hours do you need?' she enquires.

'I'm sorry,' I state with glacial pomposity, 'but I am *not* a machine.'

'Pity,' she remarks and pulls me down. Kneeling over me, she sets her mouth to work. Perhaps her husband being old and permanently tired has made her expert. She is definitely effective. Three minutes and she is satisfied by the state of the nation. 'That will do,' she decides and is back on her back.

I protest. 'Look, Mrs Von Stilling . . .'

'Baroness . . .'

'Gerda! Jesus!' Flapping my arms like a gale-blown scarecrow, I stutter on, 'I mean – well . . .' and in desperation, 'Fuck!'

'That's what I'm here for,' she points out. 'It isn't happening.' She gives my prick a glance that would curl a cactus and adds, 'And if you're not quick, it won't.'

'It won't,' I state and leave the bed.

'Where the hell are you going?'

'To make coffee,' I say and stalk through to the kitchen with none of my dignity left only to discover the French girl seated at the table looking miserable.

'What the fuck are you doing here?' I demand. I *deserve* to lose my last ball for that remark. Jesus! what a shit.

'I can't get the door open,' she says.

And there are billions of nice straight workers of the world who complain about Monday mornings. They don't know how lucky they are! 'Look,' I say, 'I'm sorry, right?' I open the door and attempt to give her a gentle good-bye kiss except she shudders away from me like I've got the plague. I understand.

Depressed and ashamed, I head for the stove and put the percolator on. Waiting for the water to boil gives me time to calm down and get my act together. The problem is that acts are never together – though I *think* mine is.

Cool and collected, I bring the coffee, set the tray on the bookcase and enquire politely, 'Gerda, what is it you want?'

She gives me a sweet smile over the top of the book she's picked up. 'To get fucked.'

'Laid,' I suggest.

'Laid . . .' She gives a twitch of her shoulders. 'What's the difference?'

I flip. 'Look,' I screech, 'will you put down that Goddamned book.'

She doesn't put down the book but she does continue smiling. 'You mean something's going to happen?'

There are a dozen bright remarks I can make. I could also try violence such as throwing her out along with her clothes and boots. What would be the point? Defeat's not difficult to take – not once you accept it as inevitable. So I smile back and ask politely, 'Sugar?'

'One.'

'Cream?'

'Please . . .'

I almost drop the jug. 'What did you say?'

'*Please*,' she repeats – the bitch – and has the nerve to laugh.

What the hell . . . I sit down on the bed and pass her coffee. She looks beautiful sitting there sipping at her cup like a green-eyed cat. She also looks desirable. There's no point in my pretending otherwise. 'That poor kid was sitting out in the kitchen all this time,' I tell her.

Miraculously, she looks dismayed.

'Can't be helped,' I say.

We study each other. Gerda finishes her coffee and puts the cup back on the tray. Then she slips down the bed so she's flat on her back. She gives a tiny gesture of her hands which is not even close to supplication but is a kind of asking, and she grins up at me. 'Please . . .'

I smile back and say, 'With pleasure . . .'

Next moment we're giggling like two kids in each other's arms. It's not great but it works – though there's no hanging about. Up she gets and off to wash herself out. I cross over to the window.

Her father is sitting in one of those plastic Citroen jeeps. The top is off the jeep and he is only three floors down so I can see him clearly. He looks unhappy. He is peering anxiously up at my studio and is biting at the nail on the little finger of his right hand. I turn to watch Gerda reappear from the shower. She looks pleased with herself.

'What does your father do?' I ask.

'Do?' For an instant she looks nonplussed. 'Nothing . . .' and she shrugs like it has no importance. 'Looks after our house.'

'Your house?'

'My husband's.' She flicks a hand in the direction of where she presumes the village of San Miguel to be. She is a few degrees off but I understand.

'Oh,' I say and she smiles with a little mischief showing in the way the corners of her eyes crease.

'Are you going to let me out?'

I let her out.

'Tomorrow's no good,' she says at the door. 'See you Wednesday.' No kiss.

I go back to the window to watch. She doesn't say a word to her father. Just gets into the passenger seat.

Very weird, I think and head back to bed.

Wednesday it's the same six o'clock in the morning routine, except that I'm wise enough this time to have no one waiting for Gerda to throw out. Once again I look out the window. Dad is there.

'Is he your alibi?' I ask of Gerda as she yanks on her boots.

'Not exactly.'

I think of asking not exactly what? but decide Gerda is not the kind of lady to give information merely because someone asks. I see her to the door and say, 'I hope your husband likes fish.' Now there's a tacky remark.

'He's on a low cholesterol diet,' Gerda tells me. 'See you Saturday.'

Saturday Dad is again on sentry duty. I have begun to feel sorry for the old man. It can't be fun for him sitting down in the jeep while his daughter gers herself laid upstairs.

Gerda comes Monday and Tuesday. Thursday she flies home to Dusseldorf with her husband who I have learned is Germany's equivalent of Henry Ford II except Baron Freidrich Von Stilling is the Tenth. This information has not come from Gerda but from a creepy German real-estate agent I've seen bowing before them one morning in the Monte Sol. The realtor tells me Gerda has been married to Von Stilling three years.

'And before that?' I ask.

He gives me a smile packed with pornographic innuendo and says, 'This and that.'

'What's this and what's that?' I ask.

'Modelling,' he reports. His leer suggests she's done most of her modelling in the prone position. I feel like hitting him in the face but don't have time. Nor do I have time to elicit any further information. The realtor has spotted a prospective client and is off like a dog after a rabbit. Nor do I care that much for Gerda, really. I merely dislike the real-estate agent. In fact, Gerda's flying to Germany feels like a holiday time to me. Not that she's been work. You get paid for work. But her morning visits have made me nervous of casual encounters. Gunshy!

It is a definite drag being gunshy two weeks after Easter with the hunting season so recently open. A good part of the pleasure of living in Ibiza is the casual life pattern. Ladies arrive, ladies leave. We share a few days of fun and joy and no one gets hurt – or that is the intention – and that is how it was for the rest of the week. Sunday morning a Uruguayan lady returned to the island. Maria Jesus . . .

Chapter Eight

Maria Jesus skied with me in the Pyrenees for almost two months that winter. We first met as I was driving off the Barcelona ferry. The quay was blocked by a mail truck loading sacks of Christmas thank-you letters. A young lady strolled over. She carried a pack on her back and I had three sets of skis strapped to the roof of the beat-up 2CV Citroen.

'*Hola*,' the lady opened with a toss of her head at the skis. '*A donde vas?*'

'Aragon,' I replied. '*Tu?*'

Her grin and the flip of her shoulders told me she had no idea and didn't much care. Nice mouth, I thought; warm . . . but her eyes looked short on happiness. Grey-green eyes. She wore jeans, a cotton T-shirt and a brown wool cardigan. The cardigan was light weight.

'You have anything warm?' I asked with a nod at her pack.

'Sweaters.'

'So get in,' I suggested like it didn't matter if she did or didn't. Keep it casual, is my motto; that way you can't get put down.

The mail truck cleared before she had time to think. Immediately the driver in rear of me hit his horn. He was plump and Catalan, according to the registration on his Mercedes sedan. Decked out in a dark-blue suit and regimental tie he looked bad-tempered and arrogant as well as rich. Possibly he was angered by the injustice of a young lady approaching a five-year-old Citroen with rust decorating its wings in preference to his twenty-thousand-dollar power symbol . . . and possibly Maria Jesus shouldered her pack on to my rear seat as a revolutionary gesture. Ten years of those crazy Colonels has switched most Uruguayans under thirty into potential Che Guevaras.

There might be other reasons for a young lady getting into my car that early on a winter's morning. But who wants to risk an unpalatable answer by asking? She could be broke and have no other place to go, or maybe I look harmless. Or maybe she thought I had a nice smile.

Winter in the mountains is great for getting to know a lady. The village where I winter is short on night life so you spend the evenings nursing your bruises in front of the log fire. Mostly Maria Jesus rapped while I listened. Finally she had to go to meet her sister who had flown in from Montevideo.

A week later an Argentinian macho type hit the slopes. There must be nice Argentinians. Maybe they stay home in Argentina. This one was so into his muscle power, you would think he was trying to murder the snow. A lousy way to ski. Also he talked as if he were in training for the Sun Valley Olympics which failed to add to his popularity. He recognised me from Ibiza where he'd kicked around a few months flexing his biceps on the beach. He presumed this made us bosom friends. '*Hola*,' he greeted me, 'I hear you had Maria Jesus staying a while.'

'A while,' I said.

'Nice chick,' was his comment. 'You get it in?'

Gentlemen don't talk is how I was reared (how about writers?). I looked blank. 'Get what in?'

'Well,' he remarked, 'she's a dyke.'

I countered, 'Yeah? She forgot to tell me.'

This was a lie. Maria Jesus had told me – not that she was a dyke (ugly word), but that she'd been crazy in love with some lady back home for a couple of years. The experience had left her sad, uncertain, and a little scared. Perhaps her weeks in the mountains was my usual service as a transit camp. I didn't bug her about her past. We would lie in front of the fire, she with her head in my lap and both of us reading till the atmosphere became relaxed and tender enough for her to risk speech. By the time she split for Paris I judged her in fair shape.

Now that she was back she came directly to my studio from the boat. I had given her a key the day she left the mountains. My studio and my life are too small to contain much worth hiding, and having a key in her purse can give a young lady confidence while she is out checking the world.

The squeak of the hinges woke me and she called out, '*Hola guachito . . .*' Coming through to the front room she discovered me in bed. 'What's new?' she asked as we embraced.

'You stink,' I cracked.

She sniffed at her armpits. 'Train sweat.'

'So try the bathroom,' I suggested. She did.

Showered, she returned with a breakfast tray and sat cross-legged at the foot of the bed. She was twenty-one years old plus four months – one of those end-of-December Capricorns who keep everything tidy in neat little boxes (Aquarians prefer trays) – but seemed younger with her hair wet and perhaps because of her breasts. They were small – more like buds. Tentative at coming out into a rough world was how I saw them.

'How was Paris?' I asked.

'Still beautiful and outrageously priced,' she confirmed and recounted how she had found work waiting tables at a fellow South American's meat restaurant.

'So you're rich?'

'Huh!' She snorted and laughed. 'Ever know a Frenchman to leave a tip?'

'Only for cops,' I agreed. My reward was a smile. 'Anyway, you look happy,' I told her, which was true.

She raised her shoulders a half-inch, her smile wry, and inspected my studio. 'Why not?'

So my key had been of help. 'Great,' I said, 'and love?'

She blew a rasperry. '*Nada.*'

'Tough.'

She gave me a look which suggested she'd given up on the search and, laying the tray aside, slid in under the sheet.

Her neck muscles were as taut as bow strings so I set my fingers to work. Finally she relaxed and snuggled her nose into my shoulder the way we used to sleep in the mountains. A black and white rabbit I kept as a child did the same. The rabbit saved me from despair through a lousy first year at boarding school. Give a rabbit salad leaves, bread and clean straw for bedding along with a little affection and you have yourself a contented friend. Maria Jesus was more complicated.

She wasn't in need of physical love. I had a feeling she had come searching protection – though from what, I had no idea. Perhaps talk would have helped except I tend to be monosyllabic. Anyway, bodies are more truthful than words.

We rested a couple of hours before stopping off at the Cafe Monte Sol for a second coffee. The sidewalk tables were all taken so we joined a Bolivian painter and his Dutch girlfriend. A tall, rangy looking French lady strolled by with a striped beach bag slung over her shoulder. Halting at a table of other French, she leaned down to kiss some man on the cheek. The sun, striking her hair, transformed the long auburn waves into a gilded curtain through which her face glowed like that of a Madonna in a stained-glass church window.

Maria Jesus let out a tiny gasp. Sensing me watching her, she met my eyes. She looked shy rather than embarrassed.

'I'll get the check,' I said. The French lady came in while I was paying at the bar. We had met a couple of times. '*Ça va?*' I asked.

She stuck out her lower lip in that French way of describing life as a drag.

'So come have dinner tonight,' was my advice.

She accompanied her 'why not?' with a flick of her left shoulder – body language which suggested she was dislodging a tiresome fly. If I'd been pimping for myself and didn't know the French I would have told her to forget the invitation. I do know the French. What would be extreme rudeness in any other race is their normal way. 'Sos Solito,' I invited. 'Nine o'clock.'

She turned up fifteen minutes late.

Watching Maria Jesus those first few minutes awoke memories of my own tentative teenage dating. Back then I expected to be thought a slob. It took a few years for me to accept that a lady does not normally date a man she dislikes . . . or not unless she has a profit motive.

Florence was the French lady's name. Her eyes were an almost violet blue and her mouth was broad, the lower lip firm but slightly protruding . . . the sort of mouth you knew would be warm and sharing. High cheek bones gave her a

Slavic look. Epstein used a model with the same bone structure, I recall thinking as Florence threaded her way between the tables. Maria Jesus sat tensed up like an overstrung guitar. I laid a hand on her shoulder as I rose to greet our guest.

Florence was slim – one of those ladies you can't fit easily into an age bracket. Early thirties? She was reputed to be mistress to some rich Parisian businessman happy to pay her expenses. Ibiza is a small island. You hear all sorts of gossip. Most of what you hear, even when accurate in detail, is irrelevant. How people feel and behave towards each other is what matters rather than the source of their cash flow or their sleeping arrangements.

I had no idea how Florence would behave towards Maria Jesus. She was a very sophisticated lady. In comparison, Maria Jesus appeared innocent and vulnerable. My fear for Maria Jesus probably explained Florence being uptight and prickly the first quarter-hour. A double vodka with tonic while we scanned the menu helped her relax. By the time we'd eaten *raie au beurre noir* washed down with two chilled bottles of white wine the three of us were getting on fine, except for the language problem. Florence spoke some Spanish but not much and Maria Jesus was little better in French. Having me there to find words for them helped at first but a translator ends up as a barrier, so I excused myself before the dessert on the pretext that I was expecting a caller.

Maria Jesus came up to the studio an hour later. I was already in bed and feeling a little weird wondering how she would feel about sharing my bed. You don't know much about ladies who like ladies except from novels. Admittedly, Maria Jesus hadn't found me repulsive in the mountains . . . but then she hadn't been on the verge of love. With this spinning my head, perhaps I should have opened with more than a flip smile and a casual, '*Hola ninita . . .*'

'*Hola,*' she said. She looked great . . . a touch of pink to her cheeks and eyes bright enough for you to suspect she'd discovered a cocaine distillery.

Kicking off her sandals and jeans, she dragged her T-shirt over her head and stood poised naked by the bed a moment, her arms above her head and a big grin on her face. Then she bowed forward from the hips as if about to touch her toes. Instead she kissed me bang on the mouth. Her fingers dug into my ribs. '*Guapito,*' she teased, '*o qué guapo . . .*' with me wriggling all over the bed like I remembered my kids did when they were playsize and I was playing with them. This was a lousy thought which Maria Jesus immediately recognised.

'*Qué pasa?*' she whispered. Her body flat on mine and her head back, she pinned me to the bed with my arms outstretched so I couldn't look away.

'*Nada,*' I told her.

'*Nada!*' She gave my face a shake in mock ferocity. '*Nada! Nada! Nada!*' Then she was off the bed and heading through to the shower.

By the time she returned I was pretending sleep. She wouldn't have that. Possibly being on the edge of love had given her extra strength because, up till then, I had been a sort of father figure . . . or was that only how I saw myself?

So we made love. Maria Jesus did most of the loving. Probably she was trying to prove to me that all the crap in my head was crap? Which may also be crap? A hospital bed is a tough place to try and work all this out. Also, memory of that night has given birth to the first erection I've had in three days.

I must check with the Pathan as to whether an erection is liable to further damage my ball or merely retard its progress towards good health. That's a flippant thought from a frightened man. This is crazy! Three days of lying here in good humour and reasonable contentment and now the sweat is spurting out my pores faster than it would in the hot room at the Turkish baths. Reaching out for a glass of water, I knock the two notebooks I've already filled with these scribblings off the bedside table. The unopened letter from Sister Bear flutters to the floor along with the notebooks. Nice!

Some people get in trouble, they shut their eyes. I am behaving the same way by not opening the letter and by being flippant with the surgeon instead of getting him to tell me what the hell is really wrong with my ball. Strange that I should be more frightened of knowing than not knowing. Nor is it that I'm scared of dying. My first mescalin trip cured me of that fear.

I was lying out on Big J's terrace looking up at the sky when my body peeled open and released whatever the 'I' is, so that there was no me any longer but simply a joyous acceptance of being one with creation. I came out of the mescalin certain that death would be the same: a return to the tranquillity of eternal oneness. Lots of people have stated this concept better and without the aid of hallucinogens, but I am no Guru. However, this certainly eradicated my fear of death.

I remember strolling through the woods in Afghanistan late one night close to where an American nurse had been murdered the previous week. There were two of us: myself and an Italian. Suddenly I *knew* a couple of Afghans armed with axes were waiting in ambush for us. This scared me for a moment till I thought, so what was the worst that could happen?

They could jump out and hit us over the head.

We would be dead, but so what? The world would go on. This logic led me to thinking how crazy it was to consider our deaths could have any importance . . . so humorous that laughter burst out of me loud enough for the echoes to come rebounding back off the hills.

'What's funny?' my companion asked.

'There are two Afghans with hatchets about to chop our heads open,' I managed to gasp.

The Italian failed to find this amusing. In fact, he got so paranoid he refused to speak to me for a week.

Of course I was stoned then and merely contemplating death. What scares me now is becoming a eunuch.

Will my voice screech up into a high soprano?

What happens to my beard?

Will the texture of my skin soften so that everyone will immediately know?

Will I put on flab and sprout breasts?

Why should a man who considers it hilarious to have his

head chopped open with a hatchet find these questions scary?

I am afraid because leaving the hospital will be like stepping out into emptiness. There will be no continuity with my past. I feel cold and empty. I feel as if everything has been scooped out of me. Was it Herodotus who first wrote that there is nothing to fear but fear itself? Perhaps it was Socrates? I don't recall what happened to Herodotus but Socrates ended up being forced to drink hemlock as punishment for preaching too much political philosophy and too much love. It is easy to see how political philosophy would be considered dangerous, but love? Why not? There are enough people scared of it . . . which brings me back to Maria Jesus.

She reached for the makings to roll us a joint while sitting cross-legged so she could study my face. I grinned up at her sheepishly – God knows why the sheepishness – possibly because the sex had obviously been good for us both and I was feeling pleased at that but embarrassed at showing my pleasure in case she should think I had my head into a male conceit trip.

Playing football at school was the same. You scored, then you had to run back as if it wasn't anything special you'd achieved and you weren't even particularly pleased it had happened.

How much of this she read in my grin I don't know, but she regarded me with seriousness and said, 'You know, I really love you.'

'Yes?'

'Yes,' she said. 'You're such an idiot.'

'Thanks.'

She said, 'For nothing . . .' and waited.

There were lots of thoughts in my head but they refused to come out. I was happy for her and scared for her and worried whether Florence had ever made it with a woman or would want to make it with a woman and that, despite all this concern, I felt great to be with Maria Jesus . . . so I said, 'Great.'

'Jesus!' Sticking the joint between my lips, she gave a slow shake of her head. '*Great* – is that the best you can do?'

'Well I care,' I tried.

'Care!' she groaned, 'that's what you feel for dogs. Shit!' she added and sucked dope into her lungs. 'I mean, you're forty-five.'

I knew that. I also knew she was twenty-one and heading into a crisis. I tried putting a hand on her thigh but that wasn't much of an answer so I said, 'Yes . . .'

'Yes!' She took a deep drag at the joint and held the smoke down while looking me straight in the eyes. Then she blew the smoke in my face. 'I give up. I mean . . .' and her shoulders rose as if there was nothing more she could do. 'Two months in the mountains,' she said, 'and you know everything I've ever done – as for you . . .' Grinding the joint out, she glared at my desk – at the rows of books. 'You speak three languages like a native. How come you bothered to learn?'

Fair comment, I think and look up to see Babette coming down the ward. She's meant to have left for Tunis. I work a grin on to my face. '*Ça va?*'

'*Oui,*' she lies, 'I missed my flight.'

She drags a chair up close to the bed and spots the two notebooks on the floor. She scoops them up, sees the letter, remarks it is unopened and gives me a hard look. 'Cold feet?'

'Short on time,' I correct.

'*Quel con!*' She checks the stamp. 'What's she doing in England?'

Now how the hell does Babette know who the letter is from? All we have done is sail together a few weeks, during which time I may have mentioned Sister Bear a couple of times at most . . . or so I think.

'Anyone else,' Babette says, 'and you'd have read it by now.'

My ball gives me sufficient pain. 'Look,' I ask, 'did you stay on just so you can fuck my mind?'

'What mind?' Babette enquires with a sweet smile. 'Your image of yourself is a big prick.'

'Small prick.'

'There's a difference?'

'Three inches,' I retort, pleased at scoring.

'*Merde!*' She fakes disgust while toying with the letter.

Her fingers are so itchy to open it I am surprised she can hold off scratching. Instead, she brushes the hair back out of her eyes and says, 'These Indian doctors . . .'

'Pakistani . . .'

A movement of her shoulders dismisses two wars, a six hundred mile frontier and two religions. 'They know their job?'

'Mine does,' I say.

'So what's wrong?'

Lousy question! 'I've got a swelled-up ball.'

'And a bed in the surgical ward.'

This is a piece of logic I would be happy to avoid. It is tough keeping my head straight without having to deal with her worrying. I lay my notebook aside as a hint that my patience is running short. 'Because there are no other free beds.'

Babette looks unconvinced. '*C'est vrai?*'

'*Vrai*,' I assure her and smile with confidence. If I am not careful she is going to surrender to illogical and unearned guilts and will stay by my bedside instead of flying to North Africa to spend what remains of her holiday working on her tan while getting laid on the beach. This in mind, I insist, 'A couple more days on antibiotics and they'll let me out.'

'Sure?'

'Certain.'

She appears reassured. 'Thank God . . .'

'Or the Pakistani medical school,' I suggest.

'Yes, well . . .' She runs her tongue over her bottom lip. 'There's nothing I can do?'

I look thoughtful and finally propose, 'Not unless you can find time to pick me out one of those wicker birdcages in Tunis. One of the big ones,' I add so she will know she is into future hassle. Thought of dragging a five-foot birdcage around should absolve her of *any* guilt . . . though what the shit am I going to do with a birdcage?

Perhaps she understands my involved way of thought because she smiles and calls me a cunt.

'That's all that's worrying me,' I tell her and finger my chin. 'I get castrated, does my beard moult or only slow down its growth?'

'Moults,' she says and kisses me on the cheek. 'Till Paris . . '

'Or Ibiza.'

'One or the other.' She lays Sister Bear's letter on my lap. 'Should I hold your hand while you read?'

'Later,' I say and proffer the current notebook as evidence that I'm working.

'*Bien,*' she judges and gives me a second kiss. This one is both reward and farewell. '*A bientôt* . . .'

Women understand the necessity for work. A few ladies have left me over this; three weeks of fun in the sun and they get scared. 'Don't you have any work?' they ask. Or, 'Isn't there anything I can do?'

I don't and there isn't – not in Ibiza. Writing requires solitude so I keep that for winter and the mountains. As for lady guests, what *can* they do? I enjoy cooking, a neighbour comes in every noon to clean and a retired lady of pleasure has washed my clothes for the past fourteen years; a lady who would get uptight at finding a stranger's iron marks on my pants. Laundrywomen are scarcer than bedfellows . . . a piggy thought, I admit, as I watch Babette disappear out of the ward and temporarily out of my life. Her departure leaves me with Sister Bear's letter and a head full of memories. For the moment they are memories of Maria Jesus.

As I return to my scribbling, I acknowledge that her relationship with Florence acted as a catalyst on my life. Without Maria Jesus, there would be no letter for me to fear.

She, Florence and I had a fine time the four days following our first dinner. The three of us would be off to the beach each day: picnic, spear-fishing, borrow a sailboat . . .

Maria Jesus was extra phsycial with me as if proving to Florence in advance that the way she felt for the elder woman didn't mean she was in any way weird. This was how I assessed her manner. Of course it is possible she was extra loving to me because she felt so Goddamned happy and had to let that happiness out on someone or explode.

I did my best to get them off by themselves with excuses of how I had to go fix a friend's water pump before her garden dried up. Three days this went on (not the pump – but the fun) and the fourth day a young Ibicenco dropped by to ask me to come visit his house. It was an old farmhouse his father had abandoned in preference for a concrete horror built down the road. Ten years of tourism and the dirt road had become a throughway and the concrete house got so hot in July you could bake eggs on the living-room floor. The son wanted ideas on how to modernise the old farmhouse without spoiling its charm. The two of us spent all day up in the hills with tape-measure and paper – good work but tiring. I got back around nine o'clock.

Maria Jesus arrived with Florence two hours later to find me reading on the bed. Maria Jesus knelt to hug me and I felt her arms tremble. I tried to search her eyes for what had happened. She had the same look I remembered from my kids when they'd come rushing into the house full of some fresh adventure they had experienced except Maria Jesus controlled her tongue.

'There's champagne in the refrigerator,' I suggested with a welcoming smile for Florence. '*Ça va?*'

She thrust her hair back with both hands and laughed. '*Superbe.*'

Well that was fine – except I felt I ought to leave them alone. Unfortunately, splitting immediately would have seemed impolite. On the other hand, having me rap might be a drag so I gave what I hoped would sound an appreciative chuckle and waited for Florence to open the conversation.

The cork exploding out of the champagne bottle in the kitchen saved us. Maria Jesus called through to ask if I wanted coffee.

I called back, '*Si, gracias, ninita,*' and heard her put the kettle on.

Watching me fiddle with my book, Florence suggested the equivalent in French of, *You want to read, read,* and departed to help Maria Jesus.

By the time they had coffee brewed I was deep into my book. It was restful curled up in one corner of the bed with these two down the other end rapping at each other in a mixture of struggling French and stumbling Spanish – warmer and more comforting than having the radio play. A half-hour passed before my subconscious registered a sudden heightening in the intensity. I tried to keep on reading but they fell silent and I glanced up.

They sat facing each other in the full lotus. This was all they had in common except for both being beautiful and even their beauty was different. Florence had no curves left. Perhaps this is the difference between beauty and prettiness. Beauty lasts and has strength . . . is this merely a memory of that evening? Because Florence certainly looked strong; not tough, which is physical and pugnacious, but calm and oddly detached: like a general, I thought; a battle-hardened general viewing from a hilltop the marshalling of his troops.

Maria Jesus seemed a child in comparison. She was all nerve ends. Head bowed, she sat picking at a frayed cuticle on her index finger. I could hear the tick of the travelling clock on my desk and was aware of the sweat seeping out of my palms. Possibly my worrying for Maria Jesus was impertinent. It was certainly a waste of emotional energy . . . but then I hadn't taken a risk with my own heart in years. Transit camps are sited well back from the battle front. I was so scared for her I tried to think up some crack to lighten the scene. Fortunately Florence saved me from error.

She reached forward to still Maria Jesus's fingers. Her touch shot a shiver through the younger woman . . . like getting touched with a hot iron, I thought, except Maria Jesus had sufficient courage not to leap back. Instead, she slowly raised Florence's hand, holding it cupped in her palms as a child might protect a fully open rose from the breeze. She hesitated . . . like a skater poised on the bank of a newly-frozen lake. Know that feeling? The ice will be firm out in the middle but you have to cross those first few metres. You can tiptoe or take it at a rush. Maria Jesus tiptoed.

Head bowed, she gently brushed her lips to the older woman's hand. It was so delicate and so gentle a kiss and yet so strong in its commitment that nothing else existed . . . like time sometimes stops when you are on acid or in fairy tales.

Is it crazy to write of someone else's experience with such emotion? I look over at my neighbour in the hospital ward As far as I know he is unconscious, but does this mean that he has nothing going on in his head? Perhaps he is dreaming of the life he is about to leave. I doubt if death worries him. Ceasing to be a flower bed for plastic tubes would be a relief. But does he have regrets? Regrets for the chances he passed up, the joys he missed, the pain he caused . . . ?

Back then I felt pain. I found myself praying into their silence; praying that Maria Jesus wouldn't get hurt. She looked up at Florence, Florence's hand still cupped in hers. The French woman showed no emotion. She sat there immobile and tranquil as a stone Buddha abandoned to the Thailand forest for the last two thousand years. The Buddha accepts. She was like that. And Maria Jesus worshipped.

Please, I prayed, and very slowly Maria Jesus rocked forward out of the lotus position on to her knees and, kneeling there in front of Florence, gently kissed her on the lips. The kiss was a feather brushing. It was so perfect and I felt such relief that my stomach seemed suddenly empty the way it feels when you have ridden your bike fast into a curve only to be faced with a truck hurtling straight for you and on the wrong side of the road. You survive by instinct and miracle – but *do* survive and feel so Goddamned thankful but also sick enough to throw up.

This was *my* emotion. As for Maria Jesus, she slipped back to sit on her heels and looked round at me. There wasn't a line on her face. All her nervousness had vanished. Regarding me out of giant grey-green eyes, she said quietly, '*Gauchito*, you're crying.'

'Yes?' I raised a hand to my cheeks. She was right. 'You don't want me to cry,' I said, 'then don't make me feel like I'm about to walk up to the altar for my First Communion.' You can make this sort of statement to a twenty-one-year-old South American lady. South American Spanish (except when spoken by Argentinians) is all music and diminutives and endearments as with Maria Jesus's habit of addressing me as *Gauchito guapito mio*.

My pretty little cowboy! This sounds neither normal nor sane when translated into Anglo-American; particularly considering I am forty-five years old, grey in the beard and am wearing my reading spectacles. Right? Also I hate horses. They have a quarter the brains of a mule, a tenth of the stamina and demand ten times the attention.

It is also perhaps neither normal nor sane that a man's embarrassment at his own emotions should get him writing on how he feels about horses! So back to Maria Jesus . . .

She smiles at my First Communion sally and says, 'Baptism is more your need.'

I grin. 'At my age – who'd bother?'

'You could try looking,' she suggests. There is concern in her eyes as she offers me her glass of champagne. The concern strikes me as odd considering I have spent the last quarter-hour in a sweat of fear over *her* situation.

'Not right now,' I say to the champagne.

'*Seguro?*' she presses.

I know what she is asking is not whether I want a drink but whether I want to be part of their act. I already am a part of their act if only in the way a good audience participates. Perhaps this is my role. It is certainly draining enough. '*Seguro*,' I assure her.

We have lost Florence. Her limited command of Spanish doesn't extend to the niceties Maria Jesus and I are playing. Also she has lost her tranquillity. For a moment I wonder whether she has picked up on Maria Jesus offering her glass, but this is nonsense. Florence is far too worldly wise for the idea of a threesome to bug her. She is fully capable of saying no. So what has destroyed her poise, I decide, is having Maria Jesus so blatant in her love. You get loved that openly by someone, your normal defences get shattered. With all this spinning my head, the best I can do is smile at her, pat my shirt pocket and remark, 'Shit, we're out of cigarettes.'

Neither Maria Jesus nor Florence smoke tobacco but Maria Jesus knows there is a half-full carton of *Ducados* in the kitchen. 'You should quit,' she says as I clamber off the bed.

'Maybe tomorrow,' I reply with an anxious look at the clock. 'Anyway, I have to meet a man . . .' I check out the Moroccan jar in which we keep the household hashish supply and toss the remaining fragment from hand to hand so Florence can see we are really short. Any lady should understand you don't break a date with your dealer. 'He's got a few ounces of Grade A Afghani,' I tell her with a grin and split for the street.

I returned two hours later to find the bed made and them in it. They were asleep and facing each other, each with her upper arm lying loosely across the other's body above the sheet: bronzed shoulders, bronzed arms, delicate hands open and defenceless, and these two heads resting on the pillows, hair loose and dark with sweat at the nape of the neck as their eyelids were dark with sleep.

Quietly I shifted the easy chair over to the window, set the reading lamp to focus and seated myself with my book. Every few pages I would look over at the bed. Each time I got the same kick in the guts. They looked so vulnerable. Perhaps it was arrogance on my part to feel so protective for something I was not even part of any more except that it was my bed they were in.

I had this sense of being both a privileged witness and a guard. Some memory nagged to the surface. I kept on trying to read but the need to remember destroyed my concentration. Finally giving up on the effort, I sat watching over their sleep. There was a faint lightening to the east so it must have been after four in the morning when the memory finally hit: Passion Week back when I was a ten-year-old entrusted to the Jesuits and we had this rota of who would watch over the Holy Sacrament.

Sitting watching these two ladies, I recalled how it had felt to be alone in the school chapel, kneeling before the altar with the gold monstrance shining above you with its tiny window through which you could see the white wafer which was the Body of Christ.

Ten years old and at guard over the Body of Christ and now, thirty-five years later, I was suffering the same sense of privilege at watching over two ladies asleep in my bed. This is hardly a memory to win points in the locker-room after a game of golf! Would the Gay Liberation Front approve, or the Female Liberation Front? Odd – in fact very odd – because I can think of couple of Benedictine monks from my second school who would understand and be truly pleased to know that a little of their faith stuck strong enough to give their pupil two hours of joy in his middle-age. Worship is probably a truer word than joy. Certainly I was more moved than I am by a parade of braless ladies screeching slogans outside the White House.

I guess I am just a freak.

Does anyone else get confused between the Holy Sacrament and two naked ladies on a bed? Lesbians, homosexuals, gays, dykes, fairies, fags – this is the image game: two men giving each other head or fucking each other up the ass (though not at the same time of course) – a couple of ladies, one of them wearing a ten-inch rubber dildo and black net stockings. It would be nice to change track and think of how two people are making love to each other rather than how disgusting it is that they are committing all these unnatural acts to each other's bodies. I guess I have done just about everything at some time or other that a male body can do, and the only actions I can now remember as unnatural were those done without love. Of course this is hindsight and viewed from the vantage point of a hospital bed with a Pathan surgeon hovering over my remaining testicle with a carving knife.

A lot of these thoughts chased through my skull as I sat in the easy chair. The fishing fleet was heading out of port. Their big one-lunger diesel engines thumped like heartbeats – comforting sound – and Maria Jesus awoke.

She looked at me out of those grey-green eyes. Solemn eyes. I certainly didn't smile. You don't smile in Church! Careful not to wake Florence, she slipped out of bed and tiptoed over to squat at my feet. She had studied dance back in Montevideo which accounts for the way she holds herself and moves with such extraordinary grace.

She had taught me a great deal in the mountains. Reading of violations of human rights in *Time Magazine* fails to give you the same sense of evil and horror as hearing how it was from the lady you are making love with . . . of how the Colonels let their soldiers loose on Montevideo University; of how the soldiers came in with clubs and how they were grunting with excitement and were smiling and sweating so their faces glistened in the sun and how they chased the female students and rammed their nice army issue clubs up the cunts of the students they caught because, after their first few rapes, they were out of seed, and how there were teenage girls leaping from the windows, the whole University fuller of screams than a Rolling Stones Pop Festival.

Now I recall what book I was reading that night – or what book I had been trying to read. *The Honorary Consul* by Graham Greene.

I know it was *The Honorary Consul* because she took the book off my knee, glanced at its title and then laid it aside, which I recall thinking was a slightly complicated piece of accidental symbolism.

She smiled as she set the book aside, then rested her cheek on my knee. We stayed like that for a while. I stroked her hair and finally whispered how I had been thinking of sailing over to the neighbouring island of Formentera for a few days.

She looked up at me with a quick little nod which was nice because like that I could kiss her on the forehead without making a big thing out of it. Then I got my fishing gear together along with a spare pair of jeans and a couple of T-shirts.

'Love you,' I whispered.

She said, '*Tambien*,' and we gave each other a grin that suddenly turned into a two-way fit of giggles which we had to muffle for fear of waking Florence who might not have understood. Sad that I never got to tell Maria Jesus about the gold monstrance and the Body of Christ. She would have gotten high on that. Perhaps she knew anyway. Osmosis? Because Saturday, when I got back, the studio was fuller of flowers than a church decked out for Epiphany.

Maria Jesus had left a note propped on the desk. The front door key was in the envelope. Apparently they had split for Amsterdam and some music festival.

They were deliriously happy, Maria Jesus wrote, and prayed I would find happiness and that she would remember me with gratitude forever and ever, etcetera, etcetera. She had scrawled a bunch of crosses below her signature. The crosses were presumably meant as kisses rather than a hope I would get myself multiply crucified. She had also added a one word postscript. *TRY!*

A lady lives with a man a while, she likes to leave believing she has changed him for the better. Judging by her postscript, Maria Jesus felt she had failed. She was too sweet a lady to disappoint so I *would* try, I decided as I headed through to the shower . . . However, it would have been easier if she had been more explicit such as suggesting what I should try *at*.

Soap in my ears, I was still mulling over this problem when the front door crashed open. Gerda was back! She had come straight from the airport.

She strode past the open bathroom door without even a *Good morning* or a *How have you been?*

'Hurry,' she commanded, 'I'm pressed for time.'

Obviously this was true because by the time I was out of the shower and dry, she was out of her clothes and on the bed.

I took a quick peek through the window. Sure enough, her father was down there in the car busy at earning his ulcer. Poor bastard, I thought and headed for the bed. We'd balled before with Gerda in a hurry but never in this much of a hurry. Laying on top of her felt like riding a horse that is bolting for its stable with no thought in its head except to get the ride over with.

I did my duty the best I could while deciding that some time soon I would get up courage to ask Gerda what or who she was actually fucking while sprawled on my bed . . . and why? While these thoughts delayed my orgasm (to her irritation), I also decided to ask myself why I was fucking her. This was a stupid question to be asking myself because I knew why.

I was fucking her because she had to be suffering some hurt to go through with this crazy ritual; until I discovered what this hurt was, I had no right to add a new hurt by rejecting her need. Also, though I did not particularly care for her father, I did feel sorry for him. Our fucking put his future as caretaker to his son-in-law at stake and he was too old to find another sinecure. Also Gerda was a very tough lady and would certainly persecute the old man for any frustration I gave her . . . at which point I orgasmed.

Gerda rolled out from under me and dashed for the bathroom. Five minutes and she was dressed and ready to leave. Poking her head round the door, she finally noticed the flowers. She presumed the flowers were my preparation for her arrival. Not only did she throw me a smile but actually wasted a good seven seconds by returning to the bed to give me a kiss.

'Sweet of you,' she said. 'See you in the morning.'

Chapter Nine

'See you in the morning.'

The Pathan has just passed by to echo Gerda's threat to my virility. I would like to have rapped with him a minute but he was pressed for time. One of his heart-disease patients has gone into a coma and been slipped into an oxygen tent.

I wonder how the Pathan's failure rate as a surgeon compares with my failure rate as a stud. Surgeons have an advantage over studs: their failures don't talk.

This sounds like I worry over a lady telling tales. Not true. There was a period I even spread word of how I was impotent. This was back when I was naïve enough to attempt combining a writing career with life on Ibiza and expected a reputation for impotence to give me more work time and less temptation. I was wrong. Either male impotence is a challenge to the female species or my having a hot water geyser that supplies the best shower in town is too great an attraction for a lady to miss out on because she is told my penis prefers rest to erection.

Believe me, an effective shower on Ibiza is a hell of a bait, as is a toilet which can be relied upon to flush. Mid-June through mid-September even floor space on which to spread a sleeping bag is hot property and that is how I met Sister Bear.

Sister Bear sailed in on the Barcelona ferry the day Gerda flew home after a week's stay on the island. Gerda and her husband were booked to attend some Dusseldorf social function. Gerda assured me the function would be a drag. Maybe for her it was. I felt differently. There were afternoons we would meet on a beach and actually have fun, but those six o'clock in the morning calls to duty headed a different category.

You try playing two hours of tennis a day, spend four hours on the beach, dance half the night and be expected to produce both an eager erection and a welcoming smile after only three hours sleep . . . not that I would prefer eight hours on the assembly line or down the mines.

Sister Bear's problem was different, though she was equally exhausted. This was her first visit to Ibiza and her first visit to Europe. She had criss-crossed France, Italy and Spain by train on one of those Eurorail passes which give you unlimited mileage and unlimited fatigue. Landing on Ibiza, she wasted four hours hunting a hotel room. There weren't any.

Finally she accosted a plump and happy-looking Frenchman sufficiently into beads and suntan to be a resident.

He told her he maybe knew a place and led her down my street. A small pension crumbles away its existence at the end of the block. It boasts one bathroom (cold water shower) and one can. Normally neither functions.

Spotting my door ajar, the Frenchman stopped by for a smoke and to check the lady could wash up at my place if she found a room. A German painter was already visiting. The painter is great with a brush but has a skull which serves as an athletics arena for jumping beans hyped on acid.

Disconnected ideas fired at you in broken English is tough going for the morning after the week before. The Frenchman recognised my problem. Waving his lady companion to a seat on my bed, he licked six Rizla King Size into shape, crumpled an eighth of an ounce of Nepalese in with two Thai sticks and a half a Marlboro and came up with a joint the size of the *New York Times* and with a kick that would have shamed an irate ostrich.

Ten minutes and the painter's jumping beans had switched to melted marshmallow. The Frenchman led him out. I sagged with relief. Then realised the Frenchman had left a sleeping lady on my bed. What with the painter rapping non-stop, we hadn't been introduced. Nor had I taken time to inspect her. There was little to see. She was dressed kind of hippy: long dress short on shape, a shawl, a few silk scarves and a pair of boots. The scarves covered most of her face so all I could really tell was that she had black and very thick long hair. He being French and she having that hair, maybe she was North African Arab, I thought. Curled up in the corner, what she resembled most was a multi-coloured dumpling.

The painter's visit had already denied me my morning tennis. Now, presumably, I would miss out on the beach. Dumplings don't wake easily . . . also my door is complicated to operate. Ladies find it unpleasant to awaken abandoned in some strange man's apartment as if left to be put out later along with the garbage.

I had a couple of letters to write. These finished and she still sleeping, I got into a book. Every now and again I would glance at her over the top of my reading spectacles. The situation reminded me of Maria Jesus and Florence – not that a dumpling is easily confused with the Body of Christ – but she was sleeping and I was reading and Maria Jesus had written, TRY!

Had she meant I should try communicating, I wondered. If so, I was into a lousy start.

The dumpling finally awoke around eight o'clock in the evening. This says nothing for travel by train so perhaps I am writing an airline advertisement.

'Shit!' was her first word while rubbing gum out of her eyes. 'Have I been keeping you?'

American.

I answered, 'Not specifically . . .' and seeing she was still preoccupied with her eyes, added, 'Though I had been planning on going to the beach.'

'Great,' she said. Presumably she was unaware of how late it was.

'Yeah,' I said. 'Want something to eat?' I asked this because she was yawning so had her mouth open. She had nice teeth but remained a multi-coloured dumpling and I had a dinner invitation for nine-thirty so was offering her a sandwich out of politeness while she got herself together. She did not understand any of this (or perhaps she did).

Whichever, she answered, 'How about after we swim?'

'Now?' I glanced at the clock.

She ignored the clock. 'Now what?'

'Swim,' I said.

She looked puzzled but managed a strained smile. 'Swim

right after you eat, you get stomach cramps.'

My nurse told me this back when I was a six-year-old. The nurse also insisted I say please and thank you, taught me to open doors for ladies and demanded I stand up every time a lady entered the room. The door opening number was tough on a six-year-old. This situation was tough on a forty-five-year-old.

Fuck! I thought . . . but remained a gentleman. Fortunately there were two clean beach towels in the bathroom. I collected these. What else could I do? So I would be a little late for dinner, but no one has expected me to be on time for years; not if they are friends and it is summer – anything could happen.

Something did happen. I spotted her backpack skulking under the kitchen table. By then it was too late. We were already at the door.

We rode the Bultaco out to Salinas. Daytime the beach looks dirty grey and is speckled with empty coke cans, plastic bags, abandoned ham sandwiches, soda bottles and chunks of tar. Thank God for moonlight. Now what faced us was a gently curving stretch of silvery white with the sea dark and smooth as a mirror, the moon drawing a glistening path right across the four-mile straights to Formentera.

'Beautiful,' she whispered.

I agreed but walked on tiptoe for fear of slicing my feet open on broken glass. I also worried over how cold we would get on the ride back to town and over what in hell was I going to do with her when we *did* get back to town.

We must have been swimming some time before I realised I was having fun. I have known the same feeling of surprise in the mountains. You come off the lift with your feet frozen and your hands numb and the crest covered with ice plus the clouds so thick and low you can't see the tips of your skis. Fear hits. You hesitate . . . but the others are better skiers than you are and you don't want to get abandoned. Down you shoot. Suddenly you are over a shoulder and into pure powder with your limbs thawed out and the sun bursting through the cloud. The whole valley gleams below. Smoke floats up from the village, and old Pepe is clearly visible way down there with his sheep by the river bank. You can actually hear the bells ring on the lead goats' necks. Miraculous!

So it was now, except this was summer and the sea. I wasn't creating all this magic so it had to be the lady. Flipping on to my back, I looked for her as if she actually existed as a person instead of a block to my dinner date.

She had turned back for shore. She swam well, her feet churning up a wake of phosphorescence. I raced after her. We had said maybe thirty words to each other and now she was standing on the beach and did not look at all like a dumpling. She looked beautiful.

Long black hair tumbled to her ass and she had a tough little all-together body packed with muscle, which you knew would be perfect at making it over the hills if you were out trekking the Himalayas. Not that I thought much about her. I just recognised that she looked great and that I felt great.

I wasn't hot for her. Nor was I anxious for any entanglements, let alone one more in an endless stream of sexual adventures. Gerda had left that day and would be back in a week plus this was mid-June and the whole island had been balling crazy ever since the week before Easter. If anything, I wanted a rest.

She flung me a towel as I hit the beach.

'Thanks,' I said while she simply smiled as if she'd discovered heaven.

She had a broad face with high cheekbones, bright black eyes and a short hook of a nose that flared at the nostrils. Either she had spent a lot of time basking nude in the sun or had been born dusky. Her mouth was very wide with firm heavy lips. It was a tough face and matched her body. Perhaps this was why her smile was so irresistible. It was like spotting a beacon marking a reef on a dark night with the wind up and driving you towards the coast. You spot that light, you keep your eye on it, however much spray freezes your face. You'll even climb the mast . . . though, of course, what I actually said was, 'Want a drink?'

She said, 'Sure,' so we dressed and strolled back along the beach to the pension where we had parked the bike.

The bar is in the garden patio. Two fishermen were at the

bar. They were several drinks ahead of us and happy, so the evening turned into a typical island rap session: recollections of how the sea used to be full of fish and is now full of tar and sewage from the hotels.

Back in my first years on Ibiza supplying dinner for eight entailed a ten-minute swim off the rocks. In those ten minutes you would see a dozen fish. Finally you would spot a meru the right size. Sorry friend, you'd think, the fish gulping at you out of his cave patiently as a geriatric banker with bad eyesight. Bang! and dinner was ready to be laid out on the charcoal once you'd stuffed the gut with thyme and rosemary picked fresh from the hillside. Those days are over.

So are the days of running booze and cigarettes into the beach at two o'clock in the morning, which was another topic of conversation. Smuggling used to be an island sport. Now we fuck, play tennis, and watch badly dubbed American soap operas on TV.

'Is that an improvement?' The shorter of the two fishermen demands. Deep lines drag down his mouth. He must be sixty, judging by the grey stubble on his face; one of the pre-tourist generation, he gets himself shaved by the barber every Saturday evening.

His companion is a stocky forty-year-old into gestures more than words. He shrugs and says, '*Mierda!*'

'No adventure . . .' This is my contribution.

'*Claro*,' the old one says while the barman nods and gives me a wink in acknowledgement of the two years he knows I've spent in jail.

'Some people do all right,' he says. In his late twenties, he is six inches taller than either fisherman; one of the benefits of tourism has been an improved diet. The fishermen ignore him.

'My childhood,' the old one recalls, 'Ibiza City was an eight-hour ride by pony trap from our *finca*.'

'Easter,' the stocky one confirms and spits at the tiles.

'That's how it was,' his companion agrees. 'The farmers came in once a year at Easter.'

'*Que viaje!*' snorts the barman. He sets up a round on the house while I recount meeting one of the island's doctors two days previously at the Cafe Monte Sol. 'Just back from Bali.'

The stocky one is shocked into speech. 'Jesus!' he says. 'My father never even got to Barcelona.'

'Nor did he get his pole wet,' cracks the barman, 'not till he got married.'

Embarrassed, I looked down at the lady sitting beside me. 'You understand any of this?'

She shakes her head. 'Though I should,' she says.

Mexican, I wonder. 'Where are you from?'

'Santa Fe.'

'Nice?'

'All right . . .' She gives a flick of her shoulders like it is immaterial. 'We moved to California.'

'Oh,' I say.

Her smile flashes back. 'You speak more Spanish. Hey,' she says as my mouth droops, 'don't worry – I dig listening.'

'You do?'

'I don't lie.' Her eyes go solemn. 'That's the first lesson.' Back comes the smile. 'Right?'

'Right,' I say.

'Fine,' she says. Slipping an arm around my waist, she nuzzles her nose against my shoulder.

The Spaniards are watching. They sense something has happened but are unsure of what. They have company! There I was whacked out and swearing abstinence and now my belly has gone warm and mushy.

'How about food?' I suggest in Spanish and we shift to a table under the palm trees.

'For all of our complaints,' the old man says and includes each of us in his smile, 'it is a good life.'

The barman's mother overhears this remark. She is five foot tall and four feet wide. Slapping a flat loaf of peasant bread on the table, she grunts, 'For those with idle hands.'

'*Venga Madre*,' protests the barman. 'Join us.'

'With sixty sheets to launder,' she snaps.

The barman raises his shoulders in apology. 'She enjoys complaining.'

'They all do,' concurs the elder fisherman.

'Life,' adds the stocky one. Clutching the bread firmly against his belly, he produces a one-blade pocket knife from his overalls and slices the loaf into slabs a half-inch thick

The lady from Santa Fe leaves us. I presume she is off to the toilet. Instead she heads for the kitchen. A barrage of Ibicenco greets her but she stays

'You have a good one there,' remarks the barman as he thumps wine on the table. Toeing a chair back, he slumps into it and drags a forearm across his face. 'Shit!' he says, 'we served six hundred lunches.'

'*Pesetas*,' says the stocky fisherman – perhaps he has a mortgage to pay off.

'Who cares?' The barman looks up the road to where he can see the lights of the two other Salinas *pensiones* shining through the trees. 'We used to be friends,' he recounts of their owners. 'Now . . . shit! We look each other in the eye and all we can see is competition.'

Glum-faced, the fishermen nod. 'As bad as the Civil War,' the elder remarks.

Nice philosophy, I think as Miss Santa Fe returns with a big bowl of salad topped with black olives. Her smile prods the party back into shape. Anyone that happy is a tonic. We watch her carry two glasses brimming with *Marques de Riscal* off to the kitchen. We hear the old lady cackle. We look at each other. God alone knows how those two women are communicating. We men grin at each other sheepishly. Two women without a language in common, and all the heavy male rap we've been laying down seems suddenly less important than the froth on a glass of beer. I am so conscious of this that I stand up as the old lady appears with a platter loaded with fish.

There's a problem in standing up: what in hell do you do with yourself? The old lady supplies the answers. She looks me up and down the way a butcher inspects beef on the hoof. Head tilted, she throws Miss Santa Fe a wink and cackles, 'Not bad for a blond.'

Miss Santa Fe grins – not that she can understand the words – but the old lady's meaning is plain as is the way she slaps the fish platter down. '*Venga cabrones*,' she orders, 'Did we work for nothing?' Forking fish on to our plates, she nods at Miss Santa Fe to serve the rice.

I sit down. Miss Santa Fe seats herself beside me. She is obviously enjoying herself. So am I.

'Great,' I mumble through a last mouthful of rouget.

She rewards me with a smile before pushing her chair back. As she passes the old lady, the old lady attempts to rise. Santa Fe holds her down.

'As for those pigs of bankers . . .' the elder fisherman complains and we are off to another favourite topic: how the local bankers have ripped off every land-owning peasant family on the island along with at least half the foreigners who have attempted property development.

We are still on this subject when Miss Santa Fe returns bearing cups on a tray along with a pot of coffee. She gives me a kiss on the left ear before setting the tray in front of the old lady. Cackling at the kiss, the old lady slips an arm around the American's waist.

'Tell her,' she orders me. 'What chance! Back in my day the men worked so hard, the only night they were useful was Saturday and *then* they were drunk.'

I grin. 'We're better?'

'An old one like me, how should I know?' she chortles and rubs her thighs while the three Spaniards rock with laughter. She pats Miss Santa Fe on the rump. 'She'll tell us.'

I regard my evening's companion.

'Well?' she asks.

'The old lady says things are better than they used to be.'

'What things?'

'Things,' I say.

The old lady guesses I've chickened out. 'Hah!' she snorts. 'Men!' With a slap on the ass, she drives Miss Santa Fe back to her seat. 'So tell her in bed.'

The ride home is as cold as I had suspected it would be. Miss Santa Fe shivers. I spread my arms in hope of keeping the wind off her. 'You all right?'

For answer she snuggles closer against my back.

We park outside the studio. I chain the bike to the ring set in the wall and open the door. Entering ahead of me, she halts by the kitchen table. For a lady who has appeared so confident all evening, she looks surprisingly uncertain.

I lock up and say, 'After that ride, you need a drink.'

'Thanks . . .'

'My pleasure,' I assure her with a smile, and head through to the front room where I keep the spirits. 'Brandy or rum?'

'Whichever's easiest.'

'Easiest . . .' The booze shelf is at knee level so I have to look up. She is standing in the doorway. Without her smile, hands on her hips and draped in the shapeless dress, she has switched back to being a dumpling. Perhaps she thinks I am about to put her out. 'What's easiest is what you want,' I tell her. 'Maybe you'd like a shower?'

This makes her happier.

'Get the salt out of your hair . . .' Passing her a brandy, I warn, 'It takes a couple of minutes for the water to heat.'

Off she goes with her glass while I unroll the bedding. A clean lady deserves a clean sheet, so I find one.

'Do I leave the water running?' she calls.

I say, 'Please.'

Out she comes wrapped in a white bath towel. The white looks good against her tan. She has her hands full of our beach towels which she has rinsed. 'There's tar on one of them,' she says.

I say, 'That's the Mediterranean for you.'

'So where do I hang them?'

'Balcony,' I tell her. 'There are pegs on the line.'

Returning from the shower, I notice she has left her pack under the table. The straps are still fastened. She has turned the lights off in the front room before opening the curtains to go out on the balcony and is still out there. Her hair is pulled forward each side of her head so I can see she has a nice neck and nice shoulders. She is watching stevedores load a small container ship that does the Valencia run twice a week.

Joining her, I say, 'They make quite a noise.'

'Nice,' she answers, 'this end of the port. It's not so touristy.'

I say, 'Right,' and put an arm around her shoulders. She leans her head against me and we stand like that for a while.

The moon is so bright we can see not only the outline of the hills the far side of the bay, but also a difference in tone between the wooded areas and open terraces. A car weaves its way up the track towards the crest. Back in my first year in the studio the car would have been George and his wife driving home from a dinner date. There were only two houses on the hill in those days and George owned the only car. Now it could be any one of a hundred people.

We hear the thump of a diesel engine and a mast-head shows swaying beyond the sea wall. The fishing boat surges in round the lighthouse at a good twelve knots. As the skipper cuts back the engine revolutions, the boat gives the impression of slumping into the water like a fat duck making a landing on a lake. Breaking along the mole, the bow wave curls towards us. It is a long curl and capped with foam – a fair curl sparkling in the dock lights, and I realise my wife has slipped into my head.

'Beautiful,' Miss Santa Fe murmurs.

I nod and raise a hand to the owner of the fisherman's bar. He has come out on to his terrace and looks up at us.

'Need anything before I close?' he shouts.

'*Nada, gracias,*' I call back. '*Buena nite.*'

'*Buena nite.*'

'You live alone?' she asks.

'More or less . . .'

She waits . . . then, 'What does more or less mean?'

'There's a lady,' I tell her. 'She's away till the end of the week.'

What a shitty half-truth to have told, I think now as I lie here in this hospital bed. I have told worse. But it was a stupid half-truth and cowardly as well as unkind. I knew she was lacking in confidence at that moment; that she felt alone and a little lost. There was no need for the lie.

Lie?

I seem to have trapped myself. This is the risk to writing memoirs. You write fast enough, you have insufficient time to raise your defences. The truth seeps out.

Some idiot once said that sticks and stones may break your bones but names can never hurt you. Of course this proverb predates airmail, but can you imagine quoting such insanity to kids?

Fortunately Sister Bear has big bold handwriting, I think as I finger her letter: there can't be that many names on one sheet of paper. But even a few names, if they are well chosen.

will cause me more pain than I am now suffering with my ball.

She spotted I had only one that first night. 'Does it make a difference?' she asked. We had made love and were resting peacefully on the brink of sleep – or I was.

'I don't know,' I said.

'You try very hard.'

'Yes?'

'Well not at conversation,' she admitted with a sniff of laughter and struck a match to the candle above the bed. 'So I can see your face,' she explained. 'If I don't see, I'll think I'm talking to myself.' She smiled. 'But you know what I mean . . .'

For answer I produced a grin and waited.

'Jesus!' she said. 'How about a smoke?'

'Great idea.'

She sat cross-legged. I watched and hoped the time she'd take rolling a joint would give her mind space to change track. Of course this was our first night together and I didn't know the lady. Her assurance had returned with our lovemaking. Hair falling forward over her shoulders, she looked tough, calm, competent and very beautiful. She was rolling a joint but could as easily have been sewing mocassins. 'Out of a western,' I murmured.

'Squaw?' She hadn't bothered to look up from the dope tray.

'That's right.'

'Dead right,' she said. 'Navajo and Apache . . . my Dad's the Apache.'

'Oh,' I said . . . and seeing this seemed a good time to ask, 'Do you have a name?'

She grinned. 'Sister Bear.'

'Jesus! That's your given name?'

'First name?' She was too taken up with rolling to recognise my horror. 'Alice Jane . . .' She wrinkled her nose in disgust. 'Euch!'

'So how come the Sister Bear?'

'My brother played half-back,' she recounted. 'They called him Bear. I got to High School, it was Sister Bear.'

I could understand this could happen with their being

Indian. 'But it won't do here.'

She looked up and looked cross. 'Why the hell not?'

'There's a writer over the other side of the island,' I told her. 'He wrote a novel entitled *Sister Bear*.'

She still looked cross. 'That gives him a monopoly?'

'Not a monopoly,' I said. 'But he's more of a success than I am, which is a drag to be reminded of.'

She scratched at the back of her head. She looked young doing that. 'Is this for real?'

'I could learn to live with it,' I said.

'Before the end of the week?'

Karma! Lies always catch you out. 'I could try.'

'You *do* try,' she said. 'That's what we were talking about.'

True Karma! But what can a man do? 'How about a drink?' I suggested.

She said, 'Shit on your drink,' and lit up. 'Here . . .'

I dragged while she watched. 'Take another poke,' she said.

'Trying to get me stoned?'

'Loose,' she retorted while studying my face. 'How old are you?'

'Forty-five.'

'Twice my age.'

'So maybe I should retire.'

'Not from this conversation,' she told me. 'I mean, look . . .'

'I am.'

'And stop playing games.' She took a deep drag as if hoping the smoke would organise her thoughts. 'I orgasmed five times . . .'

'Nice.'

She grinned. 'I'm not complaining.'

'So?' I shot – which should teach me not to try being sharp.

'So it was kind of like being worked on,' she said. 'Know what I mean?'

'Professional?'

'Kind of . . .' She had another go at the back of her head. 'You have beautiful hair.'

'You're changing track.'

'And you're Bogarting that joint.'

'Bogarting – shit!' she complained. 'That's early fifties.'

'My generation,' I pointed out. 'Look, maybe I just don't want to talk.'

'Because we've only just met?'

'Maybe . . .'

'Crap!' She grinned. 'But like the sex, I'm not complaining.'

'No?'

'No.' Unfolding her legs, she stepped over me and disappeared into the kitchen. 'There's no fruit?'

Fruit at three in the morning! Next she'd have me eating brown rice. 'There's half a bottle of wine open in the refrigerator.'

She returned with a tray on which she'd set two glasses of wine and a plate of cold turkey she'd sliced off the remains of a bird Gerda had left. I had told Gerda once that eating cold turkey in the middle of the night got me horny. 'Have fun,' she'd said as she left the bird, 'but you'd better be in shape for when I get back.'

Sister Bear set the tray on the bed and clambered over to her side with a pleased smile on her wide mouth. 'No,' she said. 'What I mean is, it makes it interesting trying to find out.'

The way she could hold on to a conversation reminded me of how the Apaches used to set their kids hanging on a pole. The ones that let go were dead. Or was that the Spartans? Three o'clock and my memory tends to lapse. Age? 'By the end of the week?'

'If it takes that long,' she said, 'and if I stay that long?'

I grunted as if she'd hit me in the belly. 'Tough lady!'

'Tough enough,' she agreed. 'Now eat up – an old man needs to build his strength.'

'For you?'

'For you,' she responded with a complacent smile. 'My five to your one, time to even the score a little.'

Sister to a football player! 'Great,' I said, 'but I'm out of poppers.'

She whisked the sheet back. 'When I'm finished, you'll

be out of more than poppers.'

The lady was correct – though failing to even the score by a wide margin. She certainly tried.

'Jesus!' I finally gasped.

She ran her tongue over her bottom lip. 'Nice.'

'But enough . . .' I closed my eyes as she pinched out the candle. 'God!'

With a puff of laughter, she snuggled in against my side. 'See what I mean?'

'Absolutely,' I assured her.

Chapter Ten

The anchor clattering through the ferry's hawsepipe woke me three hours later. Four of us play tennis weekday mornings from early spring to mid-November. It was cool for one of us to miss a game now and again, but not two mornings running. There has to be some discipline to life.

Of the three, one is Chilean, one is French and one is Dutch. They started out as painters and settled on the island way back, with the intention of escaping the real world money hustle so they could devote their lives to art. They did escape the money hustle for a few years and even got to paint a few pictures. Now each of them is married to a lady with a boutique on the *Calle Mayor*.

This street, till recently, was a continuation of the fisherman's quarter. Now it is the closest you get to a bazaar without visiting the Middle East or North Africa. Every damn house is a boutique and the Mayor's Office has banned traffic to make room for street stalls. The stalls sell nothing but junk-jewellery and forget-me-pleases. The boutiques are better – though outrageously priced, Gerda complains. She should know.

I don't complain just so long as I get to play tennis. At my age, you need exercise to keep in shape. Balling is insufficient – nor is it good for your game – or so my three partners had been accusing ever since Gerda started in on her six in the morning routine. They certainly made a lot of cracks that first morning of Sister Bear. They said my service was getting weak.

I had scrawled Sister Bear a note saying I'd be back around half-nine and was (miraculous for an Aquarian). She'd been out shopping I saw by a vase of red roses set on the kitchen table. Her pack had disappeared from under the table. 'Hi,' I called.

'Through here.' Sitting cross-legged on the bed, she was sewing the hem on a skirt. 'Good game?'

'Great.'

She raised her face for a kiss. 'I'll get breakfast while you wash up.'

You can divine most of a woman's future intentions the first morning. There are those who loll in bed while you serve them coffee. If they are still in bed after the second cup and you are cooking eggs, then they are definite transients. The same goes for toothbrushes. A lady who carries a toothbrush in her purse intends staying overnight but will be gone by ten in the morning.

For some men, the worst is to spot a lady polish the dust off her boots on the sheets. I have had this happen. There is no need for concern. The lady will be leaving directly and won't be back unless she has accidentally left her car keys on the bedside table.

No, the ones you have to watch out for are the ladies who wash the ashtrays. This is a sure sign they are moving in. Sister Bear was definitely serious. Not only were the ashtrays gleaming but she had hung my pants in the wardrobe as well as working out how and where to stow the bedding. She had also stowed her pack. Where, I had no idea . . . but, for sure, she now knew whatever lady I claimed to have was a lady who lived off the premises.

I am not against domesticity but merely suspicious of what tends to accompany it. I am also suspicious of men who protest they hate domesticity. Stand them under a hot shower after a game of tennis and let them listen to the sounds of a sweet lady setting the breakfast table! This makes me a male chauvinist pig. Possibly. But I have never demanded of a lady that she cook, sew or clean. It is the lady's choice.

Sister Bear appeared to be having a ball. 'Can you imagine?' she announced as I left the shower, 'I've no train to catch.'

Those Eurorail passes! To get full value out of them you have to keep on the move: Vienna today, Florence tomorrow with time in between for a rushed visit to two cathedrals and three museums. Also the train windows are usually too shitted up for you to see much of the countryside.

Knowing this, I grinned. 'The museum's closed and the

ceiling's fallen in on the art gallery.'

'Great,' she said.

She had fresh orange juice, toast, coffee and buttered eggs on the table. I finally protested at the third slice of toast. 'Steady, I have to watch my weight.'

'Age or vanity,' she mocked.

'Probably both.'

'Such honesty!'

'For a change . . .' I smiled, though a little uncertainly. She looked great and it felt great to have her there, but the thought of those ashtrays had me suddenly freaked. 'You like to cook?'

'Some,' she said. 'Why?'

'Because . . .'

'That's better,' she teased with a big grin. 'There was a moment there I got scared you might string more than three words together. More coffee?'

'Please.'

'So why the question on cooking?' she asked as she refilled my cup.

'Thanks,' I said.

'To the coffee or the query?'

Her baiting was knocking me out of stride. 'Goddamn it, will you shut your mouth.'

She seemed pleased. 'Polite,' she said, 'and that's seven.'

I was lost. 'Seven what?'

'Words,' she said and stuck out her tongue. 'You're doing fine.'

'Jesus! *Look*,' I finally managed, 'I spent two years in jail.'

She showed no surprise. 'Dope?'

'What else?'

'Yes,' she said, 'my brother's in now.'

This made it easier. 'Then he'll understand,' I said. 'You come out, you hate for anyone close to you to be doing what they don't like.'

'Ah . . .' She gave me a wise nod and a cool stare. 'And *you* don't do anything *you* don't like?'

'That's right,' I said.

Whistling through pursed lips, she looked school age. 'Wow! So this is our conversation.' She grinned happily.

'I'd bet· make the best of it.'

'You ılready have,' I said from the vantage point of being twice her age. Also this was my house. 'The subject's closed.'

'Like *shit* it is.'

Cup raised, I smiled complacently at her over the rim. Her eyes suddenly sparked with more energy than the transformer at a nuclear power plant.

'So what happens if what I want isn't what you want?' she purred with the sweetness of a cat about to pounce.

'Exactly,' I said.

'Exactly what?'

My shoulders rose.

'You mean we split?'

'Would there be much point in staying together?'

'Not here,' she agreed with a deliberate look around the small kitchen. 'Not enough space. I guess it's designed that way?'

'Perhaps.' Uncomfortable, I added, 'I was married once.'

'And that was enough? You tell me that,' she warned, 'I'll call you a lying son of a bitch. You're one hundred per cent marriage bait. And what's more,' she finished, 'this is a shitty conversation to have started after you've known me one night so you can do the Goddamn dishes.'

This said, she looked suddenly so delighted with herself, I was left wondering whether I *had* started the conversation. Maybe I had been manipulated . . . all that teasing to set me off? For a moment I considered getting angry but this would have been another victory for the lady. Also, it was too great a day outside to waste on an indoor argument – particularly one I would lose. At least there was one point I could win. 'No dishes,' I said. 'There's an old lady comes in. She finds them done, she'll get scared for her job.'

'Huh,' said Sister Bear. 'She have a key?'

'Right,' I said.

'Oh . . .'

Pushing my chair back, I left the table. 'Let's get down to the Monte Sol.'

'I thought we were going to the beach . . .'

'We are,' I said. 'The Monte Sol's an obligatory stop.'

Strolling down any waterfront is fun. Ibiza waterfront is close to earthly paradise . . . for me, that is. After nineteen years on the island there are few faces I don't recognise – I write of the Ibicencos and residents, of course. Mornings, not that many tourists visit the port.

Walking hand in hand with Sister Bear was a great accompaniment to this sense of belonging. It would be more polite to write that this sense of belonging was a great accompaniment to our walking hand in hand but would be untrue. Nineteen years against one night and a good breakfast, what can you expect?

Three trading schooners lay alongside the far end of the quay close to the slaughterhouse. All the schooners are motorised now though a few still carry steadying sail. The skipper of one of the schooners was a friend I hadn't seen in a while so I led Sister Bear over. We chatted a few minutes. Sister Bear let go of my hand so she could slip her arm around my waist.

The skipper smiled. 'You've found a pretty one.'

I agreed.

Strolling on, we met a young German lady in shopping from the far end of the island out San Juan way. In Ibiza we all kiss each other. Kissing is a good greeting just so long as it is summer and there are few people suffering head colds.

Perhaps there had been other kisses. I don't recall. Anyway, Sister Bear suddenly stopped dead on the sidewalk. I presumed she had spotted something of interest so checked before looking down at her. She appeared cross more than pleased – also a little uncertain. 'Mind telling me now many keys there are floating around the island?'

I looked surprised.

'Not that it matters,' she said. 'Just so I know who's a burglar and who has rights.'

That was fair, I thought. Maybe the German lady and I exchanging a few words in Spanish had made Sister Bear feel out of it. 'No one has rights,' I said. 'Except for you, me, and the cleaning lady.'

'Till the end of the week . . .'

I shrugged. Why meet problems ahead of time? 'Look,' I said and gave her my warmest smile, 'the sun's shining, right? So let's get to the Monte Sol before everyone splits.'

She hesitated.

Perhaps I looked impatient . . . a forty-five year old with only how many summers left? She could go along with my trip or collect her pack.

Now, as I write, I'm thinking this out of *her* head, not out of mine. I wasn't impatient. If she had said, 'Why don't we go off somewhere by ourselves?' I'd have said, 'sure' and fetched the bike. Funny what odd moments turn out to have had importance in your life. At the time you don't even realise there's a decision . . . not one that matters.

Sister Bear made ours by returning my smile. 'You're right,' she said, and slipped her arm back around my waist.

The Monte Sol was packed. There were lots of smiles and calls of 'Hi, Tobias, what's new . . . ?'

Both sexes checked out my companion. In winter the male eyes might have betrayed an acquisitive interest, the female eyes suspicion. Mid-June there's none of that.

'Who's ready for the beach?' someone suggested and started the drift.

It was a good day on the beach. So was the next and the next. The nights were fine, too. Sister Bear made a lot of friends. Ibiza society is easy that way.

Friday came and she was still in residence. It was my residence and I was twice her age so the responsibility for discussing what came next was mine. Looking back from the vantage point of my hospital bed, I see this. Sister Bear presumably saw it then and waited for me to say something or other about Gerda's return. I nearly did a couple of times but decision making has never been my strength. If I had a point of view, it was that we were having fun. Why risk wrecking the fun by getting into a heavy rap?

Friday morning a cable came as I was leaving for the tennis club. Gerda wired that she was flying in at six that evening and would be unaccompanied so I should meet her jet.

I left the cable on the kitchen table presuming Sister Bear would read it and broach the subject over breakfast. She did read it but did not broach the subject. Nor did I. Probably I was waiting for her to make my mind up for me. She failed to do so. Instead we strolled down to the Monte Sol and rode out to Salinas. After swimming, a bunch of us ate a late lunch at the French restaurant back from the beach.

Sister Bear sat opposite me.

There is a vague idea in my head that I tried to manoeuvre her into sitting beside me so I wouldn't have to meet her eyes; this is probably present guilt rather than fact. It was a fun lunch. Full moon would be in five days and we were recollecting full moon parties out of early history; acid parties up on Mount Atalaya – that sort of thing.

'You riding home first,' Sister Bear finally asked, 'or are you going straight to the airport?' We'd finished eating and were drinking coffee. She looked happy enough. I presumed she wanted to get home so we could decide what to do about Gerda.

'Guess I'll change,' I said.

She stood up with a smile. 'Good, then you can drop me off at Marie Ann's.'

Marie Ann is wife to Pierre, the French member of our tennis quartet. I would have probably said *at Pierre's*, which is a difference in the sexes. What I did say was, 'Fine.'

Gerda stayed five days. The afternoon she split, Sister Bear moved back in. This routine happened twice. Sister Bear didn't seem to mind and it was turning out to be a vintage summer. There are no bad summers, but some are just that much better than you could possibly expect or forget. The whole island hits a high. '63, '68 and '72 were the best. Incredible!

It was soon after Gerda split the second time that Sister Bear and I got into our next rap. We were out with Black Tim on his cabin cruiser. Tim had a lady for company . . . a blonde Dane who looked sixteen though people said she possessed a sexual repertoire that would have put a retired lady from Madame Claude's back into first-year kindergarten. Madame Claude supplies pleasure to Presidents amongst others, so her Parisienne ladies are on the up.

As for Black Tim – a suspicion floated around for a while that he was a narcotics agent. Perhaps he is. If so, he is too nice a man for anyone to care. Probably, like Big J, he is merely in the inheritance business. Even the black community is permitted a remittance man. He and I ski together most winters, though, once he's in training, Tim moves to the Alps. I can't afford the Alps. Two dollars for a cup of coffee isn't worth the snow.

This day we were after a grouper I had spotted under a rock earlier in the month. Groupers tend to be homebodies. This one's home was a rock-head half a mile out from the South West point of Es Palmador, which is a small island lying between Ibiza and Formentera. The rock was about twenty metres down. Deep for me. Tim is twelve years younger and his lungs are in better shape.

Tim swam off to check out the fish while the three of us remained on the boat. A sun-bed covers the motor. Sister Bear and I were on the bed while the Dane had spread herself on the bench seat. I was lying on my belly so I could keep an eye on Tim, when Sister Bear remarked, kind of musing, 'That stuff about wanting me to do what I want . . .'

Having a joint in my mouth, I merely nodded.

'You mean that?'

I had to remove the joint to say, 'Yes.'

Unfortunately her feet were the same end of the sun-bed as my head; otherwise I would have checked her eyes. She hadn't sounded heavy. Anyway, she was silent a while . . . dreaming, I presumed. A load of temple balls had hit the island that week – expensive but good dope – and the joint we were sharing with the Dane was strong for a sunny July afternoon.

'So what happens if I want to fuck some man,' was Sister Bear's next question. She still sounded cool. 'You don't care?'

This question has come my way so often that I have the answer pat. 'Not if that's what makes you happy,' I told her. 'Like, if I love you, then I ought to be happy about your being happy.'

'No jealousy?'

'What's there to be jealous about?' I reasoned and took another drag.

'Sounds fine,' she said – though something sounded like it wasn't fine. Her right foot tapped the mattress.

I glanced back over my shoulder. Storm clouds were

building in her eyes. More out of hope than expectation, I passed her the joint. Tim had surfaced. He jerked a thumb up to tell me he had spotted the fish. I waved.

'Some people would say you just don't give a shit,' Sister Bear remarked.

'About what?'

'Anything . . .'

The Dane had heard enough. Grabbing for a mask, she slid over the side. I would have preferred joining her to continuing the conversation. 'What the fuck do you want me to say?' I asked. 'That you fuck some man, I'm into agony?'

Tap tap went her foot. 'That would be nice!'

Her foot pissed me off. 'For you or for me?'

'Shit!' she snapped. 'We get into a rap, you start playing games.'

'What games?' I put a placating hand on her thigh 'Look . . .'

'At what?' she interrupted. 'All I can see is your Goddamned back.'

'So sit up,' I said. 'There's a man out there I have to watch.'

She did sit up. 'Exactly . . .'

She had me lost. Keeping an eye on a diver is sufficient work without having to follow an argument. Normally I would have sheltered in silence but we'd had a great month.

So, 'Exactly *what*?' I enquire pacifically. This was a mistake.

'Any one of your Goddamned Ibiza gang,' she charged, 'means . . .'

Familiar ground from past years! 'More to me than you do?' I finished for her and continued coolly. 'Right now Tim *needs* me more. There's sixty feet of water sitting on his head.' I reached for the joint.

'It's out,' she said and flicked the butt into the sea. It hadn't been out.

Having spent two years in jail for running dope, I view wasting the stuff as a social crime. 'That was mean.'

'Mean!' She gave me a glare that should have shaved my scalp and followed the butt into the water.

For a moment I felt relief . . . but experience told me we weren't through.

Back she swam after a few minutes.

I said, 'Hi,' with a nice smile. 'How's the water?'

'Like it's been all fucking month.' Resting her arms on the gunwhale, she inspected me with less enthusiasm than she would have shown a jelly fish.

Maybe the best I could do was try. 'Well it's just that the other doesn't work,' I said with an inadequate wave at the distant beach. This didn't sound right. 'Look,' I attempted, 'it's not that I want you to fuck some other man . . .'

'But you don't much care if I do.' Perhaps she meant this as a question.

'I want you to feel free,' I said.

'Thanks!'

So I'm bad at explaining, then the lady should make an effort. I mean, I *did* care for her. You don't have someone share your house for a month for no reason. 'Look,' I said, 'I love you, right?'

This didn't help. 'Love! So I split,' she shot back, 'and you love someone else. How many people do you get to love in a year?'

What can you say to a question like that?

'Look,' I protested, 'this is my life, right? You come into it, what do you want?'

'Some Goddamned abstract oneness,' she retorted, 'not part of that and that's what you're into. Jesus!' She threw an arm wide as if to encompass the three islands. 'You don't give a shit more for me than you do for the Goddamned rocks.'

Before I could get a word in she added, 'Yeah, so you'll tell me you love the rocks.'

Nice! 'Maybe I do,' I said and grinned hopefully. 'Aquarian?'

It was the wrong moment for a joke.

'Fuck your planets . . .' She heaved herself on to the deck. 'Your life – shit! I mean, for someone who's so fucking free and easy you come up with a lot of Goddamned ultimatums.' She glared. 'Know that?'

I could hear the young Danish girl swimming up from

back of me. This was her third return to the boat since we had started arguing. If we didn't finish soon, she'd drown, which might irritate Tim. He'd found her on the port that morning and hadn't had time yet to check her talents. This was a shitty joke to have had in my head but Sister Bear made me desperate.

'Like what ultimatums?' I demanded.

'Like like your life or get out.'

'I never said that.'

'Said! You never say a Goddamned thing,' she shot. 'You're too much of a fucking coward to speak and you're too much of a fucking coward to risk relating. Jesus!' she swore in disgust and grabbed a towel. 'One Goddamned marriage goes wrong and you hide in a fucking womb the rest of your life . . .'

This was too strong. 'Now wait . . .' I began, but Tim surfaced from what must have been his twentieth dive. He waved frantically so I'd see he'd lost his gun. 'Get that girl on board,' I rapped at Sister Bear and leapt for the anchor warp.

'Got him,' Tim gasped as I eased the boat alongside, 'but I can't get the mother free.'

Shoot a grouper in his hole and he puffs his gill bones out like a bunch of spikes. Once he's done this, he is hell to shift.

Tim looked beat. 'Man, I really tried,' he said as I hauled him on board. 'You want to look?'

'How about from the rear?' I asked.

'A noose?' Tim shrugged. 'Man, there's no space.'

Tim stands six four and weighs two hundred pounds. 'Maybe I'd fit,' I said.

He just, 'Just so you don't get stuck.'

'I get stuck,' I said, 'you can pull me out.'

He grinned, 'Yeah . . .' and looked at Sister Bear. She didn't say anything so he asked, 'Want to fix me a rum?' And to me, 'Give me five.'

I keep a wire noose in my fishing sack along with a bunch of extra weights and spare harpoon tips. The noose fits on an aluminium pole. I got the noose out and the pole, then knotted the weights to a line.

Tim watched the knotting. 'In a hurry?'

'Kind of,' I said.

'Yeah . . .' He'd got his breath back. 'Well, like I said, just don't get stuck.'

'Right.' Rinsing my mask, I dropped over the side with the extra weights left balanced on the side-deck.

Tim looked at me in the water. 'You'll get your back cut to shit without a suit.'

'And I won't get in with one on.' I hung there on the surface venting my lungs till he was ready. You don't go into a hole unless there is someone watching, not if you're me and enjoy life.

The rock was about ten metres wide. From under one side of it came Tim's line stretching through his gun and up to the yellow diving float he'd been trailing. There was small point to inspecting that side. If Tim couldn't shift the fish, there was no way I could.

Tim dived in to join me. I gave him a wink through the face plate, jack-knifed and jerked the extra weights off the boat. The weights shot me down. The groupers rear entrance was as Tim said: tight. I had a good look. A couple of small rocks lay beneath the main rock. These might shift. I tried and they did. The hole remained small.

Each dive you make cuts your wind. At my age it takes time for you to get your wind back. This depth and I either made it now or gave up. On the other hand, if I *could* get the fish, fine; no one is going to give a man a hard time if he has boated a big grouper – not even Sister Bear.

I decided going for the fish might be easier than having to surface to an argument on how I lived my life. Sticking my head under the rock, I wriggled in with the noose on its pole stuck out in front. I was in to my waist before I saw the fish.

There is nothing difficult to holding your breath. All you do is count. You say to yourself, ten more seconds and I'm coming up. You hit ten and say to yourself, alright, so ten more and this time it is definitely up. You do this three times and count slowly so you know you aren't cheating and you've gained forty-five seconds. Of course your ears may pop a little. Some people say they don't have time to get scared. I always have time to get scared. I got scared shitless under that rock, but I did get the noose on the fish and I did get him free.

The moment I was out, I hit my belt clasp and dropped the belt. This saved me a few seconds. Tim was already half-way down, bent on dragging me free. He grabbed the wire as I went past. All other highs are shit in comparison to that first breath as you surface. You blast the water out of your pipe and drag the oxygen in like it is every known pleasure drug under the sun.

Sister Bear greeted my victory with a disgusted shake of her head. 'Now I've seen everything.'

Helped by the Dane, she dragged me on board where I collapsed like a burst inner tube. Probably I looked disappointed.

'What did you expect,' Sister Bear demanded, 'a hero's welcome?'

A little peace, I might have answered. The pressure down at sixty feet had got at the nerve beneath a loose filling. Hand clamped to my cheek, I don't suppose I looked a hero – not even to a sixteen-year-old Danish schoolgirl.

'Look at him,' Sister Bear said. 'Forty-five and he'd rather get himself killed than face up to a discussion.'

And rather wait on losing my ball than face up to her letter . . . at least I show consistency. So does life in its attitude to my manhood: one long saga of attempted castration. The Pathan has been by in the last half-hour. Apparently pumping huge doses of antibiotics into my ass has proved ineffective.

A male nurse unslung my ostrich egg.

'Hmmm . . .' commented the Pathan.

I have a distaste for *Hmmms*. They scare me. 'Where did you train?' I ask.

A black eyebrow shoots up. 'Why?'

'People say I should fly to London.'

He grins at my ball. 'And pay overweight?'

Dispatching his Maltese minion in search of an unnecessary roll of cotton wadding, he sits himself on my bed and says, 'Actually I was Senior Consultant at Manchester General before returning home.'

I am not impressed by this being one of the largest

hospitals in England. It is the man who impresses rather than the qualifications. 'I wasn't doubting your competence.'

'Just as well,' he says, 'because we're going to have to take a little look at this testicle.'

'You are?'

'Afraid so.'

'Leave the fear to me,' I retort.

He smiles.

'And you *are* a Muslim?'

Again that eyebrow shoots up.

'Don't get insulted,' I interject. 'It's just that I'd hate to have anyone who believes in Karma get his knife between my legs.'

The eyebrow drops and his smile flashes. 'Then you've come to the right side of the border.'

I manage a smile of my own. 'And I've always believed Kashmir should be Pakistani . . .'

'That should keep my hand steady,' he says and hoots with laughter.

Laughter is a crime in banks, churches and hospitals. A passing priest scowls disapproval and even my fellow patients frown. I merely lie here thinking about having no dinner tonight and off to surgery in the morning.

Why read Sister Bear's letter before I come out of the operating theatre . . . with ball or without? If it is without, my mother may be pleased. She once accused me of consecrating my life to sex. She considered this disgusting. Possibly she was suffering a jealous pang. She was certainly suffering that female presumption that any male who is getting laid is privileged. Getting laid, she considers, is the height of a man's ambition. It is also his greatest pleasure and always a pleasure. Sister Bear felt the same about my balling Gerda.

'Want to go to Palma?' I asked her, once I'd recovered my wind. 'I have to get to the dentist.'

'So what's wrong with here,' she snapped, 'no anaesthesia?'

'No appointments,' I growled and caught the evening flight.

‘Stay away a week,’ was her parting shot, ‘Gerda will be back for you to fuck.’

Sweet! I did stay away six days, but only because the dentist discovered a tooth his bank account told him he should cap. I returned to a cable from Gerda saying she would be ten days late. Sister Bear was gone. It was unnecessary to ask where. One coffee at the Monte Sol and ten different creeps delighted in telling me she’d moved in with a Sicilian I dislike. He owns a country house beyond San Carlos.

Perhaps country life would suit her, I thought, and rode over to the yacht marina in time for a day’s sailing with the friendly owner of a thirty-foot catamaran. The wind was perfect.

Chapter Eleven

Sailing is great sport so long as you don't suffer from seasickness. I don't suffer from seasickness but my wife did. Perhaps it was this recollection that pushed me into memories of our marriage that day on the catamaran. The sails set and the owner at the helm, there was nothing for me to do, so I sprawled on the forward trampoline, the spray flicking at my back and memories chasing each other through my skull like dolphin pursuing flying fish. It is easy knowing what caused the break-up of a marriage. What is tough is working out the causes of the causes of the causes of the causes and so on *ad infinitum*. Introspection is a waste of time but I got trapped that day.

Perhaps Sister Bear having split was the catalyst.

Or Maria Jesus?

Maybe it was being forty-five . . .

Or the way the owner handled the cat. His last boat had been a monohull with enough weight in its keel to carry the hull on through the waves when thrusting to windward. Catamarans are light. Punch them into a wave, they stop dead. We stopped dead every few minutes. Shyness stopped me going aft and telling the owner he should pay-off a few seconds earlier. This was his boat and no owner likes to be lectured on how to sail, however tactfully the lecturer puts his points.

So we went on getting stopped dead which is what happened to Joan and my marriage through a failure in either of us to communicate our knowledge of what was wrong. We were not equipped to talk about what really mattered though we were great on literature, politics, the children . . .

We both had fantasies (know anyone who doesn't?) but could never discuss them.

We tried. Jesus, how we tried. We would always end up in evasions. Sometimes I would think we had the children as an excuse to get out of bed and go feed them or find out why they were crying in the middle of the night so the conversation would end before it got too deep.

Of course the reason for the children crying in the middle of the night was not that they were hungry, but were straight unnerved by all the tension and frustration in which Joan and I co-habited.

Both she and I had married fantasies instead of people. The fantasies kept us going for twelve months. Then the fear stepped in. We were scared of having to face up to whom we had actually married and were scared of being discovered ourselves.

Two years of this fear and we were stuck in a vacuum. There was no fantasy left and no reality. Problem is you can't fuck a vacuum. Friction is absent.

Women have a slight advantage over men in these situations. They can at least fake it while lying there praying for some miracle to bring fulfilment.

A man can't even get an erection – or can get an erection but knows it is one dollar to a thousand he will lose the erection before he can get inside. This is worse than not getting an erection. You lie in bed with your erection pressing against your lady-love's back because, even if you can't ball, you can still sleep with mutual tenderness.

You know your lady-love feels this erection. You know she longs to get balled. You want to ball – but you are scared of what will happen if you *do* try to ball. This situation fills you with guilt. You know your lady-love takes not balling as a rejection because you obviously could ball; she feels the evidence cradled against her spine.

You both lie there in the dark in misery and silence till finally one or the other of you try to talk. The talking is so fucking difficult. What can you say? You have lived together for what seems a like a long time. Through all this time, you have been living a pretence of love – pretence because you can't *love* someone you don't know.

All this pretence and untruth has created an armaments industry which would shame the USA and the USSR at their most productive. Any conversation may tip the balance of power. This is an unacceptable risk because, behind all these barriers you have mutually constructed, you believe there must exist someone you actually *do* love or *could* love; you would not be so stupid as to be living this way simply out of masochism

But each day of silence strengthens the barriers.

Silence becomes a habitual refuge. So does reading late into the night, smoking too much dope, drinking too much booze, filling the house with acquaintances, friends and relations so you are never alone together long enough to risk having to rap.

You set up situations where you can quit the marital couch at dawn to avoid the morning risk . . . as I used to do. Off I would go to my studio at five in the morning for the pleasure of falling asleep over a typewriter. I would awake from my typewriter to fantasise what was wrong between us (Joan rather than the typewriter) and why it was that I was incapable of fucking my beautiful wife.

For a while I blamed the birth of our first child. Joan went through eight hours labour before being sliced open by a Spanish surgeon. I was present. Slice went the knife and I stood there looking into this huge bloody cavity of pain too vast for me ever to fill again with my limited ability to love. This is how I felt at the moment. Joan was on gas so felt differently. She felt joy and achievement and relief. Without the gas she would have felt joy and achievement and relief plus a little pain.

I was not interested in how she felt. I knelt beside her bed, tears running down my cheeks, while out from my mouth poured these promises of how *I* would never let *her* go through such suffering again.

How about that for a fine piece of Male Chauvinist Piggery? It was my pain at her pain which provoked the promises.

Anyway, all this crap about birth was a cop out.

What really hung us up was this simple little problem of our both being incapable of lowering our sexual defences sufficiently to communicate.

Joan knew this.

I knew this.

Unfortunately we had both been reared wrong. As I

have already written, we could discuss politics, theology, sociology, literature, music, painting . . . and even how best to educate children so they would grow up happy and capable of communicating. But we could not discuss how best to ball each other with joy, humour and a little ecstasy.

Every few months one or other of us would suggest, 'Hey, how about getting away by ourselves for a few days. No kids. Pure holiday.'

'Yeah, but who's going to look after the kids,' would shoot back the other – which query we both could translate into, *I'm too fucking scared.*

We did get away twice. Both holidays were sexual mayhem. The first was at my mother's. Matters started off well. We not only got to ball but balled before dinner. Unfortunately, my size eight feet kicked the bedside lamp off the bedside table ten strokes before orgasm. The bedside lamp was a stand-up miracle of Venetian glass carefully preserved from somewhere around the seventeen eighties. Its shattering ended our copulation, added a new guilt to our lives and provoked a new problem in communication, though this time with my mother.

Tough hatching an explanation of why a valuable antique has ended its life shattered against a wall five metres away from the table on which it is meant to stand in pristine glory. I mean, what the fuck were my feet doing up that end of the bed?

The second effort took place in a chaste uncle's Swiss chalet. His chasteness is an assumption based on the draggy character of his wife and on there being no double beds in the chalet. Despite being married to a harridan, he has maintained a sweet character and had lent us the chalet for a fortnight. Two weeks had to be sufficient for us to get it on (or get it in).

We were determined. Twin beds were no hindrance. It was this time or never. We knew this for sure – not (naturally) that we had discussed the matter. We had to come to the right country.

The Swiss are so square they make pissing feel like an orgy. The atmosphere had us rampant. No single bed would be near big enough for what we were going to do with each other.

The beds were Swiss and had Swiss castors on their legs. Swiss castors are like Swiss watches. They function. You could shift these beds with your little finger. While Joan bathed, I lashed them together with the only string I could find. My penis erected during this lashing, which was definitely promising since I am not a bed-leg freak even though an aluminium wheelchair did once turn me on.

Out came Joan from the bath and down we drove to a grand restaurant to dine and dance by candlelight so as to attain not only the mood for, but total and inescapable commitment to physical love and romance. This was back in those bad old days when couples danced together rather than ricocheting their separate comet tails through the galaxy. We danced cheek to cheek, breast to breast, erection to vagina. Our eyes shone with expectation. Back we drove to the chalet, Joan fondling our erection and both of us feeling as proud as the parents of a child genius.

We nursed our erection from the garage to the front door and up the stairs to the bedroom. The log fire glowed in the grate. Two fresh logs and a bottle of champagne from the refrigerator had us ready.

Stripped for action, we were as sure of ourselves as Richard Millhouse Nixon is righteous.

We were so sure of ourselves that we risked all sorts of preliminaries, though nothing weird: a little mutual tongue loving and light finger work. I recall the tongue loving well. Joan lay across both beds with her ass on the edge while I knelt on the carpet. Thinking back now, I wonder if this made her nervous – I mean my erection being out of her sight. But the erection was still in existence. Finally, not only was it in existence, but in Joan. Imagine our joy!

We were so crazy confident we took our time . . . slow and easy for starters, then a little speed and Joan actually orgasmed with our erection inside her for the first time in God alone knows how long.

If this continued, we would be risking an approach to relationship with truth sprouting out of our mouths. Bliss.

More speed . . .

And more speed . . .

Thumpity thump and we were actually looking into each other's wide open eyes, the log fire flames flickering rose light over our sweat-glistened bodies.

Joan's legs were up over my shoulders. 'Now!' she managed to squeak, 'NOW! NOW! NOW!'

What perfect timing – except right at that moment the string snapped with us balling crossways across the two beds. The beds slid apart.

Slid? They fucking flew apart.

Thank God we were in a Swiss ski resort.

Where else in the world could you call an osteopath at three o'clock of a January Sunday morning? And so ended our marriage. Of course we tried again – though never in Switzerland and never with hope. We both accepted the odds were too long on success.

Strange product, impotence. There is more of it around than there used to be. Few men discuss the subject except in textbooks. Modern women novelists do. They write on how it affects them; on how they feel rejected, frustrated, humiliated, insulted – all of which is Female Chauvinist Piggery. It includes neither understanding nor consideration for how the man feels.

Often the man feels too fucked up to discuss his problem. Often he simply blames the lady for not turning him on – which is Male Chauvinist Piggery. Sad – perhaps we are still too young in our experience of sexual liberty to drop our male and female defences sufficiently to accept we would be happier as allies rather than enemies.

Sprawled out on the catamaran's trampoline I was mulling over all this with the sun hot on my chest and the spray cooling my back. I recall thinking how alliances only work when there is mutual knowledge and acceptance of each partner's strengths and weaknesses. You have to know what is going on in your partner's head. Joan and I never knew. We guessed, and having guessed, tried to relate to whatever we had guessed at. All this guessing produced more chaos than understanding.

Even thinking about it got me uptight, so I gave up on being polite and clambered aft in hope of instructing the cat's owner on how to helm his boat. He failed to get irate which was nice. Instead he left me the helm. We had a great sail.

Catamarans are one of my passions along with ski-ing, diving and hang-gliding. All four get your head integrated with your body. I learned this lesson while I was married.

One whole summer got wasted with my trying to write. Every time I cleared my head to see what would flow out of my imagination, all I got were plans of how to quit being married. The snow came and I left for the mountains. The first day up on the crest found me with a mouth full of smoked ham and a skull full of the same old crap when I should have been screeching with joy at four inches of fresh powder coating the *piste*.

Sandwiches eaten, down I headed with my head still spinning. I was so deep into introspection that I failed to notice the sign off to the right for the Blue run and went straight on to find myself on what felt and looked like a precipice. There were a few dozen ants on skis at the bottom of the precipice. But for those ants looking up at me, I would have probably taken off my skis and tried walking back the way I'd come. The first fifty feet committed me to no return. A further five hundred feet and I found a mogul to rest on while I got some air back into my lungs.

Thank God for padded pants. Without the padding every skier on the mountain would have heard my knees knocking together from a combination of fatigue and terror – mostly terror! As for the introspection, my skull was clear as a white diamond.

Recognising this made me over-confident, which was an error. I shot the last five hundred feet on my face straight into a beginner's class with the instructor screaming at me to pay attention.

How do you pay attention when hurtling down a precipice on your skull?

But at least, despite the bruises, I had learned how to free my mind of the circling syndrome common to so many members of our modern sedentary society. Read many of our best-selling American lady novelists whining their sexual problems at the audience and you should pray for them to give up writing and take up ski-ing. If you don't pray for these novelists to take up ski-ing and, instead, continue reading their endless stream of egomaniac complaints over the condition of their clitori, then you are in need of the Tobias Therapy yourself.

This advice is free.

Hang-gliding is fine, too, as are diving deep and sailing cats. Crazies recommend parachute jumping. I don't. But sailing a catamaran is definitely sound treatment. You can sail a monohull without paying too much attention. The keel keeps you from capsising. All that keeps a cat from capsising is the helmsman's sense of feel. All that keeps a relationship stable is telling the truth about where you are at. Of course it is easy to sell a lady on fantasies, but once reality takes over, the relationship is finished. I had not tried to sell Sister Bear on fantasy. If she objected to the reality, then that was cool with me, but I still felt sad over her moving out.

Back from sailing, I dropped in on the Calle Mayor in search of my tennis partners. Half an hour before closing every husband and lover of a boutique owner is strutting the street having checked the day's take.

Seeing them, you would guess it a pimp's parade. The men practice that bow-legged swagger. Head well back and a slight sneer for lip decoration, they eye each other out of slit eyes. 'How did yours do?'

'Two hundred thousand.'

'Yeah . . .'

Of course it is all lies. One hundred thousand pesetas is probably nearer the mark.

I met Pierre first. He was counting thousand peseta notes into a lizzard-skin billfold for his competitors to envy. One eye on his cash, he reported Sister Bear and her Sicilian were in town. He also said Sister Bear was a very nice lady and that I was a Goddamned fool.

Strange how marrieds always try settling their friends into a permanent relationship . . . particularly when they don't much like being settled themselves.

Pierre was correct both about Sister Bear being an exceptional lady and that she and her Sicilian were in town.

We bumped into each other at the corner of Market Street.

'Hi,' I said happily and gave her a big hug.

Returning my hug, she said, 'Hi yourself, when did you get back?'

'This morning,' I told her.

'Great,' she said.

I asked, 'Having fun?'

'So so,' she answered, 'let's go eat.'

The Sicilian appeared irritated by this exchange. His muscles were balled up ready for the scene he expected me to start. I hate to disappoint a man but saw no reason to start a scene. This further irritated him. *He had stolen my old lady.* That I showed no anger hurt his ego. This is a recurring problem for men who are into owning women. Whichever way things go, they always end up insulted. He sulked right through dinner at Sos Solito while Sister Bear and I rapped joyfully.

Dinner over, she asked whether I had bought a fresh bottle of brandy. I had forgotten, so she went next door to the fisherman's bar. Returning with a bottle of *Ciento Tres*, she said to the Sicilian, 'Julio, can you drop my things by next time you're in town?'

That night she and I really got it off in bed for the first time. All we said of the Sicilian was my 'How was it?'

And her, 'The country was great, but he was kind of a drag.'

The next morning was the same except I was awakened at three o'clock in the morning by some man trying to start his motorcycle. He kicked it for about fifteen minutes. A lady was with him. She was drunk and giggling which angered him more than the bike did. But for Sister Bear, I would have been out someplace going through the same routine. Knowing this, I rolled over carefully so as not to wake Sister Bear. Her face glowed faintly red every eight seconds with the lighthouse sweeping the curtains. Her eyes were open. I felt good about this. It was perfect being there . . . not touching, nor talking.

I lay back with my head a foot from hers. I could hear her breathing now that the Swiss and his lady had finally departed minus the bike. Her breathing was slow and relaxed. After a while her hand slid across the sheet and into mine. A further five minutes passed before she murmured, 'I love you, Tobias.'

There was no big deal to this announcement. Unemotional, it was a statement of fact. No future was implied. There was no guarantee. Nothing was involved except the two of us at that precise moment in time.

I felt as if she had thrown a pre-heated electric blanket over me. Even now in this hospital bed and waiting for the morning and the operating theatre, I feel the same sensation of glowing all over. I also feel real fear. What happens if the operation fails? Will I have heard those words for the last time? Or is this an insult? And, if so, against whom is the insult directed: myself or the women I may meet?

I don't know . . . but I do know that I am frightened of a life in which there is no expectation of again hearing those words. They are not words which get said that often . . . or not to me. Sure, at moments of passion and while two of us are out of control. This does not count. Also sometimes by ladies who feel guilt for what they have just done or for what they are about to do or for what they are thinking or have been thinking . . . though this happens less than it used to.

Today's ladies are freer agents. They do more of what they want than ladies of my youth ever could or thought they could. Back in the fifties there was far more calculation in relationships. That's why it is so important that women should be independent. Independence gives them the possibility to be honest. This never used to be the case. Female liberationists recall those days as the days of women's servitude to man. Perhaps . . . but men were meal tickets.

An odd error exists in much of Female Liberationist thought. The error is that men like to work. Some men may, but most don't. Nor do most men expect as their right a vocationally satisfying and upwardly mobile career, which is what many women I meet demand of their new-found liberty. Men work because they don't know any other way of supporting themselves and a possible wife and kids. Men also presume their wives are living out the perfect dream

This is what a man asks when he proposes. 'Honey, is your dream to be my wife, keep my house in order, fuck Saturday nights and have two decimal three kids?'

The lady says *Yes*, the man believes her. Unfortunately, he may be in error.

The lady may simply prefer the idea of marriage to working an eight-hour shift. If this is so, she will end up very discontented with married life. She will complain that she is her husband's servant, divorce him for mental cruelty, attach half his salary in way of alimony, make it difficult for him to see his children and bitch to all her lady friends over how hard she was done by.

He, poor son of a bitch, will simply continue to go to work each morning . . . not that any of this was in my head that night.

That night I gave Sister Bear's hand a squeeze of gratitude and said something truly romantic like, 'That's nice . . .' And a little later, 'Very nice . . . thanks.'

'My pleasure,' she answered and drifted back to sleep while I lay there thinking how very comfortable it was to have her sleeping beside me – not at all like a typical July fuck-and-forget episode. I started to consider all the ladies I had ever balled – right back to that first lady on the ship who took my precious virginity. There were a lot of them to consider, which was all right; except I wondered how many of them I had really wanted to ball. I mean wanted so badly that it would have hurt if I hadn't. This cut the hell out of my list.

Next I considered how many of these few remaining ladies had truly deeply desperately wanted to ball me.

One hand was enough for the counting.

This was a slight shock to my ego.

It was also a considerable jolt to my life-style.

If I was correct in my memories, then I had been wasting a great deal of time and might do better rethinking my way of life, though this would be a drag because I was definitely enjoying my life. I would also have to consider why I had been balling all these ladies and why all these ladies had been balling me. If it was simply the exercise plus a five-second kick out of orgasm, perhaps I would do better working on my tennis game. The tennis would definitely be better for both my figure and my health and would probably improve my bank balance. I might also get to beat Pierre after six years of trying, and I could read more because a lot of the ladies who pass through the studio get insulted if I pick up a book. This is understandable as they are only there for a short time and expect attention . . .

But then I thought, *Yeah, but this is night time thinking.* What happens when the sun comes up and when it is springtime and the first of next year's ladies come tripping down the companionway off the Barcelona ferry with sun in their hair and desire for adventure showing in their eyes and in the way they sway their hips despite carrying heavy packs on their backs?

This train of thought produced an erection.

Sister Bear stirred in her sleep and shame for my erection stirred in my breast.

Next spring I might well not be available – not if the way I was thinking was correct.

But was it correct?

For centuries men have been educated to believe that all they really want is to get that skirt up and their pricks in. Back before the Pill most men were not getting it in often enough to discover that perhaps the whole chase is overrated – at least as a full-time pursuit.

Part-time might be all right.

Yes, part-time, I thought in memory of spring and in memory of how those ladies' asses look in their tighter-than-tight blue jeans as they hit the quay, and in memory of how they smile with joy in their eyes at how the island really is as beautiful as they've heard (despite the concrete sprawl of apartment blocks that has grown up around the Old City). Yes, indeed, springtime. But . . .

In fact, I was into one of those nights of deep philosophical bullshitting with myself which happens to all of us now and then. However, I awoke with my head still in much the same direction. Sister Bear was in the kitchen.

Propped up in the doorway, I watched her prepare breakfast. I *enjoyed* watching her. I found the way she moved beautiful and her shape beautiful . . . not exciting, though she was naked, but simply beautiful. And her eyes turned on me. They were relaxed (almost lazy) and yet very watchful at the same time and with a permanent trace of mischief lurking in the background; eyes to keep you on your toes because you knew, if you said something crass, she would say something real quick back which would destroy whatever male dignity you had erected as shelter for your ego.

Looking up from the stove, she presented me with a nice wide good-morning smile.

'Hi,' I said. 'I've been thinking . . .'

'Yeah?' While juggling boiled eggs, she switched her smile into a grin. 'Sounds an improvement.'

'Most of the night,' I insisted and pushed myself upright off the doorpost. 'Like first I love you and second, I need to play more tennis.'

'Shit!' She had burnt her fingers on the coffee pot handle, where the plastic insulation had cracked. This was unfortunate: both the burning and her exclamation. My wife had cried 'shit' the moment of my marriage proposal.

We had been in an ancient taxi cab driven by an equally ancient driver. The cab had lousy suspension and the driver lurched into every curve of a bumpy mountain road as if scared we would never make it. The combination of bumps and curves upset my wife-to-be's stomach. Her surprise at my marriage proposal was the final straw.

'Shit!' she exclaimed and yelped at the driver to pull up so she could throw up.

See?

My declarations of love produce unfortunate consequences.

Remembering how it had been to be married, I said nothing more to Sister Bear except, 'Yeah, I'll have to get another coffee pot.'

Not even, '*We'll* have to get another coffee pot.'

Jesus, just how shitty can a man get?

Such moments of betrayal truly fuck your life. I mean, I *knew* she was waiting for me to say something – Sister Bear, that is. My wife had given up on waiting; not that our marriage had been conducted in silence. To the contrary. We had said so much to each other by the end that all our conversations came interwoven with rubber shock cord set to catapult each word back and forth through the entire range of marital memory

This was a bad way to live

Every part of our lives had become a weapon from how the eggs were boiled for breakfast to how the kids behaved. We had even graduated from accusations over past events and present events and were into accusation of what she or I might do in the Goddamned future.

With all this in mind, I sat down in silence that morning to breakfast with Sister Bear. This says much for the efficacy of all the crappy philosophising I had been doing the previous night in the clammy privacy of my skull.

Sister Bear was hip to all this. She watched me shovel egg and finally said, 'Yeah, well, tennis is cool but how about getting into a little writing?'

How was Sister Bear to know that my writing and my not writing when I said I was writing had been a prime weapon in the marriage arsenal? She smiled in case I should take her too seriously. 'Well, isn't that what you're meant to be?'

'I might just do that,' I said, as her smile sunk without trace into the bog of my paranoia.

'Write?'

'Right,' I said.

She studied me a moment. Then she smiled again, but more at herself than in friendship. 'I was thinking I might go stay a few days at Marie Ann's. She and Pierre are dyeing silks this week for the boutique.'

'Should be interesting,' I said while concentrating on buttering a piece of toast.

Propped in the doorway ten minutes earlier, I had presumed we were headed fast for earthly paradise. Instead, Sister Bear headed for the shower.

'Tobias,' a voice shouted from below the window. I scurried on to the balcony. It was Tim with a gunny bag of diving gear slung over his shoulder. 'Hey, man, how's things?' he called.

'Just fine.'

'So you want to go fishing?'

'Be right down.'

I keep mask, flippers and wet suit in the shower where the salt gets washed off the rubber without any effort on my part. Sister Bear was under the shower. In I went with a brave face. 'Tim wants me to go fishing.'

Please note, *Tim wants* . . . as if this wiped out all responsibility I had for my own actions.

Sister Bear smiled sweetly. 'Have fun.'

'Yeah, well . . .' I mumbled. Pretty, don't you think? You can see why I would hate for any surgeon with faith in Karma to get his knife between my thighs.

Shovelling gear into my diving bag, I unslung the compressed air gun from behind the door and trotted down to the port.

One six-kilo corbo and an equally small meru was a bad catch, but Tim and I dived all day for it. Six o'clock in the evening we eased into Formentera harbour for a quick beer. A lady drove by the bar in a 2CV. Spotting us, she called out, did we want to go to a party on the other end of the island. We found this a fine idea so she gave us a lift. The party was still in progress the following morning, which was good from my viewpoint. Partying keeps you out of your head.

We got back to the boat around noon. There had been no balling at the party. Formentera houses are too small and the ground is nothing but rocks. These circumstances had left Tim frustrated because he'd had a week of the child-Dane and the Dane had had the clap. Having paid for her cure, Tim had given her a lecture and shipped her home on a Scan Air charter.

'Goddamned kids,' he complained on telling me the story. 'Know what?'

'What?'

'Man, that little bitch had skipped school three fucking months. Jesus!' he whistled with a disapproving shake of his head. 'Can you imagine – her folks didn't even *know* she was in Spain.'

My thoughts on the subject were less objective. You have a black stud for a friend and he suddenly hits the father trail aged thirty-two! If this was happening to him, where was I at? So when he said, 'You want to go see what's happening on Midjons Beach?' I heaved a sigh of relief.

Fishing ladies is easier than fishing fish in Balearic waters. We had the anchor down a bare five minutes before two young Swedes swam out. Hanging on to the side of the boat, they grinned up at us as if we were dentists conducting a high-school dental examination.

One of them knew enough English to say, 'Hullo.'

Tim said, 'Hi,' and we heaved them on board. They giggled as Tim hit the starter motor.

It was a real fun day except I kept thinking it would be more fun if we could communicate. 'Good?' we would ask.

'Good,' they would answer, giggle, and nod their pretty heads like a couple of China dolls at a toy fair.

Diving was the answer to non-communication. Face down in the water you are safe from fruitless attempts at conversation. Tim shot one fish while the ladies and I collected sea urchins.

They are a drag to open, sea urchins – all that scissoring their tops open and all the mess of spines and shell you get left with. We set the ladies to work on a flat rock which the waves would clean up the next north wind. Then we balled with reasonable enthusiasm and headed back to Formentera to see if the party was still active. It was and we were welcome.

A bunch of kids were playing livish music in that desultory way that makes you suspect a macrobiotic diet, but there was lots of good dope circling. I had fun despite the occasional streak of black thought. Two more days of fishing and Formentera and I might have gotten the whole Sister Bear emotional number sorted out of my head . . . or so I thought at the time.

Our hosts produced brown rice sewn with stewed vegetables around three o'clock in the morning. Served up in a big shallow earthenware pot, the food looked like a mock-up for a mangrove swamp, so we caught a lift back to the boat.

The Swedes came with us. The communication cut-off had us uncertain where they wanted to be, but they seemed contented enough. Tim suggested we anchor in Es

Palmador Bay for what remained of the night.

I said, 'Fine.'

Off we motored, dropped hook, had a swim, wrapped ourselves in towels and studied the stars. There were a lot of stars.

Finally Tim made one of those remarks that come out when you are stoned and forget that whoever you are with may not be following your thought pattern considering you have been silent for the last quarter-hour.

'Yeah,' he said, kind of wisely, 'she's a real nice lady.'

'Right,' I agreed with equal wisdom.

'Yeah,' Tim repeated after a heavy pause and rolled his head so I could see his eyes. 'Tobias, man,' he advised, 'you should get that on . . .'

There we were rocking gently on the blue Mediterranean Sea at quarter to four in the morning with these two nice Swedish ladies (one of them brewing rosemary tea) and we had said not one word to each other in two days except about fishing or currents or where to drop the anchor . . . now this! Brotherhood is the name for it.

Thank God for Brotherhood because, in this new society we have to find new forms of relationship. All that shit about no man being an island unto himself is correct.

We left our blood families back the other side of the hill because we have great difficulty in conversing with them This is not because we have taken too much acid or suffered an Eastern religious experience or hate holding down a regular job, but is because we live by a whole different set of rules. There *are* rules, but they are our rules – our moralities Like not dealing junk as an obvious example; and coming down heavy on anyone who *does* deal junk; and helping each other even when we don't specifically approve of where the one who needs help has his head at that moment (which is why he needs help).

We all, some time or other, need help. This is what families are for. Nor do you necessarily have to like each member of this new family you belong to. It is not a question of liking. It is a question of hanging in there together. We are a nomadic tribe and the only way we are going to survive is to support each other when the need arises.

I think this out now with the fear of tomorrow's operation strong in me. The operation fails, I am going to need a lot of help. Tobias the Eunuch . . .

Back then on the boat Brother Tim had decided I needed help. It was a weird conversation considering I had the head of one Swedish lady cradled in my lap. We meant no offence to her. One hand playing through her hair, I returned to studying the stars and continued studying the stars till the tea hit the deck.

Smiling gratitude at the bearer of the tea, I looked over at Tim to find him watching me. I said, 'Yeah, you're right . . .'

Some dialogue – I mean, DYNAMIC! But it was sufficient.

Tim reached out a hand which I shook.

'Great,' we agreed.

Decision made, we drank tea, smoked a joint, then played desultory sexual games till the sun rose. The only problem remaining was how to rid ourselves of the Swedes without causing umbrage. Running them back to Midjons, Tim shooed them into the water while caroling, 'Bye bye, Bye bye . . .'

The ladies got the message and I got a reminder of my children.

Tim threw me a grin. 'Yeah . . .'

We plucked us a sack each of sea urchins and shot across the straits. Ibiza looked the same but my studio was empty and depressing. I checked the wardrobes. Sister Bear had left one shirt. The shirt was red silk and her favourite. Presumably this was positive.

Having washed the salt out of my hair and draped my diving gear under the shower, I bought a big bunch of flowers at the market and rode out to Pierre's with the sack of sea urchins. This was not as friendly a gesture as it may appear. Where would they clean the urchins? In the garden? So they could get spines in their feet for the next six months? Fortunately it is the thought that counts, not the thoughtlessness.

Sister Bear lay in the sun beside Pierre's pool. She was into a game of chess with the household's fourteen-year-old son. The son is crazy about bikes and rides well, so I left mine running with a suggestion he take it up the hill.

I then squatted down in front of Sister Bear with a slack grin on my face – the sort of grin ten-year-olds use to say, *So I'm guilty, Ma, but could you pretend I'm not?*

Sister Bear showed little interest in my grin. Instead she jerked her head at the chess board. 'I was going to win . . .'

I checked. She was full of shit. Pushing the boy's white bishop three squares to the left, I say, 'Try.'

She frowned at the move. 'He wouldn't have thought of that.'

'Crap,' I said, 'he's been beating me since he was six'

This cheered her up. 'He has?'

'Yeah,' I said. '. . . I brought flowers.'

'I saw.'

'You did?'

'Seeing you're holding them,' she said, 'I'd have to be blind. What's in the sack?'

'Sea urchins . . .'

'So go sit on them,' she suggested with a sweet smile.

'That's why I brought them,' I said. 'I'm into comfort.'

'You're into being full of shit,' she replied. Romantic!

I said, 'Yeah, well, I've been thinking.'

She came back fast, 'Which is where we left off the day you split.'

You can recognise truth by the way it hurts. 'So I'm sorry,' I said.

'Big fucking deal.'

'Yeah . . .'

We locked eyes.

'Jesus!' Suddenly giggling, she flipped on to her back. 'Come here you stupid prick.'

I did. A little later my pants were off. We had forgotten Pierre and Marie Ann. They came out of their house while we were playing Mummys and Daddys. 'Charming,' Pierre drawled, 'but expensive on flowers.'

Somehow the flowers had gotten under Sister Bear's ass.

Marie Ann had meanwhile inspected the sack. 'Any time you're free,' she remarked, 'the Bear knows where we keep the kitchen scissors.'

'But don't feel pressured,' Pierre added. 'There's no hurry.'

This kind of barracking, you can't hurry! However, once our hosts had left us in peace, we did get to finish. We also cleaned the urchins, ate dinner and rode home.

Gerda marched in on us at seven the next morning. 'Hi, said Sister Bear. 'We never met.'

Gerda looked surprised. I probably looked embarrassed Sister Bear looked happy. 'But right now we're busy,' she remarked, 'so if you'll just leave the key on the table . . . ?'

Exit Gerda.

I got out of bed and crossed to the window. Dad was waiting in the jeep. As usual, he looked scared. 'Poor old sod,' I said. 'Gerda's going to give him hell.'

Sister Bear said, 'Serve the motherfucker right for pushing her into marrying rich so he could have a nice place to live

'Yeah?' I glanced back. Sister Bear was wearing a smart-assed grin.

'Why do you think she's been fucking you?' she asked 'For your looks?'

My head doesn't function without coffee. All I could manage was a weak, 'Nice . . .'

'That's why she has him wait. She's paying him back, said Sister Bear as I watched Gerda stride to the jeep. 'She gets caught, he's out of a job.'

I couldn't hear what Gerda said but her Dad flinched and shifted ass to the passenger seat. 'Jesus,' I said.

'Jesus is right,' said Sister Bear. 'Jesus, sometimes you're dumb.'

Chapter Twelve

Ibiza is where the hip people live. In straight society, ladies marry and have two kids before hinting it is time for the move to suburbia where the schools are good, the neighbours white and where the grass grows green for kiddies' play time.

Ibiza ladies are way ahead. They step off the boat in search of an instant mate and they start dropping hints of need for a move within weeks of achieving co-habitation. Nor do they plan on moving to some nice country house convenient to the road. No, they demand the true primitive style of water coming out of a well and none of that electricity crap.

Behind them lies the Big City and the status-money hustle of America's upwardly mobile middle classes. The status-money hustle is their parents' bag. Their parents are welcome to it. For the Ibiza lady, joy lies in her fantasies of the simple life.

Fantasies are stronger but also shorter lived than reality. I have seen the Ibiza route run too many times to hold illusions on this score. I have seen the route run by men who should have known better. I have even seen it run by men who did know better but allowed themselves to be swept onward by the fantasies of a lady they loved. So here is my warning and I write it from a male point of view because I remain a man despite Dr Rahman's threats; and it was from a male point of view that I warned myself of the dangers when faced by Sister Bear's first hints.

The route starts out in summer which is the first mistake. A *finca* that looks like paradise under the summer sun can be grim in mid-winter.

Once the lady is installed in her *finca* she will feed her mate brown rice and slices of wholemeal granite she fantasises as bread. She will wear long skirts, walk barefoot and treat crapping in the cactus patch with the same enthusiasm shown by Darwin on discovery of the Galapagos Islands.

Of course she will also get bored shitless after a while and will complain that she never gets to see anyone. You, her mate, presumably besotted, fail to point out the choice of *fincas* was hers. Thus commences the dinner party period of your relationship. All the other *finca* ladies will bring their men to your *finca* so they can sample your lady's brown rice, bread and home-grown carrots . . you will then be dragged off to all of their *fincas* to sample their brown rice and bread.

The competitive vegetarian and natural health trip is a total drag. Because of it, your lady will nag at you to give up tobacco and will frown on all alcohol except 'country wine'. Country wine is a euphemism for a sticky red sludge brewed by the local farmers. No one but a *finca* lady or an Ibicenco peasant could drink country wine.

Be warned, however. Do not point out that the grapes for good wine are also grown in the country. Suggesting this will earn you an argument. The lady will tell you good wine is commercial. Victorious from the argument, your lady will insist on a hot bath to relax her nerves and you will have to pump water and hew firewood for two hours.

Next your lady will demand you buy a car so she can visit her lady friends without having to drag you along when you should be repairing the roof. You protest that you can't afford a car.

'Yes you can,' your lady will retort and produce your latest bank statement she has accidentally discovered at the bottom of six heaps of letters you are due to answer except you have too little time what with cleaning the oil lamps, whitewashing the walls, cutting timber and pumping water.

You will admit to having bread to buy a car but to having insufficient bread for repair bills which will be numerous and costly considering *you* live and all her *friends* live the far end of goat tracks capable of knocking shit out of a trail bike, let alone a 2CV Citroen or a Renault 4L.

This conversation will resurface every few days and will give birth to the first irritation period of your relationship Dragged by the irritation, you will finally buy the lady a car

You will also repair it for her which is good for the soul but a drag unless you have unfulfilled ambitions of being a motor mechanic Also you have to pump water by hand because it is a crime against nature to own a gasoline pump in the depth of the country (how about automobiles?) and you are having to irrigate all the vegetables the lady has planted the first weeks of her enthusiasm.

What with all this toil, you are not having much fun. This is good, as your lady will explain. You are becoming a serious citizen. You are also becoming a Goddamned bore through being short on balling energy, what with all the chores and thoughts of how life is a drag.

More rows start.

It looks like the relationship is over except the lady determines to rescue the situation by getting pregnant.

You ask, 'Is this wise?'

She asks, 'What are you? Scared of responsibility?'

You say, 'What responsibility? It's you who are into having the child.'

'Like I said,' she retorts, 'you're scared of responsibility.'

'Shit!' you say.

'Yeah,' she says and cries, so you carry her upstairs to fuck as the easiest way of shedding your guilt for her misery.

Of course she has quit using the Pill and that fuck is the one that sows the seed. Life becomes truly joyful down your goat track. Your lady is into natural childbirth.

Her lady friends are into natural childbirth.

Your male friends are into telling you horror stories of what happened when their old ladies started haemorrhaging at three o'clock in the morning with the rain pissing down and the 2CV refusing to start.

When I was young, it was the ladies who worried over the dangers of childbirth.

Situations change. And certainly your situation changes once the baby arrives. All your lady's ladyfriends bring their babies over to see your baby. You come in from pumping water, watering the garden and repairing her car to find the living-room kin to a dairy. Breasts bounce at you from every corner, there are babies crying and yelling, and toddlers tearing at your prize shirts and destroying the first fifteen thousand words of the horror novel you had started while waiting for the pregnancy to culminate. There is spit-up on every cushion and shit on the floor because pinning babies into diapers is unnatural.

Your lady now feels imprisoned at the end of the goat track with a baby to look after and gives you hell for not getting back on time from the shop to which she has despatched you for canned baby food. She has discovered canned baby food is easier to prepare than the natural variety though you are still forced to eat brown rice and granite bread. Paradise!

Because you are responsible for your lady's imprisonment, her lady friends view you as a vicious criminal. Your lady also views you as a vicious criminal; after all, it is always the man's fault. This has been well established in divorce jurisprudence. Each time you enter the house from repairing the car or pumping water or cutting wood for the fire, you are greeted by silence so you know you have been the subject of discussion.

You are also accused of taking no interest in your child Interest denotes feeding, changing and washing the infant, particularly in the middle of the night.

You explain how you are already overworked from all your other chores – to which your lady snaps, 'Don't give me that shit – you never wanted a child in the first place.'

Winter comes round for the second time and all the free ladies are off to buy junk jewellery or silk batik in the Far East. All the free men are off to Poonah to check with Rajneesh on how to hang loose. This exodus gets your lady jealous as all hell because, with the baby, she can't go anywhere . . . all your fault.

She weeps some and you take her upstairs for a balling session in hope of cheering her up. Unfortunately you do not ball her that well because, frankly, she has become a drag with all her weeping and problems and all her friends hating you and she hating you. You lose your erection (or don't get an erection) and she shouts, 'You don't love me'

'Yes, I do,' you say.

'No you don't! No you don't! No you don't!'

Please note the question of whether *she loves you* is never raised. A lady can love who and where she wishes, having no erection to betray her tastes.

This non-balling and negative conversation happens a few times till finally you either say, 'Yeah, so I don't love you,' and stamp out of the house or you work on her car hard enough for her to be able to get around the island . . . your hope being she will find some other man with whom to fall in love and will therefore leave you to the misery of having to return to a heated apartment on the waterfront with a hot water shower that functions and a can that flushes.

Sister Bear showed first signs of prenatal *fincancy* one week after Gerda's expulsion . . . though perhaps her side trip with the Sicilian was the true start.

Being an old hand at the game gave me the advantage during her noviciate.

'Hey,' she said with a quick smile one breakfast. 'How about we don't go to the beach?'

Glancing up from a plate of eggs, I eyed her with perfectly disguised suspicion. 'Too much sun?'

'Too much people.'

'Want to try the rocks?' I asked. 'We might get a fish.'

Sister Bear had lost interest in fish. 'How about a ride in the country?' was her suggestion. 'I made sandwiches while you were playing tennis.'

'Any place special?'

'San Carlos way,' she said. 'Marie Ann says there's a great track through the hills.'

Four hours later found us lying on a rug on a hill. We had settled on this hill through my allowing Sister Bear to give directions from a map she pretended to ignore.

Below the hill a track cut through a valley studded with almond trees and olives. The valley rose in gentle terraces towards an arched farmhouse. A swimming pool glistened on the terrace below the house. The pool was protected on three sides by dry stone walls. Honeysuckle spilled over the walls and ivy-leaved geraniums tumbled like green waterfalls flecked with crimson spray from crannies between the stones.

The honeysuckle perfume drifted up to us through the hill scent of pine and rosemary. Bellies down, we had been regarding the house for close on half an hour before Sister Bear remarked, 'That was yours.'

'Yes,' I said.

She gave me five minutes grace, then asked, 'So what happened?'

There were so many answers to that question. I had been running through them while waiting for her to broach the subject. 'Cold War casualty,' I suggested. 'Know what I mean?'

'Should I?'

'Maybe not . . .' Content with my effort, I sheltered in silence.

'Yeah,' she said after a while. 'Living with you, I should have trained as a dentist.'

I smiled. 'So roll a smoke.'

'For learning you're a Cold War casualty?' she said. 'Do your own rolling.'

I roll lousy joints. 'Free World,' I explained. 'Dulles, that lot . . . know how close it was?' With a shake of my head, I looked down at what had been my married home. 'Crazy!'

It had been crazy. There was a day in Germany when all troop officers of our regiment were taken out to the banks of a river to choose positions for our tanks should the Russians break through.

If war came (and it looked imminent), our task would be to hold the Russians the forty-eight hours needed for NATO reserves to get into position behind us.

Sister Bear gaped. 'You were an officer?'

I said, 'Yeah, well, it was a long way back.'

'I can't imagine . . .'

I suffered her inspection with a shrug.

'Were you good?' she asked.

'The worst – half-way through I turned pacifist.'

'True?'

I considered. 'Yeah . . .'

My conversion occurred the day of the tank positioning. A brief inspection of the river told me we couldn't hold shit let alone the Red Army. We would kill a few hundred before getting killed. That was all – and there didn't seem much point. However many we killed, the Generals would finish by using nukes which would be the end of Europe, if not the end of the world.

'That's being a Cold War casualty,' I said in the longest speech I have ever made to a woman. 'They get set to blow the world up in defence of your freedom, you get to believe your freedom had better be genuine.'

Sister Bear's look presupposed my insanity. 'Is this for real?'

'You asked,' I countered.

'Come on,' she said. 'No one leaves his wife over the Cold War.'

'They don't?' I scratched my head. A man raps abstracts, there is always a lady ready to demand a detailed inventory of daily life. 'You want what we fought about? Well, mostly we fought about my having a bad attitude.'

Sister Bear smiled. 'That I can understand.'

'But you don't care to know where my attitudes come from?' I grinned. 'Kind of a waste considering how much thought I've given the subject while waiting for you to suggest we move.'

She acted dumb. 'Move?'

'Yeah,' I said. 'To a *finca* with a leaky roof and no heating.'

'You're not here in winter.'

'Too Goddamned right I'm not,' I said. 'But what happens with the baby?'

'What baby?'

'The one you're planning.'

Her eyes flashed thunder. 'You've got nerve.'

'Experience,' I corrected.

'Shit!' she said.

'Look,' I said. 'Sister Bear, do you think we hit on this hill by coincidence?'

Changing tactics, she essayed a smile. 'You mean you're not that dumb?'

'No,' I said, 'I'm not *that* dumb.'

'And you don't want a baby?'

'Can't afford a baby,' I corrected firmly.

'Bullshit,' she said. 'What's wrong with you is you're scared.'

'Scared is right,' I admitted. 'I've *had* living in guilt.'

'Guilt for what?'

'My attitudes,' I said. 'They're fine for a transit camp but lousy for a home base.'

'Yeah.' She flipped on to her back to study the sky. 'I believe you.'

Faced with her finality, I reached for the dope. Rolling reminds me of jail. Tailor mades were too costly on a prison librarian's pittance. Is this why I roll so badly? Subconscious refutation of the past? If so, she had brought me to the wrong hill. Sufficient memories remained in that house to have me refusing any action more dangerous than a visit to the ice-cream parlour.

Checking her profile, a surprising wave of tenderness momentarily washed away the knots in my belly. 'Sister Bear . . . ?'

'We're still talking?'

'Trying,' I said. 'Look, I already have two kids.'

'So?'

'So I know what they cost.'

'Clever,' she said. 'So now you're a computer?'

'Calculator.'

Head proppped up, she regarded me coldly. 'So big fucking deal. Ever thought of getting a job?'

'Back running dope?'

'There are other ways to make bread.'

'Such as?' I asked. 'Sweeping streets? A dope sentence is a shitty reference.'

'You could write.'

'I do write.'

'Not since I've known you.' She sat up. 'You don't have to give me an argument, Tobias. You don't want to, you don't want to.'

'Maybe I want to climb Everest,' I said. 'Wanting's not going to get me to the top.'

'Trying might,' she said and looked down at the house.

Trying . . . that seemed to be this summer's advice for Tobias. Unfortunately I knew what the house cost. Thirty kilos landed in New York would pay the bill. I would need a new passport, preferably Canadian, plus eight thousand in the bank. Tim would front me the remainder. So I'd finish in jail with a second lady left holding the baby. The family suffers more than the imprisoned. Justice says the lady should have chosen better.

Yes, dope dealing was a definite negative. Writing? Experience has taught me writing is a solitary occupation. You split your head into different characters, you don't want to put your head back together every few minutes for a lady who demands you relate. Nor am I talented enough to view writing as a serious source of income.

As for Sister Bear . . .

'What brought you to Ibiza?' I asked.

She had been lost in her own thoughts. 'Huh . . .?'

'I mean, this is a lousy place to come hunting a man wedded to a straight job.'

She almost smiled. 'I didn't hunt.'

'So you got dumped,' I agreed. 'Look, I make about six thousand dollars a year doing what I like. That's how come I'm relaxed. I start doing things I don't like, you're going to find me a drag to be around.'

'Yeah?'

'Experience,' I assured her.

'There's more in life than having fun.'

'Such as?'

'Achievement'

So we were on to that one. I know it well. Fortunately I come from the aristocracy My inheritance is an expertise in leisure.

Trade Union leaders demand the right of their members to work and organise strikes against automation that would put their members out of work. Many intellectuals support Trade Union officials Intellectuals believe the average worker has insufficient intellectual ability to enjoy leisure. I believe this is a lot of crap. It is a hell of a lot easier learning to enjoy leisure than learning to enjoy a five-day week on the assembly line.

Of course, Female Liberation does not demand the right for women to work on the assembly line. They demand the right of women to have worthwhile, upwardly mobile and self-expressing careers. Men should do the rest.

'There's a secret I have to tell you,' I told Sister Bear. 'Most women are full of crap.'

She was already pissed off so I wasn't risking much. 'Yes?' she said, her eyes spitting icicles.

'Yes.'

'So how come you hang out with so many?'

'I don't,' I corrected. 'They hang out with me.'

'Jesus!'

I held up a hand to cut her off. 'Also most women don't listen.'

'Is that an attack?'

'Not specifically.' I grinned. 'Depends whether you listen.'

'To you,' she interrupted. 'I'd go to sleep waiting.'

I look up from this notebook to see the night nurse smiling at me. She is the night nurse of my first day. Have I flipped the other one into a nervous breakdown? 'Hi,' I say. 'What happened to your holiday?'

'Nurse Mintoff went sick.'

'My fault?'

'Perhaps.' She straightens my sheet. 'Now be sensible. You have an operation in the morning.'

'So give me a pill.'

Her smile returns. 'What kind would you like?'

'How about a Mandrax?' I suggest.

She attempts to look shocked. 'You shouldn't know so much about drugs.'

'Nor should you,' I tell her.

'You'll go to sleep?'

'Promise . . .'

Off she hurries and back she comes.

The pill she's brought isn't a Mandy but beggars can't be choosers. I smile sweetly. 'How about a kiss?'

My suggestion takes her by surprise.

'Look,' I explain, 'this is my last chance of kissing a lovely lady before losing my manhood.'

She smothers her laughter in her hands. 'You should trust Dr Rahman.'

'I'd rather trust you,' I tell her.

'Well.' She stoops to brush my forehead with her lips. 'You promised . . .'

My right hand steals around her waist. I smile and say 'All's fair in love and war.' Some pacifist!

My hand fails to disturb her. She has probably been bored sitting alone in the office. Smoothing my hair back, she asks, 'Do you have a wife?'

'Not in a long time.'

She ponders. 'You mean you're divorced?'

I nod while watching her fiddle with the tiny gold crucifix she wears strung around her neck. Presumably she is thinking Catholic thoughts on the sanctity of marriage. She studies me for signs of mortal sin. 'Oh dear . . . don't you have a house?'

'An apartment.'

'Who looks after you?'

Do I look that old? 'Whoever has the time,' I say with a smile. 'When no one has the time, I look after myself.'

'Where?'

'Ibiza.'

This gives her room for thought. 'They say it's very beautiful.'

'Very,' I agree.

She stoops and kisses me lightly on the lips. 'Sweet dreams.'

'Of you,' I assure her.

She smiles and disengages my hand. 'Now, be good . . .'

You may not recall, but your mother instructed you to be good while she changed your diaper, you having just peed in her eye. It is an instruction that permeates the male experience. Teenage dating was a procession of *Be Goods*. I have overheard elderly gentlemen receive the same instruction from young ladies in nightclubs. As for marriage, the words changed but the meaning was identical.

Nowadays I try to be myself. Whether this is good or not is in the eye of the beholder and depends in what direction the beholder is attempting to push me.

My wife tried pushing me into being a good husband and a good father. I considered this odd. After all, she had married me in preference to some straight young man with a career. Why change me? But then why did I try changing her? Guilt is the answer.

I suffered guilt for not enjoying the daily routine of marriage. I also felt guilt over my wife having to support the daily routine of marriage. This was my error. Perhaps I had read too much Female Liberation literature? Perhaps my wife had read insufficient Female Liberation literature? Perhaps she simply found the idea of marriage and a house and kids sufficient ambition and sufficient pleasure.

Being a passionate traveller myself, I tried getting her to take trips to the oddest corners of the world. She hated travelling. 'So have an affair,' I would suggest.

'I don't want an affair.'

'So what do you want?'

'You.'

'Oh . . .'

'Oh what?'

Oh help! Because I did want to have affairs, not for the sex or the sense of conquest, but because life is like that – or mine is – and I like for life to be like that. I enjoy watching a lady seat herself at the neighbouring cafe table. I enjoy the moment of our first shared smiled and the initial rap in which we sound each other out to discover whether we interest each other and whether we have something to give each other.

I enjoy knowing that, having given, we will part, each having gained a little warmth and a little joy from sharing – not sexual sharing (though this tends to occur), but simply a sharing of ourselves; a momentary opening up to each other in which we recognise the unlimited alternatives for love and affection that exist in life and make of life an adventure.

To me this is an innocent desire. To others it is amoral. To my wife it gave pain. Perhaps I should never have married her. Certainly she should never have married me and certainly I should have left her earlier than I did, so as to call a halt to her pain. I was too arrogant to leave her and too selfish. I thought my leaving would give her more pain than I could bear to watch. So I tried getting her to leave me.

'Would you believe it?' I asked Sister Bear that afternoon on the hill. 'I ate my way up to ninety-eight kilos in hope of her getting so disgusted she'd split for some other man.'

Sister Bear regarded me in wonderment. 'You really are crazy.'

'Yeah, I'm crazy.'

'But *really* crazy,' she insisted.

'I know,' I said.

'Yeah, but *certifiable*.' She checked my eyes for signs of comprehension. 'I mean, people like you, they lock up.'

'That's why I tend not to speak too much.'

'Shit!' She shook her head like it was full of bees. 'And you loved her.'

'Still do,' I said. 'I didn't quit because I didn't love her, I quit because I couldn't stand to be trapped in guilt for not wanting to feel trapped.'

Eyes slightly glazed, Sister Bear reached for the dope. 'Weird! Like all this time I've been pushing you to rap was maybe a mistake.'

'I don't know,' I said. 'I mean, now that I'm into it, it feels all right.'

'Yeah?' She lit up and drew deep. 'Phew . . .'

She looked a little punch drunk was my opinion. 'There anything else you want to know?'

She smoothed her dress down over her belly as if she'd eaten too much and was scared of developing a paunch. 'Your kids . . .'

My kids? Shit! I think and grab for her letter. It can't be . . .

But it is.

> Hi gutless,
>
> Here we go. London is a drag and I am two months pregnant. Do your own calculations. It could be the Italian. My ticket expires the twenty-third except I don't have bread to hang on so long plus paying for an abortion.
>
> Seeing you take decisions slow for a tortoise, I will hang on as long as I can.
>
> All right?
>
> The decision is yours.
>
> Love.

She has signed the letter with a sketch of a pot-bellied bear. Under the sketch she had added, 'The love's the drag, because I really do love you – even if I don't know why.'

Jesus God! I hit the bell.

The night nurse hurries up the ward.

'Sister, are the telephones still out?'

'Out?'

'On strike?' I demand excitedly.

'Shush,' she whispers, 'you'll wake the patients.'

'Yeah,' I say. 'So are they or aren't they?'

'They are.'

'Goddamn! Look,' I insist, 'I have to catch a plane.'

'They won't let you on a plane.'

'They won't?'

'Not without a doctor's certificate,' she assures me. 'Tell me what's wrong.'

'My girlfriend's about to have an abortion,' I report, 'and I'm about to lose my ball.' This sounds so crazy, I hand her the letter.

She seems unwilling to read. 'Please,' I plead.

Crouching to the bed lamp, she scans Sister Bear's scrawl. 'You shouldn't have kissed me.'

'Maybe not,' I say.

'Oh dear . . .' She looks up at the ceiling presumably in search of God. God is on vacation. 'What can we do?'

Wait for God to return from his vacation.

'Today's the fifteenth,' she says.

'Right . . .'

We study each other's eyes for inspiration. I receive an inspiration. 'Look,' I say, 'there's three cables I have to send.'

'They won't accept cables, not with the strike.'

I have thought this out. 'Wireless,' I tell her and grab for a pad.

First to Sister Bear: DO NOT ABORT. BREAD ARRIVING. ME FOLLOWING. PRESENTLY HOSPITALISED. OUT SOON. ABSOLUTE LOVE. TOBIAS.

Next to Big J: HOSPITALISED MALTA. DESPERATE. ESSENTIAL YOU OR TIM ARRIVE SOONEST.

HELP. HELP. HELP. TOBIAS.

Next to Tim: HOSPITALISED MALTA. DESPERATE. ESSENTIAL YOU OR BIG J ARRIVE SOONEST. HELP. HELP. HELP. TOBIAS.

That about covers it, I think and pass the messages to the nurse. 'The Yacht Agency is open at nine. The lady there will get these sent from a yacht.'

Chapter Thirteen

I lie here between these nice clean hospital sheets, Sister Bear's letter clutched in my right hand like a holy talisman My testicle hurts . . . at least I hope my testicle hurts Perhaps I no longer have a testicle. No doubt Rahman will be by later to tell me which way the operation went. If he has cut it off, has he kept it for me in a bottle?

I feel sick in the belly from the anaesthesia and sick between the legs from Dr Rahman's knife. The sickness in my head comes from a blend of guilt, anxiety and frustration. Worst is the frustration. There is not one Goddamned thing I can do except lie here and wait for either Big J or Black Tim to arrive.

An hour ago they erected screens around my neighbour's bed. The priests were in and out of his enclosure like a stream of black ants. Next arrived sons, daughters and God alone knows what all relatives. They could not all have been his children and grandchildren. There were more than fifty of them. This is too many despite those crazy papal edicts forbidding contraception.

Only certain relatives were privileged to enter the enclosure. The priests did the selecting while the relatives wept. They have all gone now and the nurses are wheeling away the tube machines. Next they will wheel my neighbour away.

The ward is deathly quiet. This is a joke and I am not the only inmate of our ward to have tried humour as a lift. Nervous giggles have accompanied whispered words. Tucked away in my corner, I am unable to hear the words but I appreciate the need for us to bolster each other's courage, threatened as we are by Hell Fire Eternal.

The priests never let us forget their beloved Hell. They draw power from our fear of it. Now, with death so immediate, they strut the ward with the arrogance of Guardia Civil in the early years of Franco.

Tea time is in ten minutes. The nurses will pour tea while chattering brightly about how sunny it is outside and how warm the sea is for bathing and how we will all soon be cured.

Of course there are a couple of us who will never be cured. We know which ones and the ones know which ones. The nurses and doctors are alone in pretending not to know. Their pretence is pointless. Even if one of the ones desired to pretend to himself that he was on the way to recovery, the priests would disabuse him with their special attentions.

This is not a criticism of the priests. They have their beliefs; if they are correct in their beliefs, then their actions are right. Who am I to criticise simply because I lost my own faith back there amongst the illogicalities of a Catholic education?

A life dedicated to chastity is the sin of self-abuse; entrusting children to the institutionalised frustrated has wrecked a lot of lives over the centuries. These are my opinions.

The priests' opinions may be that I have wrecked a lot of lives with my institutionalised dedication to the lack of chastity. As for Sister Bear's opinion . . .

I imagine her pregnant and alone in London, staying in a third-rate hotel with damp sheets and insufficient hot water in the antique bathroom down the far end of the linoleum-shod corridor. The linoleum will be brown and scuffed. There are many such hotels in London. They smell of sour semolina and inadequate drains. They used to be cheap prior to the Arab invasion. Now thay are the most expensive accommodation in Europe for the low standard offered.

When I was young, the British were the wealthy. They vacationed on the Mediterranean and complained endlessly at being ripped off by greedy Latins. They also complained at the unhygienic toilet facilities found on the Continent.

Now it is the Arabs who justifiably complain at being robbed by the British and the Arabs who complain of the unhygienic toilet facilities. Thus ends an Empire. Strange that Gibbon failed to study bathroom standards as part of his *Decline and Fall of the Roman Empire*. I have read the *Decline and Fall*. I have also read two complete and authorised versions of Mao's speeches Jail gave me the opportunity We were allowed three books a week so I chose thick ones.

Fascinating though it may be to study the editing changes demanded by shifts in Maoist policies, it is more fascinating to remark how competently a well-trained mind can sidetrack off the route to unpleasant thoughts but Sister Bear always said I was an emotional coward.

Sister Bear . . .

What disgusts me is that it is my frustration at being unable to help her that causes me most pain

And here comes Dr Rahman, wizard of the knife

He approaches with a smile. 'So how are we feeling?'

'*We* feeling?' I give him a sick grin 'Do you have to be so British?'

'Part of the training.'

'Yeah . . . well, I feel depressed.'

'Post-operative,' he assures me, 'allied to antibiotics '

'You really think so, Doctor? You don't think it could be because my neighbour just died, my girlfriend is threatening to have an abortion and I can't stop her, and I don't know whether or not you've cut off my ball?'

'Wow,' he says in imitation of how he thinks I speak. 'You seem to be losing your *cool*.' He makes the 'cool' interrogative to indicate he is uncertain of the usage. 'Anyway, your testicle remains attached.'

'Yes? I've been waiting for you to bring it up in a bottle.

'Ah . . .' He strokes his moustache. 'Hence the worries over your girlfriend?'

By way of answer, I attempt a wry smile and we lock eyes. He has good eyes, dark and direct. 'If I asked you to tell me the truth,' I say, 'would you tell me the truth?'

'Probably.'

'Well, that's honest . . . so how is my testicle?'

'Still in place.'

'And functioning.'

His pondering half a second shoots my normal paranoia into the high hundreds. 'Just tell me.'

'I can't tell you,' he says. 'Not yet.'

'Jesus!'

'Try Allah.'

'I'll try anything,' I assure him. 'When do we know?'

'Three days, four at the most. I could tell you not to worry, but you'd probably get cross.'

'Probably,' I admit.

He plays with his moustache. 'Yes,' he says finally and his eyes twinkle. 'Perhaps we can find something in the pharmacy department to cheer you up.'

I can't imagine anything cheering me up but his lips twitch and he says, 'I understand your preference is for fantasy rather than oblivion?'

Hoist by my reputation, all I can do is smile. 'That would be nice.'

'Good,' he says. 'I'll have a word with the night sister. Oh, and by the way . . .'

'Yes?' I say while he tries to look stern.

'Don't persecute her. Remember the Maltese are somewhat sheltered from reality by their religion. All right?'

Embarrassed, I smile my apologies.

He accepts my smile. 'Splendid. Oh, and try keeping your fantasies asexual. Erection could be painful . . . though not dangerous,' he adds and grins. 'I'll see you in the morning.'

The man is a saint! Off he goes and I return to Sister Bear. Thoughts of her boxed up in the lousy hotel of my imaginings are too heavy. I switch her back to Ibiza and view her belly swelling naked in the sun, dark skin stretched tight and sumptuous, her face wearing that special *I am one hundred per cent woman* look ladies acquire in the last months of pregnancy. It is a beautiful look. I was a specialist on it back in my early twenties and playing the colonial adventurer in East Africa.

The first time was Mombasa. I had sailed up from Zanzibar with a friend of mine on his fishing boat. For three days I had been dreaming of a hot bath to rid myself of the fish smell.

'I stink,' I told my friend over a first drink at the port-side restaurant.

A lady was present, eight months pregnant. I knew her slightly Her husband was a senior bureaucrat with the Port Authority The lady was in her late twenties and the child she carried would be her third in five years. Catholic?

Perhaps she was simply careless, enjoyed children, or was using the wrong method – easy to do back in those dangerous days before the Pill.

She was sipping orange juice at a table with a dozen packages at her feet. Producing a nice smile, she smoothed her maternity dress down over her belly. A tiny crater showed dead centre through the thin cotton. 'If you'd like a bath, drive me home.'

I presumed she needed help with her packages. Pregnant ladies are frail, I thought, and it was a hot midday. So I carried her packages out to her car, helped her in to the passenger seat and drove her back to her house.

She told me to fetch myself a beer while she ran the water. Bathed and draped in a towel, I found her resting on her bed. She had changed into a silk robe and looked beautiful – though what fetched me over at a canter was the plate of sandwiches on the bedside table. We hadn't eaten too well on the boat.

The lady talked while I ate. This suited her. Her husband considered pregnant ladies deserving of special consideration and respect. This consideration and respect entailed his leaving her to sleep alone. Even in daytime he seldom came near her for fear of succumbing to his baser instincts.

I do not recall how much of her situation the lady clarified in the first minutes; sufficient for me to suspect she was more in want of sympathy than a chauffeur, while there I was wolfing ham sandwiches.

She watched me eat while I sat on the bed. She appeared a little impatient which I understood: she was in need of her siesta. So I said a polite *Thank-you* and *Maybe I should be getting back to the boat.*

She said, 'You're like my husband.'

Even I, in my twenty-one-year-old innocence, recognised she was being uncomplimentary. Confused, I rested back against the piled-up pillows.

She gave me a hard look and said, 'That towel's getting the sheet wet.'

The towel being around my waist, I stood up with a mumbled apology. The lady wasn't interested in apologies. 'For Christ's sake,' she said and grabbed for the towel

'Don't you understand? I want to get fucked.'

I had not understood. However, any doubts I had were banished by the speed with which she yanked off her robe. One button flew across the room and I recalled my mother ordering the gardener to get on with cutting the lawn instead of smoking a cigarette in the shade of the old yew tree; my mother had worn the same look of impatience as the bureaucrat's wife.

I enjoy mowing a lawn. Fresh cut grass smells good. The lady also smelled good but I had no idea where to start, so knelt on the bed looking lost. Her belly fascinated me. It was tight as a drum. I was about to lay a tentative hand on it when the whole mountain lurched.

The lady smiled at my fright. 'Don't be scared,' she said and laid my palm flat on a bump which had appeared. The bump was a foot according to her. It moved against my hand.

Maybe it *was* a foot. I wondered whether it was ticklish.

The lady thought it probably was. 'Try.'

Lips to the foot, I blew a raspberry. The baby gave a couple of kicks and chundled off to the other side of the belly. Beautiful! I gave chase while the lady laughed and looked proud enough to have just been elected woman of the year. She had, if only by me. This may not have been much but was definitely better than being treated with consideration and respect by her husband. He wouldn't be back for hours.

We spent a good half-hour playing kid games with the unborn kid. Judging by his or her activity, the kid got off on our games as much as we did. I gained confidence. So did the lady. Her body seemed so fertile, I expected the sun to burst out of it.

Squatting on my heels at her feet, I said, 'Your belly's like an altar.'

'So worship,' she told me. A lazily contented smile lit her face and she spread her thighs wide to accept my prayers as I bowed my head in obedience.

My hands rested on her belly and it was as if electricity was sparking through us. We were close to ecstasy. Over she got on her knees with her ass stuck up in the air. Her belly rested on my forearm and her breasts filled my hands. Full breasts

'Gently,' she murmured and mewed with pleasure.

There was no fakery. I mean, she really *liked* being fucked. This wasn't how I had learned it at my mother's knee. If *she* enjoyed getting fucked, then maybe a lot of other women felt the same way. *Great,* I thought, and exploded with confidence.

Still filled with joy, I got back to the boat in time for the owner to announce that we were sailing on the morning tide for Pemba Island.

'Not me,' I told him.

So commenced a new vocation. Perhaps I was plugging myself into a family situation without having to help out with the mortgage payments. Equally, it is possible that I am now trying to analyse after the event – a waste of energy.

My thoughts then were that *Think of the baby* is great advice except the lady has no need to think of the baby. She feels the baby inside her belly and knows the baby is getting along fine. What is not fine is her own clitoris. Her clitoris is itching the hell out of her siesta hour and is out of her reach what with all that belly blocking the path to self-satisfaction. Anyway pregnancy is definitely the wrong period for masturbation.

The lady is achieving within her body a miracle no man can emulate. She wants men to shout out, 'Incredible! Beautiful!' And she wants *her* man not only to shout out, but feel it and do something about it, such as giving unlimited head while working out fresh and delicious ways to ball.

Maybe digging this is what being a man is all about. Being pregnant is certainly what being a woman is all about.

Perhaps this reads as if I believed women to be short on brains and strong on body.

Incorrect.

My belief is that this sedentary city society has us compartmentalised. We operate on a schizoid roller coaster: one hour of body trip, fifteen hours of head trip, eight hours of slumber.

We rap too much, analyse too much and study from books too much. Reading up on how to meditate or how to fuck is no make-up for meditating or fucking. Pregnancy lifts you out of the second hand into the unique, better integration than rapping EST while jogging across Central Park.

Not that any of this philosophising helps Sister Bear. It seemed to me that day on the hill that her expectations ran contrary to her actions. Why would a lady come to Ibiza in search of stability? Marriages, partnerships, relationships suffer undue strain on the island. Few last. There are too many alternatives.

I lie here thinking about my elderly neighbour dead this afternoon. There were few alternatives in his life. For Sister Bear everything has been available: college education for the asking, options unlimited.

'You don't know how lucky you are,' her Dad rapped at her back as far as she can remember. 'You can be anything you want.'

What crap! She can only be what she has talent to be. This is her problem: having to face up to her talents. Back in my dead neighbour's youth, people found security and recompense in fantasy. They fantasise right till their death that other life they would have led if only they had been granted the opportunity. Lack of opportunity protected their fantasy.

Unlimited opportunity has denied Sister Bear the protection of fantasy. So she has smoked dope. Dope is great insulation against worries over what to do with your life . . . and getting pregnant offers a simple solution.

'That filthy shit,' is how Sister Bear's Dad refers to dope. How will he refer to her getting pregnant? Or having an abortion? What he fails to understand is that the chance to succeed presupposes the chance to fail and there were far more failures than successes even back in the bad old days of *his* youth.

Relationships are the same. For my dead neighbour it was marriage or nothing. Faced with this, he probably worked at his marriage. Why should Sister Bear work at a marriage? One argument and she will be off down the port in search of something better. She could easily do better than Tobias Cunningham-French . . .

The third day after our discussion on the hill, the Ibiza

yacht agent dropped by the studio. Sister Bear was out shopping.

'Hi,' he said, 'want to fetch a cat from Zea?'

Zea Marina is a few miles out from Athens, Greece. 'How big's the cat?' I asked.

'Forty-five feet.'

'And the bread?'

'Six hundred on top of expenses.'

I scratched my head. 'The owners in a hurry?'

'Not too much.'

'Could be fun.'

'Could be,' he agreed. 'She's a Wharam type, not fancy . . .'

'And shit to windward.'

'So there's no rush.'

'Yeah . . .' A slow voyage meant Sister Bear and I would eat free for a few weeks plus earning dollars from leasing the studio to some rich nut with sexual fantasies ten times the size of his penis.

'Have anything else on the books?' I asked the agent.

'A couple in the fall.'

'All right,' I said, 'keep one for me and I'm on.'

Relieved, he shook hands. 'Want the airfare in cash?'

Of course I wanted the airfare in cash.

'Hi,' I greeted Sister Bear who came staggering home under a basket laden with vegetables. 'Want to ride the bike down to Greece for a cat?'

'A what?'

'Catamaran . . .'

She dumped the vegetables on the kitchen counter. 'How long?'

'Six weeks,' I calculated.

She sat at the table while I set the coffee pot to heat. I had already dragged out the necessary charts. She studied the top chart in a broody way which told me her head was off someplace else . . . and I had expected her to be excited.

Finally I said, 'Look, I have to go . . .'

'You do?' She looked up, sullen. 'Why?'

'Fourteen hundred dollars,' seemed a lot of answers. I smiled. 'That's with the studio let. There's always some sex nut wanting a bed on the port.'

She glared. 'So it's another of your fucking ultimatums

'Hey,' I said. surprised.

'Hey, shit.'

'Now wait a minute . . ' This whole scene had flung me back into holy matrimony. I used to skipper yachts. That was how I met my wife. She came strolling down the quay, spotted the British flag and dropped me a smile. Three months later we were married. Probably she fantasised marriage to a yacht skipper as romantic. Reality produced a change. A lady marries a man, she wants him home nights.

Also the ease with which she had collected me made her paranoid over other ladies doing the same. She complained I was off a month at a time, which was bad for the kids.

I answered that I spent most of the winter around the house. Working men leave the house at eight in the morning five days a week. They get home seven in the evening too tired from drudgery and too discouraged by the endlessness of it all to do more than sit slumped in front of the TV. Weekends they play golf or watch football.

Add the hours up and I spent more time home than they did. Nor did we have money problems while I skippered. Once I stopped, we had nothing else. Money problems turn life into a drag.

This reads like I'm blaming the wife for my having quit skippering. The blame was mine. If she had felt more confident over my morals, she would not have been so uptight over my being away (so she shouldn't have married an easy lay). But my guilt was mostly to blame. I felt my being away was unfair on her. I also felt it proved I didn't love her sufficiently.

Perhaps I love too easily and too shallowly. This would be Sister Bear's opinion. 'How many people do you get to love in a year?' was her response to my declaration of love that afternoon out on Black Tim's boat.

I have a brother I love and a father and mother I love, despite our using different wavelengths for communication.

I love my ex-wife.

I love my two kids.

I love Maria Jesus.

And Sister Bear.

Big J and Black Tim.

The list is endless.

I love the sun and the sea and the beach and the mountains and the snow. There are flowers to love and the scent of pinewoods . . .

In fact, I love life – my life.

Or I will love my life once I am safely out of this hospital and in command of a salvaged testicle.

Back in the studio kitchen and faced with Sister Bear, all I could think to say was, 'Look, delivering yachts is how I make my bread.'

She said, 'Yeah . . .'

'Yeah what?'

'Yeah, you'd have to pick some way of keeping on the move.'

'So I like moving . . .' I spread my hands. 'You'd prefer me broke?'

'Bread's not everything.'

'No,' I admitted with more truth than originality, 'but it sure as hell helps.'

Should I have understood her hands folded over her belly? No lady in her first weeks of pregnancy wants to ride pillion from Spain to Greece on a trail bike! Not unless they want to miscarry . . .

So she should have told me she was pregnant.

So I should be the sort of man she could feel confident at telling. Presumably I am not that sort of man because all she said was, 'You expect me to be here when you get back?'

I answered, 'If that's what you want.'

'Yeah, so what the fuck do *you* want?'

'A nice happy relaxed life,' I said. 'If that's possible . . .' and slammed my way out of the studio and down the street to collect my laundry.

I returned to the studio cooled out and repentant at having yelled. Sister Bear was still at the table. 'I'm sorry,' I said.

She looked up like it took effort. 'Over what?'

'Over being a drag.'

'Yeah . . . ?'

'Look,' I said, 'why don't you come along?'

She stayed silent

I consider painting her a fantasy of the trip which would draw her out of her sulk. The trouble with spinning fantasy is people get pissed off when they find reality is different. I know this from my marriage. Early fantasy had us sailing the seas, me as Bing Crosby, Joan as Grace Kelly and the movie *High Society*.

Remember?

Bing sits in the cockpit of the *True Love*. He has one hand on the tiller and the other full of his briar pipe.

Her Royal Highness Princess Grace has her head in Bing's lap.

The moon shines, the sails draw effortlessly, Bing sings and the sailboat carves through the sea steady as a bulldozer parked on an airstrip.

Unfortunately I don't possess a singing voice and my wife would throw up crossing the harbour on an oceanliner.

So instead of painting fantasies, I said to Sister Bear, 'Catamarans don't roll.'

'Big fucking deal,' she said. 'Ever shot the Colorado?'

I looked blank.

'Well, I have,' she said. 'From when I was fourteen right up till now.'

'Yeah?'

'Yeah,' she said.

'I get the point.' Dragging a chair back, I sat facing her and ready to make a giant effort. 'Look, Sister Bear, there's something you have to get into your head.'

'There is?'

'There is,' I assured her, 'except you have difficulty believing – but we are meant to be allies. That's why we live together.'

'Live together!' She took a huge breath. 'You call living together expecting me to go stay with Marie Ann while you piss off to Greece on a trail bike?'

I stood up, rolled the charts and said, 'So find someone else.'

'Maybe I will,' she told the table top.

'Fine,' I said and stuffed clothes into a saddle bag while

feeling shitty as a pig. Sister Bear must have felt a lot worse. It is sick in a man my age to have so little ability in the communication field. I scrawled the Malta Yacht Agency address on a pad. 'You want to write, this'll find me in two or three weeks.'

She didn't bother looking at the address.

Her not looking pissed me off. No lady complains when a man tells her the vacation is over and it is time to head for the office. Why should they get uptight with me for the way I make my bread?

The confrontation is endemic to Ibiza. Ibiza is for fun and freedom rather than doing the housework and earning bread; so runs the fantasy. Sister Bear's pregnancy would have been more reason rather than less for me to sail the catamaran . . . but I would have managed to part on a better note.

Instead, 'Maybe you should grow up and learn where life's at,' was my parting shot. 'Pierre will have the studio let from the end of the week.'

Chapter Fourteen

Big J has come and gone. His arrival says much for his loyalty to friends. His departure was hastened by a dislike of hospitals.

Big J had donned his travelling gear for the trip: Harris tweed jacket and grey flannel trousers made to measure by Pool of London and a pair of brown brogues on his feet sewn by the last master bootmaker. Both the jacket and the shoes are a little tight on Big J.

He keeps the shoes and jacket because they cost so much. He insists on wearing them travelling as a reason for keeping his travelling down to the minimum. This may not make sense to you but makes sense to Big J.

I greeted him with a friendly, 'Hi, how come you came and not Black Tim?'

'The *I Ching*,' was Big J's answer.

'Yeah? What did you throw?'

'Crossing the dark waters.'

'And what else?'

'Some crap about helping others,' replied Big J with little enthusiasm.

I said, 'Great.'

Big J disagreed. He inspected the ward like he was trapped in Harlem on the brink of a race riot.

'Travel broadens the mind,' I advised. 'How did Tim do?'

'*Don't* cross the dark waters. Says he's going to haul his boat out.'

'He's got a new motor on order,' I said.

Big J glared. 'Son of a bitch!' And to me, 'So what's wrong? You dying?'

'Not yet.'

'So how about tomorrow?' he suggested. 'There'd better be something wrong with you.'

'There is,' I said. 'They're into cutting off my ball.'

Big J cheered up. 'They are?'

'They've had a go.'

He peered at the bulge pushing up the sheet. 'No kidding . . .'

'Definitely no kidding.' I passed him Sister Bear's letter. 'Read this.'

He read and frowned. 'I have to fly round the world every time you get a lady knocked up?'

'Just this once,' I said. 'The banks and phone company are out on strike.'

'*The banks!*' Big J was shocked. 'How come you got sick in such a dump?'

'I didn't get sick out of choice,' I said.

Big J wasn't sure. He suspected a plot. Anything that upsets his Ibiza routine is a plot. He has been reading religious, mystical and scientific philosophy five hours a day for twenty years in hope of discovering who does the plotting. Right now Sister Bear and I were the instruments of the plotter. 'So you want me to do something about the lady?'

'That's right.'

'What?'

'Save the kid,' I said, 'and see Sister Bear's all right.'

'Save the kid . . .' There was something a little paranoid in Big J's nod of understanding. A few drops of sweat shook loose on to the letter. 'Yes,' he said and laid the letter aside.

His *Yes* was in agreement with his own train of thought so I remained silent while he checked my pupils. 'What sort of drugs they have you on? I mean, you have to be hallucinating, right?'

It was my turn to look shocked. 'Big J, *I'm in love.*'

'Like shit you are. Look,' he said, 'you know this chick a couple of months – half the time you were into balling that Kraut while your lady was into the Mafia's answer to Anniagoni. Is that love?'

'It suggests we ought to be able to work something out,' I said. 'And she was only into Julio five days.'

'With your track record, work what out?' Big J shot. 'I mean, do you know what sort of a drag you were when you and Joan were into marriage?'

Discussing marriage with Big J is tough. His judgement is

warped by twenty years of wedlock to a lady he won't divorce for terror at how much alimony he'll have to pay. 'I'm older now,' was the best I could do.

'Not old enough,' he said.

'Yeah, well, I promise not to invite you over to eat brown rice.'

The brown rice should have won a smile. Not from Big J. He was already into anguish over what hotel to stay at if he *did* fly to London. Hotels are part of why he hates travelling. He can never decide whether to suffer discomfort or blow a lot of bread. 'The way you live,' he asked, 'how can you afford a kid?'

So these were my lines to Sister Bear. Consistency can be a weakness. 'Worst comes to worst,' I said, 'we can move out East and live on the beach.'

'And have the kid die of dysentery? Great,' said Big J. 'What's he going to grow up as? A Hindi fisherman? Or are you back into running dope?'

This last question was a heavy put-down coming from Big J. Of course he *likes* dope but, being a Republican, he disapproves of anyone getting rich quick. Wealth should be inherited, according to Big J.

I was about to point out that I had never gotten rich, but a fresh fear had entered his skull. 'What the fuck am I meant to say to her?'

'How about that I love her,' I suggested.

'We've been through that.'

'*She* hasn't,' I assured him. 'And it's true – at least in my fashion.'

He gave me a look. 'She know about your fashion?'

'Pretty much,' I said. 'She knows who I am which is more than Joan ever did.'

'Hey,' Big J warned. He has a soft spot for Joan.

So do I. 'All I'm saying is Joan and I never meshed.'

'And you and Sister Bear do? Maybe you're right,' he admitted after a little thought. 'You're both in and out of every bed you can find.'

'We also like sharing a bed,' I said.

'And that makes you a great couple?' Standing up, he peered out of the window at the blue sky. 'London, it will be pissing down with rain.'

So he was going. 'Thanks Big J. Some day I'll do the same for you.'

Head cocked, he checked me for insanity. 'You do and I'll break your neck.'

'So make do with the thanks.'

'For helping you louse up your life?'

'It's my love I'm worried about,' I said. Not that I know what love is in the classical sense. Big J is correct. I have been madly in love once and that was enough. Who wants to be mad?

Oral sex was not too common back in the early fifties and the lady in question was the first to ever put my penis in her mouth. She was European and we met at an alcoholic party on a white settler's farm in Kenya. I don't remember the meeting but we must have met because I awoke at dawn on the living-room carpet with a blanket for warmth and the lady for company. We were both fully dressed.

The blanket covered the lady's head. I peeked. She had golden hair bleached pale at the ends by the sun and sea. Judging by the way she scurried deeper under the blanket, she also had tender eyes – or so I presumed till she pried open my pants. The erection she discovered came from a full bladder.

Terror hit that I would pee in her mouth! *Her!* Who was she? And why was she doing this to me?

My penis was dirty.

Disgusting.

Immoral.

Yes indeed, the priests and their teachings were still in my skull. No lady could be doing to me what this lady was doing to me out of pleasure.

Frenching was what we called giving a man head. *Gamarouching* was what what men did to women. I had heard of both but had an idea they were what prostitutes and gigolos did to wealthy clients.

Was she going to ask me to pay?

Not the best thoughts to have in your head when experiencing a new pleasure! Also there were prayers to be said – prayers for the successful control of my bladder.

God answered.

Thank you, God.

Finished, the lady swung her feet to the side of the bed. There was no side to the bed. She shifted ass a few inches further. Encountering no side, she groaned and retreated under the blanket with her eyes still firmly closed.

I crawled off to the can. People talk of sexual relief. How about the relief of a desperately needed pee?

The can is also great for contemplation. After a little thought, I concluded the lady had mistaken me for her husband. Now that I had seen her face, I knew she had a husband. She also had two children and was twenty-six years old to my twenty-one.

Writing this now, I *still* presume she thought I was her husband though she greeted my return with kisses. Perhaps confessing her error to herself was too painful.

Anyway, our affair blossomed from the living-room floor to the insanity of planning on running away together. She would have to discuss this with her husband and explain it to her children so could not see me for a whole weekend. By Saturday afternoon I was flipping out. Fortunately there was a neighbourhood Catholic church. In I went to confess for the first time since leaving school. Where else but a Catholic church can you find someone to listen to your tale of love? None of my friends would listen. They thought I was sick in the head.

The priest *had* to listen.

He wasn't impressed. 'How old are you, boy?' he demanded through the confessional's grill.

'Twenty-one,' I said.

'A lot of nonsense at your age,' was his next comment. 'Pull yourself together, boy, and go say three Our Fathers and three Glory Be's in the Lady Chapel.'

How *dare* he dismiss our adultery so lightly? Refusing his penance, I knelt at the High Altar and prayed God to help the lady and I to a life of shared bliss.

God must have thought that I was too young. Why else did he let me discover that the love of my life had spent the weekend, not with her husband and children, but in the arms of a stuntman playing stand-in for Tarzan.

Off I drove to kill myself in my Mark 7 Jaguar. The prime spot for suicide was the top curve on the escarpment road. The drop was four thousand feet.

A friend spotted my erratic driving. He hooted a couple of times, became concerned that I might be drunk, and cut me off.

The lady was impressed on hearing the story. She even found my jealousy flattering for a few weeks. Then she very rightly became bored and brought our affair to an end.

However, the situation was interesting if you consider the Jaguar. The Jaguar was my one love up to the moment the lady put my penis in her mouth. Nobody but me was allowed to drive the Jaguar. Nobody was even allowed to wash or wax-polish its bodywork. In fact, my love for the Jaguar was as possessive as my love for the lady.

Would I have killed myself *and* the Jaguar?

If so, I was really sick.

Suicide is an interesting speculation. Do you earn oblivion or a quick trip into the after-life? And why should Swedes be good at it while Africans remain non-runners?

The first dead body I ever touched was that of an African lady. I was sixteen years old and put my hand on her breast to see if she was dead. This was during my first job. The job was trainee stockman on a Rhodesian cattle ranch and I got paid ten dollars a month plus board and lodging. I also got to play table tennis after dinner with the ranch manager while his wife listened to the BBC World Service and knitted her husband woollen socks which he never wore.

He said wool made his feet smell.

After fifteen years of marriage, you would expect his wife to have given up. I wonder what happened to the socks.

As for the black lady, she *had* given up. Nine months pregnant, she had walked five miles for water. Lifting the filled four-gallon can to her head killed her.

I was shocked at how casually everyone took her death, blacks and whites. To my teenage eyes death was a special event. *Everything* was special except for work. Work was normal. Everyone did it – or so I had been taught.

The casualness shown by my elders towards the lady's death made me query their attitude to work. If *my* death would be considered equally unimportant, then I was wasting my life for ten dollars a month.

Having thought this out, I resigned my job and have never held a straight job since. There are millions of people who long to work but are unable to find work. As I do not long to work, it would be immoral of me to deprive someone else of the chance.

Critics ask what would happen if everyone behaved as I do. I answer with the teachings of the priests. At school we were taught that true happiness comes from living in a state of Grace. As work brings me no happiness, presumably there is no Grace in work.

The priests also taught us that suicide would be punished by God with Hell Fire Eternal. As a child, I found this unfair. Why should someone driven desperate by suffering be further punished?

Now that I am middle-aged, I understand.

God is forever. Why should he want a bunch of sufferers sharing his cloud? They would depress him with their tales of woe.

God has given us life as a test. Enjoy life and God will be pleased to see you. Just don't tell him ethnic jokes.

Fortunately I have specialised in enjoyment and enjoyment promises to be a growth industry. Perhaps I should say that I *have* been a specialist. The future is less clear.

Dr Rahman has just dropped by with a promise that I can check out of the hospital the day after tomorrow.

'So I'm all right?'

'As far as I can tell,' he says.

'How far can you tell?'

Smiling sympathy for my concern, he spreads his hands. 'We have to wait for the bandages to come off.'

'Like patients who have had an eye operation?'

He gives me a second smile. 'Except the answer won't come to you as a flash of light.'

'So how will it come?' I ask. 'You get a nurse to strip and we wait for an erection?'

'Not quite.' He gives my knee a gentle pat. 'Try not to worry.'

'While praising Allah?'

'If that helps.' He nods at my notebooks. 'Writing should keep your mind off other things.'

The good doctor is ignorant of my subject matter. Jail was easier to bear than the hospital. In jail my only worry was a nightmare that recurred with increasing frequency the closer I came to release.

A suitcase in each hand and dressed in my dope dealer's best grey flannel, I awaited my release through the prison doors. The doors were huge, wooden and studded with iron nails.

A guard stood beside me. He was an old man, short in stature and close to retirement. He carried a bunch of old-fashioned keys. He fitted the biggest key into the door, turned the key and pulled the door open a couple of feet. Then he smiled at me in commiseration.

I was panicked by his smile.

'Out you go,' he said and gave me a shove.

The door thudded shut as I stepped out into nothing. No world.

From my hospital bed I can see enough through the window to know the world is still there. Having no need to worry over the world, I worry over my health and over Sister Bear and over how Big J is getting on in London. I also worry over what happens if Big J succeeds in his mission.

What will life be like with Sister Bear?

What will life be like with Little Bear?

Little Bear will be no problem. I shall love, cherish and obey him or her with happiness.

As for Sister Bear, she will probably decide I am too old, too idle, too non-communicative, too selfish and too short on the capacity for love to be worth sharing her life with . . .

Chapter Fifteen

Dawn has brought me a cup of weak tea, a bed bath and a return to good spirits. The good spirits can be attributed to the stirring within my bandages occasioned by the light touch of the night nurse as she washed the sweat off my thighs.

She spotted the stirring and I spotted her spotting the stirring. Our eyes met.

'You're feeling better.'

'Looks that way, I said and we smiled.

Perhaps I should feel guilty over my good spirits as there is still no news of Sister Bear. However, my being miserable wouldn't help her so I might as well enjoy feeling good.

If I had known that my gloom would lift I would have accepted Dr Rahman's fantasy pill last night. Instead, I chickened out and had the nurse change it for six hours of Mogadon-induced oblivion.

Weird, but in jail I was never scared of fantasy pills. A friend living in Marin County, California, used to write me every time he got really out of his head. The letter would come with coded references to what part of the letter I should eat. His being out of his head at the time of writing didn't make for clarity or effectiveness. Sometimes I would eat the whole letter and end up with indigestion. Other times I would nibble a corner and be spaced out for a week.

Jail is a safe place to take hallucinogens. The windows have bars and there's no chance of anyone breaking in on your dreams. The other advantage to jail is the leisure you have to study yourself. What you see may not be great but will be *you* rather than the normal projections and inter-projections of social encounter.

This is not advertising copy for serving a prison sentence. A Buddhist monastery will do fine, though avoid the Himalayas – lamaseries are short on central heating. My father, fortunate in having bread, would suggest a suite in a five-star hotel.

As for a stay in the hospital, these scribblings began as a method of keeping my mind free of the fear of losing my ball. Now that I have six notebooks filled, I *think* I have gained a few insights into myself and know I have gained a callous on my index finger.

A wise man could concentrate on the callous.

Concentrating on the insights leads to dangerous presumptions of wisdom. Psychoanalysts are specialists in this error. Their insights persuade them into acting as surrogates for God. Act God to a patient with emotional problems and the patient will become dependent on you. Unfortunately the dependency is invalidated by your not being God.

I learned a little of this on leaving jail.

Freedom found me tranquil as a monk fresh from navigating the perils of male menopause. I was met by various ladies determined to experience the imagined backlog of two years chastity.

My attempts at recounting how chastity had not been part of my sentence were ignored by the ladies. They were too busy getting out of their pants.

I fled to a house way out in the Ibiza countryside. A very beautiful German lady lived there with an English Baron of impeccable lineage. The Baron was tall, blond and slender, blue-eyed and owner of a Roman nose.

The house was the Baron's.

So was the lady.

This is not a male chauvinist comment. She *was* a possession and a possession by her own choice. The Baron had no desire to own her. He wanted her to leave but lacked the balls to tell her so. She was a drag in the Baron's eyes.

The lady *was* a drag. Of course she hadn't started out as a drag. Her dragginess came from living all these months with a man who didn't want her.

The Baron was as miserable as the lady. He and I were friends from our schooldays. My arrival delighted him. I was someone to talk to. Any man would have done. The German lady was also delighted. She presumed my two years of abstinence would have left me receptive to women.

Like many Ibiza houses, the Baron's had been built at the turn of the sixteenth century by a landowner frightened of pirates. Sculpturally the house was beautiful. It wasn't so good for living. The windows were too small. Designed to keep out pirates they also kept out light.

The Baron and his lady found the gloom great for glowering at each other, but I had picked up a heavy reading habit in jail, so the Baron lent me the guest house. This was modern and comfortable and let in lots of sun. It would also have been tranquil if the Baron and his lady hadn't been so determined to air their relationship to a new audience. I heard both versions in two hour excerpts from whichever one hadn't driven into the village to shop.

Their problem was difficult to understand.

The Baron wanted the lady to leave and the lady hated being there. All they needed to do was admit so face to face. This would have taken five minutes while here they were into their second year.

'Tell the lady,' I told the Baron the end of my first week.

'I can't,' he said.

'Why not?' I asked.

'I don't want to hurt her.'

'So what the fuck do you think you're doing now?'

Two minutes thought and he said, 'You're right.'

Pleased with myself, I went back to reading while the Baron went off to tell the lady. She wept. He said he hadn't meant what he'd said. She stopped weeping and they fucked. How long the fuck lasted is their secret but, by breakfast, they were back to armed neutrality.

I had to wait till after breakfast to hear from the Baron how he had backed down. His weakness shocked me. Now I am merely shocked by my hypocrisy because my father once gave me advice along the same lines as I was giving the Baron.

'Hear you're having trouble with your marriage,' my father opened. 'Is that correct?'

I said, 'Yes.'

He said, 'Humph! A marriage doesn't work, only one thing to do. End it.'

My father, having suffered four marriages, is an expert sc

I asked, 'Yes, but how long does it take?'

'What take?'

'Ending it.'

'See what you mean,' he said and gave me another *humph*. 'Three years is about par for the course.'

'So that leaves me another ten months,' I said. It took longer, but this didn't stop me acting the sage while talking to the Baron. 'Great,' I told him, 'You've chickened out, so now you're going to have to lay the same rap on her all over again.'

The Baron studied the floor.

'Which is fine,' I said, 'if you're into drama, but not fair on your lady. She's had enough misery.'

The Baron said, 'Damn,' and pried at a loose floor tile with the toe of his riding boot.

'You have to be honest,' I said. Two years in jail had got me hyped on honesty – honesty in relationships, that is. This was natural after two years rest and recuperation from the relationship front.

'I mean, shit,' I said to the Baron. 'What are you? A coward?'

'Not a saint,' was his answer. He gave me a scowl. 'That's what you seem to think you've turned into after two years in jail.'

Stung, I said, 'Don't cop out.'

'You're the one who cops out,' he said. 'Listen to yourself speak. You're so ashamed of being British and upper class, you've worked your accent into something half-way between a gay American footballer and a black lady homosexual teaching poetry to night classes in Denver, Colorado. Disastrous!'

'Thanks,' I said.

'Be my guest.'

'I already am,' I pointed out, 'and all I'm trying to do is help.'

'How kind of you . . .' Prying at the loose floor tile had scratched his boot. 'Damn,' he said 'Anyway tonight I won't back down.'

He didn't. However, a gentleman would have dropped by the guest house to warn me of what to expect for breakfast the following day.

Armed with two slices of buttered toast with honey, a large pot of coffee and a bowl of stewed apricots liberally coated with fresh yoghurt, I seated myself at the kitchen table. The kitchen was definitely baronial. Two slit windows with wooden bars let a little light in through the five foot thick walls. A fireplace built for burning tree trunks occupied one end of the room while a staircase led up from the other end to a balcony off which opened the doors to both the Baron's and the lady's bedrooms. Oak casks filled with the Baron's baronial wine rested against the wall beneath the balcony.

The dining table was solid pine, three metres long and four inches thick. At the fireplace end of the table stood the Baron's highbacked armchair and there were benches each side of the table for his guests. The benches were backless but reasonably comfortable if you slouched. The Baron disapproved of slouching.

Confident in my post-prison sanctity, I was about to sip my first cup of coffee when the lady appeared at the head of the stairs.

The lady stood five-ten in her bare feet. Dark hair brushed and worn loose to her waist, she peered down at me out of huge brown eyes under which she had inked an inch of solid black as advertising for how tragic her life had become.

She wore a white robe of thin silk. The robe reached to her feet and hung open for me to appreciate the perfection of her breasts, the slenderness of her belly and the triangle of satiny fur fluffed up like a dark powder puff at the junction of her thighs.

She held her arms a little out from her sides, her palms open and long slender fingers slightly spread as they are in the Titian crucifixion with the fir tree in the left side top corner (maybe it's a cedar).

She had cut her wrists.

Nothing serious – just a nice steady drip.

She peered down at me, tragic and uncertain. The uncertainty came from her not wearing her spectacles. It was a drag being unable to see what impression you are making on your audience.

She needn't have worried. The scene was both beautiful and dramatic. Despite my state of pre-first cup caffeine addiction, I was definitely impressed except for the blood. This was Saturday and the Baron's Spanish cleaning woman didn't come weekends.

'Hi,' I said. 'You're bleeding.'

She: 'I've cut my wrists.'

'Maybe you should stick bandaids on them.'

'I want to die.'

'But you don't want to get scars.'

She examined the cuts. Too short-sighted to be sure, she shot back to the bathroom in search of her glasses while I drained my first cup of coffee.

My last gulp coincided with her return to the head of the stairs. She was still dripping which I pointed out.

Now that she was sure there was no risk of her suffering permanent disfigurement, she had lost interest in her wrists. 'I've taken pills,' she announced as if we were well into Doomsday.

The Baron had forgotten to tell me there were pills in the house. Here was his lady swallowing something that might be pure magic. Racing upstairs to the bathroom, I checked.

CODEINE . . . the disappointments one survives! If the lady had looked less tragically beautiful I would have gotten cross. Instead I searched out the elastoplast. Scissoring two lengths from the roll sufficiently long to make the lady feel important, I taped her up and led her downstairs to share breakfast.

We sat face to face. She tried to avoid my eyes while I tried to look sympathetic. Finally I asked where the Baron was.

'Gone.'

'Shopping?'

'For good.' Two tears plummeted on to her slice of toast. 'He's never coming back.

What nonsense! The Baron would never leave for good – not even to disengage himself from a lady. He loved his house. It was all he had left from his patrimony. A quick gulp of coffee gave me strength to realise this. The truth was that he had removed himself from the firing line and would stay removed until such time as the lady removed herself.

Desertion in the face of the enemy – some Baron! What had the aristocracy come to?

My explaining this to the lady cheered her up. She even risked a slight giggle while I made a third pot of coffee and told her how beautiful she had looked dripping blood at the head of the stairs.

'I did?' A tentative smile lifted the corners of her mouth

'Definitely,' I assured her. 'In fact,' I added, you looked more beautiful than any lady I have ever seen

'Really?'

'Swear to God.'

'Wow,' she said and produced a second giggle.

'Also very dramatic,' I added with a grin 'Beats the movies. How come you hung around the Baron's winter palace all this time?'

She answered with perfect feminine logic that she loved the Baron.

I suggested this was untrue. What she really loved was drifting around the house with a martyred look disfiguring her face so she could split for Hamburg, London or Amsterdam once every two months and impress her friends with tales of misery.

A surprising number of women only feel important when they are suffering. The same applies to men, but men into suffering are considered drags so no one listens to them.

Beautiful women who suffer are considered romantic (at least by other women and male novelists) so can get away with their act.

Personally, I consider suffering a drag. Too many people do it without option . . . like all those starving millions in India whom the freaks consider beautiful because they sit so placidly along the roadside. Of course they are placid. What else can you be when suffering from acute protein deficiency?

The lady facing me across the breakfast table was not suffering protein deficiency but she did seem to be opening her inner eyes to how crazily she had spent the last two years of her life. Five Codeine and a pair of nicked wrists is an imperfect background for thought, but she finally smiled. 'You know, you're right.'

She took a slow look around the kitchen as if seeing it for the first time. 'Would you believe it – I was a real fun person before I moved in here?'

Sure I could believe her. Any lady capable of such speedy recovery had to have fun. 'So what went wrong?'

She thought a while. 'Maybe he's just not made for marriage.'

For reply I refilled her cup.

'Thanks,' she said and looked up at the balcony as if studying their bedroom doors might supply the answer. 'Probably I expected more from him than he was prepared to give . . .'

'*Able* to give,' I suggest. 'Maybe that's the problem. Know what I mean?'

She didn't and I wasn't sure I did. Certainly I wasn't capable of putting whatever it was I meant into the spoken word. Thinking back, I suppose what I meant was that we put too heavy a load on a single partner. Fantasising how a different partner would be able to carry the load *is* fantasy. What we need are relationships that spread the load. An expanded family is as close as I can drag out of my untidy mind.

This probably comes over as both utopian and impractical. Practical men run the world and the world is a mess. As for fantasy, I think the wide freedoms we enjoy in the West lead us into disappointment through our fantasising our fantasies as realisable.

Sister Bear and I rapped a little of this. She told me of an old man living up in the mountains not too far from where she grew up. There is no road up to where he lives, but there is a small lake with a stream running out of it. The stream serves as a trail.

The old man has built himself an adobe hut close to the lake and has lived in the hut since the end of World War II. The lake is a twelve-mile hike uphill from the nearest track. Few people can be bothered to climb that far but each year some do. It is a sort of cult passed on from one bunch of late-teenagers to the next. Sister Bear first made the climb when she was just fifteen, but she was tough for her age. She was also a virgin.

The old man fascinated her . . . or she was fascinated by her fantasies of the old man. His only contact with the outside came from the hikers. Up they climbed, generation succeeding generation. First came the kid boozers ready to break a bottle of Jack Daniels with him over the campfire. Next came the smokers. Then the acid heads.

Also the sexual mores changed and each summer there would be some young lady into a fantasy of love for the old man – not that he started out old, of course.

Listening to Sister Bear's rap got me envious of the old man. Winter would be great for him. I could imagine him sitting in front of a log fire, his feet propped up on a box and his pipe drawing smoothly. All through winter he would have the excitement of wondering what new fantasies would come tripping up the trail next spring.

'Yeah,' said Sister Bear, 'I can see how you'd dig that. You do it anyway.'

I should have answered her with a *Yeah*. Yeahs are difficult to attack if you pitch them delicately into the mid-ground between agreement and query. However, I was still immersed in my reverie of the old man so was caught off guard and asked, 'Do what anyway?'

'Relate to people's fantasies.'

'So what's wrong with that? At least it's relating.'

'Bullshit!'

'Hey,' I complained.

'Come on,' she said. 'You know Goddamned well what I mean. Your kind of relating is just an easy way out of exposing yourself. Just one more cop-out,' she said and rolled on to her side so she could study my face. We were at the beach and this was the day after the hill and the day before I split to fetch the catamaran.

It was a hot afternoon for getting heavy; also I had been enjoying the thought-drift her tale had stirred in my head. A few minutes' silence would hve been fine by me. Sister Bear wasn't interested in silence. She came after me like a terrier.

'Like the way you carry on about how old you are and how you're overweight,' she said and prodded me in the midriff. 'Two pounds of fat and you use it as a cop-out against anyone putting you down for being you. Come on,' she said, 'I mean, how many women have you balled this year?'

Silence would have earned me another prod so I asked, 'What's that got to do with anything?'

'It's got to do with numbers,' she said. 'Except you're the number. You like it that way.'

'I do?'

'Yes,' she said, 'and there's no need to shut your eyes.'

'They get sore from the sun.'

She sat up so her shadow masked my face. 'Now will you open up?'

I did. She looked great – though a little fierce for a summer afternoon. 'Hi,' I smiled.

'Hi yourself,' she said without returning my smile. 'Now do we get to have a decent conversation?'

'Help yourself.'

'There you go again.'

'Where?'

'Getting on my trip. That's what you always do,' she said. 'You'd rather get on someone else's trip than risk letting them get on yours. That's where you're a fucking coward. You're scared of hurting people with who you really are.'

Working out what she meant was too complicated for the beach. Mostly I wished she would lie down again so I could shut my eyes. As I had nothing to answer, she added, 'And that's a kind of arrogance – thinking of yourself as that bad.'

I wasn't sure I did. On the other hand, there *were* people who'd gotten hurt. 'Like my ex-wife.'

'So that's her problem,' Sister Bear said. 'She wouldn't have gotten hurt if she hadn't been into fantasy.'

'And you're not into fantasy?'

'Not in a long time.'

She looked too young to have been around for a long time. I grinned.

'All right,' she said. 'Not in a lot of men. That make you happier?'

I reached for her hand. 'Do we have to fight?'

'*Fight?* Shit!' She looked exasperated enough to hit me. 'Jesus,' she said. 'Can't you understand? I'm trying to tell you I fucking love you, Tobias.'

'Woooeee!' came from our right as Black Tim leapt up and hiked his lady of the day to her feet. *'Heavy!'*

'Yeah, and you're no better,' Sister Bear accused while attempting a scowl.

'But faster on my feet,' Tim cracked with a quick shuffle. 'See you,' and off he danced.

'So?' asked Sister Bear. She had tanned nearly as dark as Tim. They say beauty is in the eye of the beholder. Sister Bear was beautiful to me. A tune fragment tinkled out of my subconscious. I got what it was after a moment's thought. *I've grown accustomed to your face . . .*

Romantic! Unfortunately, Joan and I had hummed that tune at each other the first year of our marriage. 'This is a tough island for relationships.'

Sister Bear grinned. 'All that *the grass is greener* crap?'

'Maybe.'

'So check the grass out,' she invited, 'just so you remember there's a stable. I sure as hell will. Or would you mind?'

'If we were together?'

'That's what we're talking about.'

What *she* was talking about I correct inside my head. Tell a lady you don't get jealous, she may come back that you don't love her. Tell her you do get jealous and she will consider you into ownership.

My dilemma drew a chuckle from Sister Bear. 'Just give me the truth.'

'I guess I don't get jealous.'

'Yeah, well you don't have to sound so fucking apologetic,' Sister Bear advised, that wide smile of hers lighting her face. 'We're two of a kind.'

'Yes?'

'Yes,' she said like she was warning me. 'I mean, who wants to lie around with a head full of fantasy. I've been through that trip. You know? You're balling some man one way while fantasising you're balling some other man in another way.'

She was so serious I had to laugh. 'Sounds a drag.'

She gave me a grin. 'Too fucking true. I mean, harmony .' and she swung her head back to free her hair from her eyes. 'Everyone's preaching harmony.'

She had me lost.

'Just that you can't have harmony while you're into fantasy,' she said and checked for comprehension. 'I mean we should both do what we want and not just dream about it.'

Great argument, I thought. 'That's what I told you our first night.'

'So now I'm telling you.'

'Thanks.'

'Yeah . . .' She gave the back of her head a scratch. The beach is tough on long hair. The sand gets trapped 'I mean it's all right once you're in love.'

Had I said I loved her? Though maybe she was right. Maybe we did share the same ideas on how to live our lives . . . except for the *finca*. And even the *finca* was a cop-out on my part. It was not the *finca* that bothered me but the cash it would all cost.

So I said, 'Sounds like we're going to have a lot of fun.'

The tone of my voice must have been wrong because her eyes went flat. 'What the fuck's that supposed to mean?'

Right then Big J strolled up the beach wearing a lopsided grin. His index finger marked a passage he'd discovered in Rajneesh's latest epistle to the faithful.

Big J reads more guru tracts than anyone I know. He needs to check with his fellow gurus that doing his own thing is a legitimate way of life. His own thing is painting, the study of mystical philosophy and the bass clarinet.

I once told him he was the last of the dilletantes. As a European, I thought I was paying him a compliment. He thought I was insulting him. Amateur status is sinful in White Protestant America. As for Minnesota, think of something that isn't considered a sin.

Now, as he comes up the ward, his embarrassment tells me all I need to know. My pen falls to the floor and rolls under the bed.

Grateful for the excuse to delay giving me his news, Big J crawls after the pen. He reappears red-faced and apologetic.

'Thanks anyway,' I say. 'And it was nice of you to come back '

'The flights worked out cheaper,' he says. Head cocked and mouth slightly open, he checks my face for emotional damage. 'I guess I was what you would think of as too late.'

I say, 'Tough.'

Big J is less sure. 'She didn't sound too friendly.'

'That's understandable,' I say. 'Look at it from her point of view.'

'I tried,' says Big J, 'but it's hard since I've never had an abortion.'

'Yeah, well I haven't either.'

'Right,' he says and gives one of his loose-mouthed grins. 'Maybe it was for the best.'

'Maybe.' I try a smile. 'You want to sit down?'

He drags up a chair. We know each other too well to bother bullshitting. 'So where is she now?' I finally ask.

'Santa Fe.'

'No shit! How did you trace her?'

'A few dozen phone calls. The cops helped,' he adds with his grin gone sheepish. 'I had my old man call Washington.'

Gratitude forms more of a barrier than a link between friends so I keep things casual. 'She say she was all right?'

'Not exactly. Like I called three times,' says Big J and comes up with a chuckle. 'All I could get out of her was you should go fuck yourself.'

Sounds like Sister Bear! I can see her phone in hand, long black hair tossed back, eyes flashing and a bare foot tapping the floor. Beautiful! And also strange because, if I am truly honest with myself, this is the first moment I know for sure that I love her (whatever that means). I don't *want* her that badly and I certainly don't *need* her, but if she walked up the ward this moment I would feel a firework go off in my belly.

So what would happen if she stayed around?

Perhaps the start of a firework industry.

I grin at Big J. 'Know something? I actually *am* in love.'

Chapter Sixteen

There is a hospital rule that says I am not allowed to walk to the theatre to have my stitches out. I have to go on the trolley. As I am due for discharge in two hours time this rule strikes me as a little strange. If I argue, the nurse will get upset and I wouldn't like that. She is a nice woman, overworked and probably underpaid.

So here we go on the trolley.

I give the elevator attendant a big grin as the porter wheels me in. 'Fourth floor, please.'

'Going up,' he says with a mock salute.

Fine.

And here is Dr Rahman. I say, 'Hi.'

He says, 'Good morning,' and to the theatre nurse, 'Let's have those bandages off.' Away he goes to wash his hands.

The nurse is in her early thirties, dark and rather plain. But she has nice eyes and nice hands. I lie back while she unwinds my testicle. Having me watch might embarrass her.

Rahman comes over with a pair of scissors and a pair of tweezers. he puts on horn-rimmed spectacles and has a close look at my scrotum. 'Nicely healed.'

The nurse nods her agreement.

As it's my scrotum, I feel I should get in on the act so raise myself on my elbows and say, 'Great'.

Rahman and the nurse ignore me. He snips the stitches and pulls them free. One sticks. Without looking up, he says, 'This may hurt a little,' and gives it a tug. The tug does hurt, but not sufficiently for me to complain.

'Good,' he says and takes my testicle in his left hand. Moslems use their left hands for wiping their asses. This strikes me as funny as I ask, 'Is my ball unclean?'

Rahman straightens up, smiles, and says, 'Actually I'm left-handed. Would you cough, please?'

I cough.

'Splendid,' he says.

I wish he would put my ball down. I am getting an erection from not having had my pee this morning. Hopefully the nurse won't feel insulted at my not having erected for her. Maybe she will think I'm gay.

'You're going to have to wear a truss for a couple of months,' Dr Rahman tells me. 'And don't take strenuous exercise.' He puts my ball down and hands the nurse his instruments. She carries them off to the steriliser. Her departure gives me the chance to ask, 'How about sex?'

'In moderation. Let's wheel you out to the waiting-room.' He does the wheeling. 'We can smoke out here,' he says and produces a silver case. 'Do you?'

'Sometimes,' I say, 'But not now, thank you.'

'Yes, well, they're not good for you,' he says and strikes a match. Through the flame, he asks, 'By the way, how did your girlfriend get on?'

'She's gone back to the States.'

He says, 'Oh . . .' and studies the tip of his cigarette. 'So she had an abortion.'

I say, 'Yes.'

And he says, 'Yes . . .'

For such a direct man, he is doing fine at avoiding my eyes. Perhaps it is the friendly way he feels towards me which is messing him up. As I have a good feeling towards him, I say, 'Look, you'd better tell me.'

He says, 'Yes,' and does meet my eyes. 'I'm afraid you're going to be sterile.'

I say, 'That means I am sterile?'

'Yes,' he says.

I say, 'Well, it can't be helped,' and smile. 'At my age I'd make a lousy Dad.'

He says, 'You're sure you wouldn't like a cigarette?'

'Maybe I will,' I say.

Dr Rahman lights it for me and I say, 'Thanks.'

'I'll be going home in a couple of months,' he says. 'If you're ever out that way . . .'

I watch him write his address on a prescription pad. I say, 'You've been very kind.'

He smiles and raises an eyebrow. 'Just doing my job.'

'Bullshit,' I tell him.

His laughter makes us both embarrassed at what the nurses will think. Doctors aren't meant to laugh. 'I'm sorry about the sterility,' he says. 'Perhaps I should have told you sooner.'

'It wouldn't have made any difference,' I say, and in comes the porter to wheel me back to the ward.

Dressed and sitting on my bed, I wait for Big J to come pick me up. He is fifteen minutes late. I spend the time dwelling on my sterility. It is not much to dwell on except for the irony of my having finally decided to settle down with Sister Bear and have kids. No Sister Bear and no kids. That's Karma for having led a sterile life.

And here comes Big J. The time for introspection is over. I have to get back to living, so I smile.

'Hi,' he opens with a nod at my eight notebooks. 'That all you have?'

'*All!*' I say. 'How old do you think I am?'

'What the fuck's age got to do with it?'

I give the notebooks a prideful pat. 'The memoirs of Tobias Cunningham-French.'

'No shit?' Big J shifts from being impressed to deep suspicion. 'For publication?'

'Why not?'

He scratches the back of his skull. 'So long as you don't use my name . . .'

'Would I do a thing like that?'

'You might,' he says. 'You do, my mother'll get uptight.'

'Mine too,' I admit. 'So what's happening?'

He says, 'I've been talking with Dr Rahman.'

'You have?'

'Don't echo,' he chides. 'A week in the hospital, you come on like a ventriloquist's dummy.'

'From using a go-between,' I say and raise a hand in farewell as much to my bed as to the other patients. I have been so locked into my own head, the only friend I have made is the old man with the tubes and he died without even knowing I existed.

Sliding gingerly into the passenger seat of Big J's hired car, I say, 'Easy on the curves.'

He grins. 'Yeah. Yacht marina?'

'Please.'

I got out of jail, there were all these people *free* on the streets. Now what I see is all this *health*.

I curse at the pain of Big J braking to avoid a truck.

Big J checks my face. 'Going to sail the cat?'

'I need the bread.'

'At the expense of your ball?' He risks a second glance. 'Rahman says you should rest.'

'Yeah . . . ?'

'Yeah,' he says. 'there's a Rome flight in two hours.'

'That's the one you're on?'

'Thinking of it,' Big J admits with guilt. 'That's if . . .'

'Fine by me,' I assure him. 'Jesus, the sun feels great.'

'Life's great.' He drags back his shoulders. 'That's if you keep your health.'

Big J has a blind spot on finance. It comes from visiting the bank twice a month.

He draws up by the cat. 'You're sure now?'

'Shit!' I say.

'Yeah,' he says and searches the quay for a private income to materialise for his friend, Tobias. No private income materialises. Instead the harbour master ducks out of his office to give me a wave. I know about that wave. The harbour master is waiting on me paying port dues.

'Be over later,' I shout - and to Big J, 'Coming on board?'

He inspects the catamaran. 'It's safe?'

'Enough,' I assure him.

'Yeah?' He swings carefully down on to the slat deck. The cat rocks. He gives me a hard look. 'Ibiza's a long haul.'

'Uphill,' I agree while opening the hatch to the port hull. Out drifts the familiar smell of a mushroom farm cut with rotting socks.

Steeling himself against the stench, Big J peers into the cabin. Sails and deck gear are heaped three feet deep on the cabin sole. With a slow shake of his head, Big J remarks, 'Tobias, it's time you grew up.'

'Like getting married and having a career?' I suggest with a grin. 'Want to drag that awning out?'

'I was thinking of the career,' Big J says as he gives me a hand.

We rig the awning between the masts and I haul out the bedding and deck cusions. Fresh air and sun will have them smelling sweet. Dusting my hands off, I inspect Big J. Worries over inflation and the future of the Republican party have set his eyes in twin relief maps of the Nile Delta. 'You're getting to look middle-aged.'

'We're both middle-aged,' he comes back hard. 'That's what you won't accept.'

'Oh, I accept it,' I reply. 'Middle-age is kind of late to start on a career.'

'Kind of late to be bumming around boats.'

I smile. 'Know the problem, Big J? I dig boats.'

'Yeah?' Shoulders slumped, he surveys the damp bedding. Any time he is about to raise the question of a friend's cash shortage, Big J gets embarrassed.

'Look,' he says (while I wait), and immediately studies a small yawl beating up the harbour. 'If it's a question of bread . . .'

Weird, I think: I have rid myself of guilt over how I live my life and here I am having to absolve my friend's guilt over how I live my life. 'Believe me,' I plead. 'Big J, I'm doing fine.'

'Like shit.' But he smiles. 'Well, if this is what you want . . .'

'It is.'

'And you're going to call that chick?'

'I'll give it a try.'

He spreads his hands. 'So what can I say?'

'How about *good luck*?'

'Except we have different ideas on what would be good luck.'

We face each other and suddenly laugh. 'Fuck, Big J,' I say, 'go catch your plane.'

We embrace. 'And thanks,' I tell him.

'Yeah With a return to embarrassment, he fumbles for his billfold

I tell him, How many times do I have to tell you I'm all right?'

'Sure?'

'Sure,' I say and watch him clamber on to the dock. I wave as he drives off, then open up the starboard cabin. The same stink greets me. I check the ship's clock.

Ten in the morning minus eight gives Sister Bear two hours after midnight. If she has been on the firewater she may be in a friendly mood.

A Greek millionaire's motor yacht lies over the other side of the marina. I know both the skipper and the owner. The owner is in London, but the skipper waves me up to the wheel house where I call Northforeland on the radio and ask the operator to put me through.

The telephone rings loud enough to wake the dead. Over the radio the ringing gains an echo . . . as if it is ringing in an empty house, I think. Maybe she is out with a man.

Sister Bear answers before I can hang up. 'Hi,' I say. 'Know what? I was thinking you were out with a man '

'Yeah,' she says. 'So first you say hullo. That's polite.'

'So how about admitting to feeling jealous for the first time in ten years,' I ask. 'Isn't that polite?'

'If it's true,' she says, 'I'll take it as complimentary.'

'And a sign of love?'

'*Love*,' this from the skipper. He shoves a vodka tonic into my hand. 'At your age!'

'Hey,' I protest.

'Hey *what*?' demands Sister Bear.

'Hey to the man who's wireless I'm using,' I tell her. 'He thinks I'm crazy.'

'Yeah, well I think you're a shit.'

'But a complimentary shit?'

'Like I care.'

'Look,' I say.

'Down a wire?'

'Jesus!' I gulp vodka. 'Listen, how do you feel?'

'At half past two in the Goddamned morning?' she asks. 'How the fuck do you think I feel? Tired.'

'Yes,' I say, 'but inside?'

'What the fuck's that got to do with you?'

'Goddamn it, I love you,' I shout.

'*Love!* What do you know about love?'

The remains of my drink shoots down my throat. 'Is that all you have to say?'

'No,' she says. 'Don't call in the middle of the night.'

'So when do I call?'

'You don't,' she says. 'You have something to say, put it in writing and don't bug me with any more of your Goddamned friends.'

'What the fuck else could I do?'

'You? Nothing,' she says like her opinion is final. 'Call me again and I'll get an unlisted number.'

'That's it?'

'It? It got washed down the mother fucking drain,' she yells. 'Thanks to your shit. Good fucking bye.' She hangs up.

I think of calling back. Then I think, *shit* and replace the headset.

'Want a refill?' asks the skipper.

'Thanks.' Passing him my tumbler, I look out over the harbour. The fortress walls of Valeta glow rose in the sunlight. Considering the bomb tonnage dropped by the Germans on those walls it is a miracle they stand. They also survived the Great Siege back in the seventeenth century with the Turks bombarding them day in and day out during six years. Definitely miraculous. So maybe I will survive Sister Bear's bombardment. 'Cheers,' I say to the skipper.

'Cheers.'

Two Englishmen! What else would we say to each other?

The return stroll produces a few stabs of pain so all I pick up is a six-pack of beer and a bag of ice. Back on the cat I turn the cushions and bedding for the sun to get at their undersides, then walk over to the marina office to pay my dues. Next I connect a hose to the water faucet and fill both tanks. This done, I strip to a pair of briefs and hose the deck.

Two young ladies stroll up. One of them is tall and a little plump. The other is short and slim. Both of them are deeply tanned and have dark hair. Jewish and New York is my instant judgement. 'Hi,' I say with a grin.

The short one nods at the hose. 'Looks good.'

'Cool,' I agree.

Kicking off her sandals, she reaches for the port-side

pulpit and swings on board. 'Mind?'

'Be my guest.'

Her friend joins us.

They shuck off their shirts and shorts Malta is strictly Catholic so it is fortunate they are wearing bikinis underneath. I sit down on the cabin top and watch them hose each other.

The small one whistles her appreciation. 'Jesus, that's good.'

'Great,' agrees her friend.

I say, 'Look, I'm just out of hospital. Could one of you shut off the faucet?'

The tall one does. Her friend inspects me. 'What's been wrong?'

'Some maniac surgeon cut open my ball.'

'Yeah?'

'Yeah,' I say and give her a shrug. 'Nice man, he sewed it back up.'

The lady giggles. 'How does it feel?'

'Painful,' I admit, 'and I'm kind of tired. There's a six-pack in the refrigerator.'

She drops down into the port hull and hands up two beers before inspecting the chaos. 'Shit!'

'Yeah,' I say, 'it's kind of a mess.'

'So relax,' she tells me. 'You have a brush?'

I tell her where the cleaning locker is. 'Great,' she says like she really means it.

Her friend, having shut off the water, accepts a beer and checks out what her friend is at.

'The man's sick,' the short one says. 'Castrated,' she adds with a giggle and a wink. 'Or so he says. Want to start in on the other hull?'

I go lie in the sun. I lie there on the edge of sleep and think about Sister Bear. I have this feeling we could have worked somehing out. Something that would have been good for both of us. So it hasn't worked out and I can't pretend that my life is shattered. It was a good life before Sister Bear came into it and it will probably go on being a good life. After all, I've spent years trying *not* to have kids.

The advantage to having been in jail is that you serve two

years and get pleasure out of the two years, then you know you can hack the worst that straight society can lay on you.

What you lay on yourself is another matter. Neither junk nor speed have ever tempted me and, though I enjoy good wine, I don't have a problem. As for cigarettes, a pack of Marlboro will last me three days. These being the four real killers, I can consider myself fortunate. I earn enough bread to get by and can earn more if I have to; and earn it at something I enjoy doing.

Maybe life would be better with Sister Bear and a kid. Equally, it could turn out to be a real drag. Though I am prepared to take the risk, there is no point in weeping over her not being prepared to take the risk.

This doesn't sound as if my love for her is very deep. Perhaps. But then I am still uncertain as to what is meant by love. Longing? Desire? Both words hold an ownership connotation. A desire to share sounds better. So does having respect for whom someone is.

Most people who tell me they are in love look a little crazy, either from unhappiness or from ecstasy. This is probably a prejudiced judgement on my part. Mostly what I feel is that thinking too much is a waste of energy. If you get stuck in your head, you miss out on the joy passing by on the outside of your head.

Nor will my feeling guilty over Sister Bear and her abortion do either she or I any good.

I am about finished with this train of thought when the shorter of my new acquaintances pokes her head out of the cabin. The sweat is running down her face and her long hair is a mess. 'Jesus,' she says, 'but it's hot.'

'Not up here,' I tell her.

She grins. 'Idle son of a bitch, you'd *better* be sick.'

I pluck at the top of my briefs.

She laughs. 'Show me later.'

'So a bomb drops?'

'Show me your wings.'

Clambering on to the dock, she opens the faucet. I watch her hose herself down. She is a nice lady, I decide. Very relaxed.

She leaves the hose running for her friend and squats

down by the deck mattress I am lying on. 'You sailing some place or staying here?'

She says *here* like she has had enough of Malta.

So I say, 'Sailing as soon as I've got my energy back.' She looks interested, so I add, 'Ibiza.'

'No shit! Hey,' she calls down to her friend. 'He's headed for Ibiza.'

'Great,' comes up from the other cabin. The lady appears. Whistling at the heat, she pushes her hair back out of her eyes. She looks pleased at the idea of Ibiza but irritated at having had to clean up the cabin. 'Let's go get our packs.'

The little one checks my face. 'Need anything from the shops?'

I squint at the sun. 'Maybe something to eat.'

'Booze?'

'White wine,' I suggest. 'Joe's Bar down the corner sells bottles on ice.'

Off they go and I start in thinking of Babette and Clo, the two French ladies who crewed me from Greece. They were seated in the cockpit of a sixty-foot ketch the first time I saw them. The ketch lay alongside the catamaran. The owner of the ketch was also French and had picked Babette and Clo up at the quayside *taverna* that noon.

While I prepared the cat for sea, I listened in on his rap. This was unavoidable as he had a loud and domineering voice. Most of his rap concerned the big society names he knew in Paris, the expensive restaurants and night clubs he frequented and how he owned a Dino Ferrari. Mention of the Dino Ferrari was his final error.

Both Babette and Clo were clearly *very* anti-men with Ferraris. In their eyes ownership of any automobile more powerful than a 2CV Citroen was evidence of extreme right-wing social irresponsibility.

Clo spotted I was eavesdropping. First she checked that I spoke enough French to be considered human. Second she asked where I was sailing to. Third she asked if I was alone. Satisfied, she and Babette transferred their packs to the cat.

I agree with Sister Bear on most points concerning my life. However, on her number theory I don't There's a difference between a number and a transit camp. Numbers are purely sexual.

Dr Rahman says I can ball but in moderation. So maybe I need a little luck with my new crew members.

The short one comes over as a great little lady, but I am less sure of her friend and I suspect her friend isn't that sure of me. Possibly we both suffer from paranoia. Equally, there is a look to her mouth which reminds me of my kids the times I refused their demands for candy.

Her rap is the same as her mouth. So far everything she has said has been directed at her friend. She doesn't recognise my existence . . . like when she said, 'Let's go get our packs.'

I didn't want her to ask me if fetching the packs was cool, but it would have been nice if she'd bothered to check my face for a reaction.

Maybe she suffers from shyness. Anyway, time will tell, I think, and wave to Ilsa, the Yacht Agent, who has driven by to check me out.

'Don't get up,' Ilsa says as I make an effort. 'How are you feeling?'

'Tender,' I tell her, 'but in good shape, despite the doctor's strike.'

Ilsa goes a little pink at my reminding her of her suspicions of Pakistani competence. 'Yes, well,' she says, '. . . I didn't know.'

'Nor did I,' I say. 'Maybe I was just lucky that Rahman was so good.'

'He seemed a nice man.'

'Very,' I agreed.

Satisfied we got Pakistan out of the way, Ilsa seats herself on the cabin top. 'Are you going to be able to sail?'

'Tomorrow.'

She studies me a moment. 'Is that wise?'

'I have a crew,' I tell her. And my crew have returned.

The thud of their packs hitting the deck jerks Ilsa around. She looks at them, then she looks at me. 'God!'

'Not so we've noticed,' says the short one with a smart-ass grin. She introduces herself as Debbie. Rebecca is her friend, Becky for short.

'How do you do,' says Ilsa with enough frost in her voice for me to suspect she has switched prejudices from Pakistan to Brooklyn Heights

I merely smile. 'You can cable the owners I'm back on course.'

'I'll do that,' Ilsa says. This is all she says. However the look she gives me suggests her dream is to get me alone someplace suited to a lecture on morality.

My crew and I eat our lunch, then siesta a couple of hours in the sun before bending on the sails. Next we work out a shopping list for a ten-day voyage. There are ample cans on board to cope with a calm.

'The motor's out,' I warn them. 'We hit head-winds, we'll end up going the wrong way.'

'Greece?' asks Debbie.

'Maybe.'

'Sounds fun.'

Definitely a nice lady, I think. As for Becky, she gives the motor a sour look. 'Can't it be fixed?'

'Probably,' I tell her. 'But not by me.'

'Why not?'

'Mostly because I'm lazy.'

Debbie says, 'Anyway, who wants a motor? They stink.'

She'll do fine in Ibiza – a genuine *finca* lady. I'll have to be careful. I pass her my billfold. 'There's a store over the other side of the marina that delivers.'

While the ladies do the shopping, I check the charts. Lampedusa would be a good place to stop. On the other hand, the port is a bitch to enter unless the wind's right. Mostly the wind's wrong.

Back come the ladies followed by the delivery truck. We stow the food and booze, wash up and head over to John Chu's Golden Duck for a Chinese meal. I've known John Chu for twenty years so my judgement is prejudiced in his favour, but the food is more than good according to Debbie. Becky says she's eaten better in New York's Chinatown. She probably has. However that's not my fault. Nor is it my problem. But I do wish she would show a little more enthusiasm, particularly as John's wife has thrown in a couple of extra dishes on the house.

I pay and we leave. Out on the street, Debbie takes my hand. We have to walk a little before we find a cab. The walking hurts my ball. I don't complain out loud but I do wonder about Debbie and Rebecca.

Back on the cat, we brush teeth on the deck. The ladies take longer than I do so I am first into bed. Debbie joins me 'Hi,' she says and gives me a kiss. She has warm lips.

'Hi yourself,' I say. 'Remember I'm straight from the hospital.'

She whips back the covers, inspects the damage and gives me a grin. 'Wow! We're going to have to treat that with respect.'

Becky has made it as far as the foot of the bunk. She has a look at my ball. 'You think it works?' Her question is addressed to Debbie.

'We'll soon see,' says Debbie and dips her head. A couple of minutes and she looks up with a proud grin. 'Sure it works.' And to me, 'How does it feel?'

'Interesting,' I tell her. 'Like it hurts but it's nice.'

'How bad's the hurt part?'

'Kind of a steady ache.'

'So what we want is a rush of pleasure – that ought to cancel things out.'

'Sounds good,' I say. 'How about you?'

'Be my guest,' she says and rolls on her back. She lies there tanned and beautiful and waiting. Not that her waiting implies any pressure on me. She is a *very* nice lady. Down I go on her only to remember how the school priests were always yelling at me in class to use my head.

I look up from between her legs and she catches my grin. 'What's so funny?'

I tell her about the priests.

She giggles. 'So you're a nut, but they gave you sound advice.'

I take the advice and we have fun. Becky joins in but without much enthusiasm. The best way of not thinking of her as a drag is to presume she is nervous at the situation. Maybe if I concentrate on her to the exclusion of Debbie . . .

Though my concentrating on her won't help if she simply

finds me a turn-off. Maybe she finds my scar a turn-off. She keeps her head well back from that region. Mostly what she does is lie flat on her back and wait for either Debbie or I to get her off.

Finally Debbie gets her off.

The off isn't much of an off but it *is* an off. Of course she may be acting. If so, it's good acting.

Debbie gives me a wink. 'You want to take over?'

I have a go with my prick but it doesn't work out too well. My trying to avoid pain has me humping too slow for Becky's satisfaction. I try a little extra speed and energy but my ball hits and hurts so I give up.

Debbie, who is watching, tries not to giggle. She and I are turning into a conspiracy. This won't please Becky. Debbie is *her* friend.

The simplest way out of the conspiracy is for me to hide my head between Becky's legs. Nothing much happens for a while other than Becky waiting for something to happen. Waiting is bad tactics. A good ten minutes pass before I finally get her off. This off gives evidence of being a physically more energetic off than her first. Whether it is in any way satisfying to her is harder to tell.

A few gasps and she turns to Debbie. 'He's not bad.'

So there's the judgement on Tobias Cunningham-French. It comes over like a consumer report in a ladies' magazine. You will find me listed after stoves, refrigerators, vacuum cleaners and washing machines.

Sister Bear was right after all. Half the time, all I am is a number.

Out I get from the bunk.

'Hey,' says Debbie, 'where are you off to?'

'The other cabin.'

Becky couldn't care less but Debbie seems genuinely concerned. 'There's something wrong?'

I don't want to hurt her. Nor do I want to lie. There have been enough lies. So what is the truth? I think a moment, then say, 'No, there's nothing wrong. Not any more. But I'm a writer. There's some stuff I need to get down on paper before I forget.'

What I needed to get down was this chapter. It is written

now and Debbie has come over from the other cabin to tell me it is three o'clock in the morning and high time for me to get some sleep. Right now she is making up the bunk.

Judging from how much my ball hurts, she is probably right about my needing sleep. But I feel great. I suggest Debbie also feels great by the way she clambers on to the bunk and snuggles herself into the pillows.

Odd. All those sexual games and neither she nor I had time for an orgasm. We were too busy trying to please Rebecca.

Epilogue

Ibiza
September 29, 1979

Diamonds used to be a girl's best friend. Man's best friend used to be his dog. Unfortunately a lady can no longer wear diamonds for fear of getting mugged and a man can no longer walk his dog without risking a heavy fine over his dog spoiling the sidewalk.

Given these circumstances, why don't we give up on the diamonds and dogs and work up a friendship between the sexes? It won't be easy. For generations we have been taught that we are natural enemies. But, ultimately, it could bring us more satisfaction than we get from the present warfare.

So there you are, Sister Bear. You were kind of aggressive on the phone (which I understand). Put it in writing, you said. I have. Seventy-five thousand words. If you find any of the words sufficiently interesting, why don't you drop me a line? I still believe you and I could work something out and would definitely dig giving it a try.

With love,
Tobias

P.S. My being sterile shouldn't pose a problem if you are still into kids. There are lots of bright and good-looking studs who'd be proud and overjoyed to oblige.

P.P.S. I'm into kids.

P.P.P.S. If you're not coming back, what did you do with the front door key?

TONIGHT JOSEPHINE

and other undiscovered letters

Michael Green

IF . . .

Julius Caesar had gone for a picnic and left the Senate to have a stab at something else

Hitler had taken his ever-loving mother's advice about his friends (especially the fat one)

Archimedes' plumbing had got him into hot water

Napoleon had had more than wandering hand trouble

. . . History would have been very, very different!

Here at last are the letters which changed the world (or would have if they'd ever been written).

'Delightfully engaging . . . could prove even more popular than his huge successes *The Art of Coarse Rugby, The Art of Coarse Sailing,* etc.'
Sunday Express

HUMOUR 0 7221 4084 3 £1.25